WOLF-SPEAKER

The
IMMORTALS
Book
II

Books by TAMORA PIERCE

SONG OF THE LIONESS QUARTET

Alanna: The First Adventure (Book I)
In the Hand of the Goddess (Book II)
The Woman Who Rides Like a Man (Book III)
Lioness Rampant (Book IV)

THE IMMORTALS QUARTET

Wild Magic (Book I)
Wolf-speaker (Book II)
Emperor Mage (Book III)
The Realms of the Gods (Book IV)

WOLF-SPEAKER

The Immortals
Book
II

TAMORA PIERCE

Simon Pulse

New York   London   Toronto   Sydney

SIMON PULSE
An imprint of Simon & Schuster Children's Publishing Division
1230 Avenue of the Americas, New York, NY 10020
Text copyright © 1994 by Tamora Pierce
All rights reserved, including the right of reproduction
in whole or in part in any form.
SIMON PULSE and colophon are registered trademarks
of Simon & Schuster, Inc.
Also available in an Atheneum Books for Young Readers
hardcover edition.
Designed by Tom Daly
The text of this book was set in Sabon.
Manufactured in the United States of America
First Simon Pulse edition June 2005
2 4 6 8 10 9 7 5 3 1
The Library of Congress has cataloged a previous edition as follows:
Pierce, Tamora.
Wolf-speaker / Tamora Pierce.—1st ed.
p. cm.—(The Immortals series)
Sequel to: Wild magic. 1992.
"A Jean Karl book."
Summary: With the help of her animal friends, Daine fights to save the
kingdom of Tortall from ambitious mortals and dangerous immortals.
[1. Fantasy. 2. Human-animal communication—Fiction.]
I. Title. II. Series: Pierce, Tamora. Immortals.
PZ7 .P61464 Wm 1994
[Fic]—dc20 93-21909
ISBN 0-689-85612-1 (hc.)
ISBN 1-4169-0344-5 (pbk.)

TO RAQUEL WOLF-SISTER,

once again,

TO THOMAS,

who has taught and still teaches me
to keep my mind flexible and
my creativity from stiffening up,

AND TO TIM,

always, each and every book,
whether I say so or not.

—————————————

ACKNOWLEDGMENTS

Normally I prefer not to write acknowledgments until the completion of a series, but this book entailed so much work above and beyond what my nearest and dearest are used to and so much real-life research that I would like to take a moment to express my appreciation.

First of all, I thank my good friend and fellow writer Raquel Starace. This book would never have been written if she had not inspired me with her own interest in and love of wolves. She lent me texts, tapes, and videos; she accompanied me on zoo safaris and bore with equanimity all those weird-hour phone calls with questions like, "Is brown the only eye color they have?" *Muchas gracias,* Rock—you can collect from me at will.

I also thank my writer-husband, Tim, who bails me out of the literary cul-de-sac to which I am prone, and who has lived for more than a year with wolves singing from our tape player, hunting on our TV, and watching him from my bulletin board. See, Tim—I *told* you they wouldn't eat you.

Thanks also are due to Robert E. J. Cripps, armsmaster and craftsman of the Celtic Wolf Medieval and Renaissance Style Crossbows, for last minute information on the proper name for the place where one places the bolt (the notch, where it is then secured by a clip!).

Most of all, I wish to thank those researchers and wolf experts whose work I plundered so freely for ideas, behaviors, and scents:

L. David Mech, for all his works, but in particular for *The Wolf: The Ecology and Behavior of an Endangered Species*;

Farley Mowat, whose *Never Cry Wolf* introduced me to that peculiar brand of lupine humor;

Martin Stouffer and his *Wild America* television program, particularly the "Wolf and the Whitetail" segment;

The Nature Conservancy;

The National Wildlife Federation;

NYSZ Wildlife Conservation Society;

The International Wolf Center of Ely, Minnesota, which works so hard for the preservation of this fascinating, endangered species.

CONTENTS

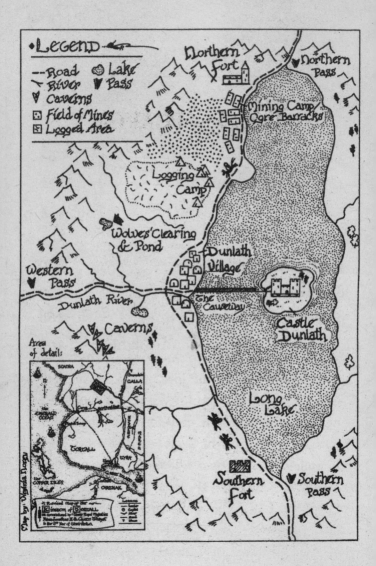

ONE

ENCOUNTERS

The wolves of the Long Lake Pack, gorged on a careless mountain sheep, slept as they digested their meal. Only Brokefang, their chieftain, was awake to see the moon rise. He sat on a stone outcrop, thinking—an odd pastime for a wolf. In the last full moon of summer, on the advice of Old White, the wolf god, he had sent his best travelers, Fleetfoot and Russet, in search of a two-legger who once belonged to his pack. Their orders were to bring her to him, to speak to the local humans on his behalf. The sight of that night's full autumn moon reminded him that winter was coming. What if his messengers couldn't find

Daine? What if something had happened to them?

He did not like "what if" thoughts. Until he'd met Daine two winters before, he had worried about nothing but eating, mating, ruling his pack, and scratching fleas. Now he had complex thoughts all the time, whether he wanted them or not.

Soft chatter overhead made him look up. Two bats had met a stranger. Clinging to a branch over his head, the three traded gossip in the manner of their kind. The newcomer brought word of a two-legger on the other side of the mountains, one who was human outside and Beast-People inside. She carried news from bats in the southwest, and if a Long Lake bat was hurt, she could heal him with her magic. She traveled in odd company: two horses, a pony, an extremely tall human male, a big lizard, and two wolves.

The local bats exclaimed over the news. Their colony should hear this, they decided. Would the visitor come and tell them in their cave-home? Along with their guest, the bats took the air.

Brokefang stretched. One new thought had

been that he could learn much if he listened to the talk of nonwolves. Now he could see it was a good thought, so perhaps the others were good, too. He was interested to hear that Daine also had learned new things since leaving the pack. Before, she could not talk directly with bats. Her healing was done with stinging liquids, needles, thread, and splints, not magic.

He stopped in midstretch as he remembered something. When Fleetfoot and Russet had gone, the pack was laired near the valley's southern entrance, where a river flowed from the lake. While they eventually could find the new den in the valley's western mountains, it might take them days to locate the pack.

He would take his wolves south and guide his visitors home.

Two days later, the girl called Daine watched rain fall outside the cave where she and her friends had taken refuge. For someone Brokefang regarded as Pack, she looked quite human. She was five foot five, slim for her fourteen and a half years, with blue-gray eyes the color of the clouds overhead. Her curly brown hair was tightly pinned up, her clothes as practical as her hairstyle: a blue cotton shirt, tan breeches, and soft-soled boots. Around her neck a heavy silver claw hung on a leather thong.

She played with the claw, thinking. She had been born in mountains like these, in a town called Snowsdale over the border in Galla. The first twelve years of her life were spent there, before she lost her family. When she left Galla to serve the king and queen of Tortall, she had hoped that she might never see the mountains again. And here she was, in a place that could be Snowsdale's twin.

Soon she would be with the wolves that had hunted in her old home. They had left soon after she did: Fleetfoot and Russet, her guides, had told of fleeing human hunters to find their new home by the Long Lake. What would it be like to see them again? To be with them again?

"What are you thinking of?" a light male voice asked from deeper inside the cave. "You look grim."

Daine turned around. Seated cross-legged by the fire, a traveling desk on his knees, was her teacher, the wizard Numair Salmalín. He wore his springy mass of black hair tied into a horsetail, away from his dark face and out of his brown eyes. His ink brush was dwarfed by the hand that held it, an exceptionally large hand that was graceful in spite of its size.

"I'm just wondering if Onua is managing the Rider horses all right without me. I know the king told her he needed us to come here, but I still feel as if I should be helping her."

The man raised his eyebrows. "You know very well Onua managed the Rider horses for years before you came to work there. What's *really* bothering you?"

She made a face. She never could distract him when he wanted to know something. "I'm scared."

He put down his brush and gave her his full attention. "What of?"

She looked at her hands. They were chapped from cold, and this was only the third week of September. "Remember what I told you? That I went crazy and hunted with wolves after bandits killed Ma and Grandda and our animals?"

He nodded. "They helped you to avenge the deaths."

"What if it happens again? When I see them, what if I forget I'm human and start thinking I'm a wolf again? I'm s'posed to have control of my wild magic now, but what if it isn't enough?" She rubbed her arms, shivering.

"May I remind you that the spell that keeps your human self apart from your magic self is one I created?" he teased, white teeth flashing in a grin. "How can you imply a working performed by your obedient servant"—he bowed, an odd contortion in a sitting man—"might be anything but perfect?" More seriously he added, "Daine, the spell covers all your contacts. You won't lose control."

"What if it wasn't the magic? What if I simply went mad?"

Strong teeth gripped her elbow hard. Daine looked around into the bright eyes of her pony, Cloud. If I have to bite you to stop you feeling sorry for yourself, I will, the mare informed her. You are being silly.

Numair, used to these silent exchanges, asked, "What does she say?"

"She says I'm feeling sorry for myself. I don't think she understands."

I understand that you fidget over stupid

things. Cloud released Daine's elbow. The stork-man will tell you.

"Don't fret," said the mage. "Remember, you allowed me into your mind when you first came to Tortall. If there was a seed of genuine madness there, I would have found it."

Daine smiled. "There's folk who would say you're the *last* man to know who's crazy and who's not. I know a cook who won't let you in his kitchen, a palace quartermaster who says he'll lock you up if you raid his supplies again—"

"Enough!" Numair held up his hands in surrender.

"Just so you know." Feeling better, she asked, "What are you writing?"

He picked up his ink brush once more. "A report to King Jonathan."

"Another one?" she asked, startled. "But we sent one off a week ago."

"He said *regular* reports, magelet. That means weekly. It's a small price to pay for being allowed to come to the rescue of your wolf friends. I just wish I had better news to send."

"I don't think we'll find those missing

people." In March a group of the Queen's Riders—seven young men and women—had disappeared in this general area. In July twenty soldiers from the Tortallan army had also vanished. "They could've been anywhere inside a hundred or two hundred miles of us."

"All we can do is look," Numair said as he wrote. "As wanderers we have seen far more than soldiers will. Even so, it's a shame the whole northeastern border is opaque to magical vision. I hadn't realized that a search by foot would be so chancy."

"Why can't you wizards see this place with your magic?" Daine wanted to know. "When I asked the king, he said something about the City of the Gods, and an aura, but then we got interrupted and he never did explain."

"It has to do with the City of the Gods being the oldest center for the teaching of magic. Over the centuries magic seeped into the very rock of the city itself, and then spread. The result is a magical aura that blanks out the city and the lands around it for something like a five-hundred-mile radius."

Daine whistled appreciation of the distance

involved. "So the only way to look at all this mountain rock is by eye. That's going to be a job and a half."

"Precisely. Tell me, how far do you think we are from our destination?"

Fleetfoot and Russet had measured distance in the miles a wolf travels in a day. Daine had to divide that in half to figure how far humans might go on horseback. "Half a day's ride to the south entrance to the valley, where the Dunlath River flows out of Long Lake. From—" She stopped as something whispered in her mind. Animals were coming, looking for her. She ran to the mouth of the cave as their horses bolted past.

Here they came up the trail, wolves, three in the lead and four behind. Two of the leaders were her guides to the Long Lake: the small, reddish white male known as Russet and the brown-and-gray female called Fleetfoot. Between them trotted a huge, black-and-gray timber wolf, plumed tail boldly erect.

"Brokefang!" Daine yelled. "Numair, it's the pack!" She ran to them and vanished in a crowd of yelping, tail-wagging animals.

Delighted to see her, they proceeded to wash her with their long tongues.

Standing at the cave entrance, waiting for the reunion to end, the man saw that the rain was coming down harder. "Why don't we move the celebration inside?" he called. "You're getting drenched."

Daine stood. "Come on," she told the pack, speaking aloud for Numair's benefit. "And no eating my friends. The man is Numair. He's my pack now." Two wolves—Numair was touched to see they were Fleetfoot and Russet, his companions on their journey here—left the others to sit by him, grinning and sprinkling him with drops from their waving tails.

Once out of the rain, the newcomers greeted Cloud, sniffing the gray mare politely. Brokefang gave the mare a few licks, which she delicately returned. The pony, the sole survivor of the bandit raid on Daine's farm, had stayed with Daine in the weeks the girl had run with the pack. In that time, wolves and pony had come to a truce of sorts.

Next Daine introduced her pack to Spots, the easygoing piebald gelding who was Numair's mount, and Mangle, a gentle bay cob who carried their packs. The horses quivered, whites showing all the way around their eyes, as the wolves sniffed them. They trusted Daine to keep the wolves from hurting them, but their belief in her couldn't banish natural fear entirely. Once the greetings were over, they retreated to the rear of the large cave and stayed there.

"Kitten," Daine called, looking for her charge. "Come meet the wolves."

Knowing she often scared mortal animals, the dragon had kept to the shadows. Now she walked into the light. She was pale blue, almost two feet long from nose to hip, with another twelve inches' worth of tail, a slender muzzle, and silver claws. The wings that one day would carry her in flight were, at this stage, tiny and useless. Her blue, reptilian eyes followed everything with sharp attention. She was far more intelligent than a mortal animal, but her way of knowing and doing things was a puzzle Daine tried to unravel on a daily basis.

"This is Skysong," Daine told the pack. "That's the name her ma gave her, anyway. Mostly we call her Kitten."

The dragon eyed their guests. The newcomers

stared, ears flicking back and forth in uncertainty, tails half-tucked between their legs. Slowly she rose up onto her hindquarters, a favorite position, and chirped.

Brokefang was the first to walk forward, stiff-legged, to sniff her. Only when his tail gave the smallest possible wag did the others come near.

Once the animals were done, Daine said, "Numair, the gray-and-black male is Brokefang." When the wolf came to smell Numair's hands, the mage saw that his right canine tooth had the point broken off. "He's the first male of the pack, the boss male." Numair crouched to allow Brokefang to sniff his face and hair as well. The wolf gave a brief wag of the tail to show he liked Numair's scent.

The brown-and-gray male with the black ring around his nose is Short Snout," Daine said. "The tawny female is Battle. She fought a mountain lion when she was watching pups in Snowsdale—that's how she got her name." Short Snout lipped Numair's hand in greeting. Battle sniffed the mage and sneezed. "The brown-and-red male is Sharp Nose. The gray-and-tawny female is Frolic." The girl sat on the floor, and most of the wolves curled up around her. "Frostfur, the boss female, and Longwind stayed in the valley with the pups."

Greetings done, Numair sat by the fire and added new wood. "Has Brokefang said why he needs you?" he asked. "His call for help was somewhat vague."

Daine nodded. "Brokefang, what's going on? All you told Fleetfoot and Russet was that humans are ruining the valley." As the wolf replied, she translated, "He says this spring men started cutting trees and digging holes without planting anything. He says they brought monsters and more humans there, and they are killing off the game. Between that and the tree cutting and hole digging, they're driving the deer and elk from the valley. If it isn't stopped, the pack will starve when the Big Cold comes."

"The Big Cold?" asked Numair.

"It's what the People—animals—call winter."

The man frowned. "I'm not as expert as you in wolf behavior, but—didn't you tell me that if wolves find an area is too lively for them, they flee it? Isn't that why they left Snowsdale, because humans there were hunting them?"

Yes, said Brokefang. They wanted to hurt us, because we helped Daine hunt the humans who killed her dam. They killed Rattail, Longeye, Treelicker, and the pups.

Daine nodded sadly: Fleetfoot and Russet had told her of the pack's losses. The older wolves had been her friends. The pups she hadn't met, but every pack valued its young ones. To lose them all was a disaster.

Brokefang went on. We left Snowsdale. It was a hard journey in the hot months, seeking a home. We found places, but there was little game, or other packs lived there, or there were too many humans. Then just before the last Big Cold we found the Long Lake. This valley is so big we could go for days without seeing humans. There is plenty of game, no rival pack to claim it, and caves in the mountains for dens in the snows.

Scratching a flea, Brokefang continued. The Long Lake was good—now humans make it bad. They drove us from the valley where I was born, and my sire, and his sire before him. Before, it was our way to run from two-leggers. Yet I do not run if another pack challenges mine—I fight, and the Pack fights with

14

me. Are humans better than another pack? I do not believe they are.

Will you help us? Will you tell the humans to stop their tree cutting and noisemaking? If they do not stop, the Long Lake Pack will stop it for them, but I prefer that they *agree* to stop. I know very well that if the Pack has to interfere, there will be bloodshed.

Daine looked at the other wolves of the pack. They nodded, like humans, in agreement. They would support Brokefang in the most unwolflike plan she had ever heard in her life. Where had they gotten such ideas?

Will you help us? asked Brokefang again.

Daine took a deep breath. "You're my Pack, aren't you? I'll do my best. I can't promise they'll listen to me, but I'll try."

Good, Brokefang replied. He padded to the cave's mouth and gave the air a sniff. The breeze smelled of grazing deer just over the hill. Looking at Daine, he said, Now we must hunt. We will come back when we have fed.

They left as Daine was translating his words. She followed them to the cave mouth, to watch as they vanished into the rain. It was getting dark. Behind her was a clatter as Numair unpacked the cooking things. Thinking about the pack and about her time with them, she was caught up in a surge of memory.

The bandit guard was upwind of a wolf once called Daine. The night air carried his reek to her: unwashed man, old blood, sour wine. Her nose flared at the stench. She covered it with her free hand. The other clutched a dagger, the last human item she remembered how to use.

He did something with his hands as he stood with his back toward her. She slunk closer, ignoring the snow under her bare feet and the freezing air on her bare arms. Forest sounds covered the little noise she made, though he would not have heard if she'd shouted. He was drunk. They all were, too drunk to remember the first two shifts of guards had not returned.

She tensed to jump. Something made him turn. Now she saw what he'd been doing: there was a wheel of cheese in one hand, a dagger in the other, and a wedge of cheese in his mouth. She also saw his necklace, the amber beads her mother had worn every day of her life. She leaped, and felt a white-hot line of pain along her ribs. He'd stabbed her with his knife.

Brokefang found her. She had dragged herself under a bush and was trying to lick the cut in her side. The wolf performed this office for her.

It is dawn, he said. What must be done now?

We finish them, she told him, fists clenched tight. We finish them all.

"I think I know why Brokefang changed so much," she said. "I mean, animals learn things from me, and probably that's how most of the pack got so smart, but Brokefang's even smarter. I got hurt, when we were after those bandits, and he licked the cut clean."

"It's a valid assumption," agreed Numair. "There are cases of magically gifted humans who were able to impart their abilities to non-human companions. For example, there is Boazan the Sun Dancer, whose eagle Thati could speak ten languages after she drank his tears. And—"

"Numair," she said warningly. Experience had taught her that if she let him begin to list examples, he would not return to the real world for hours.

He grinned, for all the world like one of her stableboy or Rider friends instead of the greatest wizard in Tortall. He had begun to cook supper: a pot of cut-up roots already simmered on the fire. Daine sat next to him and began to slice chunks from a ham they had brought in their packs. Kitten waddled over to help, or at least to eat the rind that Daine cut from the meat.

—*This is very nice,*— a rough voice said in their minds. —*Cozy, especially on a rainy afternoon.*—

They twisted to look at the cave entrance. It shone with a silvery light that appeared to come from the animal standing there. The badger waddled in, the light fading around his body. He stopped at a polite distance from their fire and shook himself, water flying everywhere from his long, heavy coat.

Daine fingered the silver claw he had once given her. She liked badgers, and her mysterious adviser was a very handsome one. Big for his kind, he was over a yard in length, with a tail a foot long. He weighed at least fifty pounds, and it appeared he could stow a tremendous amount of water in his fur.

When he finished shaking, he trundled over to the fire, standing between Daine and Numair. Seated as Daine was, she and the badger were nearly eye to eye. She was so close that she couldn't escape his thick, musky odor.

"Daine, is this—?" Numair sounded nervous.

The badger looked at him, eyes coldly intelligent. —*I told her father I would keep an eye on her. So you are her teacher. She tells me a great deal about you, when I visit her.*—

"May I ask you something?" the mage inquired.

—*I am an immortal, the first male creature of my kind. The male badger god, if you like. That is what you wished to ask, is it not?*—

"Yes, and I thank you," Numair said hesitantly. "I—thought I had shielded my mind from any kind of magical reading or probe—"

—*Perhaps that works with* mortal *wizards,*— the badger replied. —*Perhaps it works with lesser immortals, such as Stormwings. I am neither.*—

Numair blushed deeply, and Daine hid a grin behind one hand. She doubted that anyone had spoken that way to Numair in a long time. She was used to it. The badger had first appeared in a dream to give her advice sixteen months ago, on her journey to Tortall, and she had dreamed of him often since.

"Another question, then," the mage said doggedly. "Since I have the opportunity to ask. You can resolve a number of academic debates, actually."

—*Ask.*— There was a studied patience in the badger's voice.

"The inhabitants of the Divine Realms are called by men 'immortals,' but the term itself isn't entirely accurate. I know that unless they are killed in some accident or by deliberate intent, creatures such as Stormwings, spidrens, and so on will live forever. They don't age, either. But how are they 'lesser immortals' compared to you, or to the other gods?"

—*They are "lesser" because they can be slain,*— was the reply. —*I can no more be killed than can Mithros, or the Goddess, or the other gods worshiped by two-leggers. "Immortals" is the most fitting term to use. It* is not particularly correct, but it is the best you two-leggers can manage.—

Having made Numair speechless, the badger went on. —Now, on to your teaching. It is well enough, but you have not shown her where to take her next step. I am surprised. For a mortal, your grasp of wild magic normally is good.—

Numair looked down his long nose at the guest who called his learning into question. "If you feel I have omitted something, by all means, enlighten us."

The badger sneezed. It seemed to be his way of laughing. —Daine, if you try, you can learn to enter the mind of a mortal animal. You can use their eyes as you would your own, or their ears, or their noses.—

Daine frowned, trying to understand. "How? When you said I could hear and call animals, it was part of something I knew how to do. This isn't."

—Make your mind like that of the animal you join,— he told her. —Think like that animal does, until you become one. You may be quite surprised by what results in the end.—

It sounded odd, but she knew better than to say as much. She had questioned him once, and he had flattened her with one swipe of his paw. "I'll try."

—*Do better than try. Where is the young dragon?*—

Kitten had been watching from the other side of the fire. Now she came to sit with the badger, holding a clump of his fur in one small paw. She had a great deal to say in her vocabulary of chirps, whistles, clicks, and trills. He listened as if it meant something, and when she was done, waddled over to talk with Cloud and the horses. At last he returned to the fire, where Daine and Numair had waited politely for him to end his private conversations.

—*I must go back to my home sett,*— he announced. —*Things in the Divine Realms have been hectic since the protective wall was breached and the lesser immortals were released into your world.*—

"Do you know who did it?" asked Numair quickly. "We've been searching for the culprit for two years now."

—*Why in the name of the Lady of Beasts would I know something like that?*— was the growled reply. —*I have more than enough to do in mortal realms simply with keeping an eye on her.*—

"Don't be angry," Daine pleaded. "He thought you might know, since you know so much already."

—*You are a good kit.*— The badger rubbed his head against her knee. Touched by this sign of affection, Daine hugged him, burying her fingers in his shaggy coat. To Numair he added, —*And I am not angry with you, mortal. I cannot be angry with one who has guarded my young friend so well. Let me go, Daine. I have to return to my sett.*—

She obeyed. He walked toward the cave's mouth, silver light enclosing him in a globe. At its brightest, the light flared, then vanished. He was gone.

"Well," said Numair. She thought he might add something, but instead he busied himself with stirring the vegetables.

Suddenly she remembered a question she had wanted to ask. "I think he puts a magic on me," she complained.

"How so?"

"Every time I see him, I mean to ask who my da is, and every time I forget! And he's the only one who can tell me, too, drat him."

Kitten gave a trill, her slit-pupiled eyes concerned.

"I'm all right, Kit," the girl said, and sighed. "It's not fair, though."

Numair chuckled. "Somehow I doubt the badger is interested in what's fair."

She had to smile, even if her smile was one-sided. She knew he was right.

"Speaking of what is fair, what do you think of the advice he gave you, about becoming a magical symbiote?"

Most of the time she was glad that he spoke to her as he would to a fellow scholar, instead of talking down to her. Just now, though, her head was reeling from Brokefang's news and the badger's arrival. "A magical sym—sym—whatsits?"

"Symbiote," he replied. "They are creatures that live off other creatures, but not destructively, as parasites do. An example might be the bird who rides on a bison, picking insects from the beast's coat."

"Oh. I don't know what I think of it. I never tried it."

"Now would be a good time," he said helpfully. "The vegetables will take a while to cook. Why not try it with Cloud?"

Daine looked around until she saw the mare, still at the rear of the cave with Mangle and Spots. "Cloud, can I?"

"Cloud, *may* I," the man corrected.

You can or you may. I don't know if it will help, said the mare.

The girl went to sit near the pony, while Mangle and Spots ventured outside to graze again. Numair began to get out the ingredients for campfire bread as Kitten watched with interest.

"Don't let him stir the dough too long," Daine ordered the dragon. "It cooks up hard when he forgets." Kitten chirped as Numair glared across the cave at his young pupil.

The girl closed her eyes. Breathing slowly, she reached deep inside to find the pool of copper light that was her wild magic. Calling a thread of fire from that pool, she reached for Cloud, and tried to bind their minds with it.

Cloud whinnied, breaking the girl's concentration. That *hurt,* the mare snapped. If it's going to hurt, I won't do it! Try it with less magic.

Shutting her eyes, Daine obeyed. This time she used a drop of copper fire, thinking to glue her mind to Cloud's. The mare broke contact the minute Daine's fire touched hers. Daine tried it a second, and a third time, without success.

It's the same kind of magic, she told Cloud, frustrated. It's not any different from what's in you.

It hurts, retorted the pony. If that badger knew this would hurt and told you to try it anyway, I will tell *him* a few things the next time he visits.

I don't do it a-purpose, argued Daine. How can I do it without paining you?

Without the fire, Cloud suggested. You don't need it to talk to us, or to listen. Why should you need it now?

Daine bit a thumbnail. Cloud was right. She only used the fire of her magic when she was tired, or when she had to do something hard. She was tired now, and the smell of cooking ham had filled her nostrils. "Let's try again tomorrow," she said aloud. "My head aches."

"Come eat," called Numair. "You've been at it nearly an hour."

Daine went to the fire, Cloud following. Digging in her pack, the girl handed the pony a carrot before she sat. Numair handed over a bowl of mildly spiced vegetables and cooked ham. Kitten climbed into the girl's lap, forcing Daine to arrange her arms around the dragon as she ate. Between mouthfuls she explained what had taken place.

Cloud listened, nibbling the carrot as her ears flicked back and forth. When Daine finished, the mare suggested, Perhaps I am the wrong one to try with.

"Who, then, Cloud?" Daine asked. "I've known you longer than anybody." She yawned. The experiment, even though it hadn't worked, had worn her out.

But I am a grazer—you are a hunter. Why not try with a hunter? It may be easier to do this first with wolves. You are practically a wolf as it is.

"And if I forget I'm human?"

("I wish I could hear both sides of this

conversation," Numair confided softly to Kitten. "I feel so left out, sometimes.")

The man said you won't, replied Cloud. He should know. Brokefang is part of you already. Ask the stork-man. He will tell you I am right.

Daine relayed this to Numair. "She has a point," he said. "I hadn't thought the predator-prey differential would constitute a barrier, but she knows you better than I." He watched Daine yawn again, hugely, and smiled. "It *can* wait until tomorrow. Don't worry about cleanup. I'll do it."

"But it's my turn," she protested. "You cooked, so I have to clean."

"Go to bed," her teacher said quietly. "The moon will not stop its monthly journey simply because I cooked *and* cleaned on the same meal."

She climbed into her bedroll and was asleep the moment she pulled the blankets up. When the wolves returned much later, she woke just enough to see them group around her. With Kitten curled up on one side and Brokefang sprawled on the other, Daine finished her night's rest smiling.

***

It was damp and chilly the next morning, the cold a taste of the months to come. Breakfast was a quiet meal, since neither Daine nor Numair was a morning person. They cleaned up together and readied the horses for the day's journey.

The wolves had gone to finish the previous night's kill. They were returning when Numair handed Daine a small tube of paper tied with plain ribbon. "Can we send this on to the king today?" he asked.

Daine nodded, and reached with her magic. Not far from their campsite was the nest of a golden eagle named Sunclaw. Daine approached her politely and explained what she wanted. She could have made the bird do as she wished, but that was not the act of a friend. The eagle listened with interest, and agreed. When she came, Daine thanked her, and made sure the instructions for delivering Numair's report were fixed in Sunclaw's mind. Numair, who had excellent manners, thanked Sunclaw as well, handing the letter to her with a bow.

Brokefang had watched all of this with

great interest. You have changed, he commented when Sunclaw had gone. You know so much more now. You will make the two-leggers stop ruining the valley.

Daine frowned. I don't know if I can, she told the wolf. Humans aren't like the People. Animals are sensible. Humans aren't.

You will help us, Brokefang repeated, his faith in her shining in his eyes. You said that you would. Now, are you and the man ready? It is time to go.

Daine put Kitten atop the packs on Mangle's back. Numair mounted Spots, and the girl mounted Cloud. "Lead on," the mage told Brokefang.

The wolves trotted down the trail away from the cave, followed by the horses and their riders. When the path forked, one end leading to the nearby river and the other into the mountains, Brokefang led them uphill.

"If we follow the river, won't that take us into the valley?" Daine called. "It won't be so hard on us."

Brokefang halted. It is easier, he agreed, as Daine translated for Numair. Humans go that way all the time. So also do soldiers, and men with magic fires. It is best to avoid them. Men kill wolves on sight, remember, Pack-Sister?

"Men with magic fires?" Numair asked, frowning.

Men like you, said Brokefang, with the Light Inside.

"We call them mages," Daine told him. "Or sorcerers, or wizards, or witches. What we call them depends on what they do."

Numair thought for a moment. "Lead on," he said at last. "I prefer to avoid human notice for as long as possible. And thank you for the warning."

The humans, Kitten, and the horses followed the wolves up along the side of the mountains that rimmed the valley of the Long Lake. By noon they had come to a section of trail that was bare of trees. The wolves didn't slow, but trotted into the open. Daine halted, listening. Something nasty was tickling at the back of her mind, a familiar sense that had nothing to do with mortal animals. Getting her crossbow, she put an arrow in the notch and fixed it in place with the clip.

Numair took a step forward, and Cloud grabbed his tunic in her teeth.

"Stormwings," Daine whispered. Numair drew back from the bare ground. Under the tree cover, they watched the sky.

High overhead glided three creatures with human heads and chests, and great, spreading wings and claws. Daine knew from bitter experience that their birdlike limbs were steel, wrought to look like genuine feathers and claws. In sunlight they could angle those feathers to blind their enemies. They were battlefield creatures, living in human legend as monsters who dishonored the dead. Eyes cold, she aimed at the largest of the three.

Numair put a hand on her arm. "Try to keep an open mind, magelet," he whispered. "They haven't attacked us."

"Yet," she hissed.

Brokefang looked back to see what was wrong, and saw what they were looking at. *These are harriers*, he said. *They help the soldiers and the mages.*

Daine relayed this to Numair as the wolves moved on, to wait for them in the trees on the other side of the clearing.

"Stormwings that work in conjunction with humans," the man commented softly. "That

32

sounds like Emperor Ozorne's work." The emperor of the southern kingdom of Carthak was a mage who seemed to have a special relationship with minor immortals, and with Stormwings in particular. Some, Numair included, thought it was Ozorne's doing that had freed so many immortals from the Divine Realms in the first place. He had his eye on Tortall's wealth, and many thought he meant to attack when the country's defenders were worn out from battling immortals.

"Now can I shoot them?" Daine wanted to know.

"You may not. They still have done nothing to harm us."

The Stormwings flew off. Vexed with her friend, Daine fumed and waited until she could no longer sense the immortals before leading the way onto the trail once more. They were halfway across the open space when Numair stopped, frowning at a large, blackened crater down the slope from them. "That's not a natural occurrence," he remarked, and walked toward it.

"This isn't the time to explore!" Daine hissed. If he heard, he gave no sign of it. With a sigh the girl told the horses to move on. "The wolves won't touch you," she said when Spots wavered. "Now go!"

Follow me, Cloud told the horses; they obeyed. Daine, with Kitten peering wide-eyed over her shoulder, followed Numair.

Blackened earth sprayed from the crater's center. Other things were charred as well: bones, round metal circles that had been shields before the leather covers burned, trees, axheads, arrowheads, swords. The heat that had done this must have been intense. The clay of the mountainside had glazed in spots, coating the ground with a hard surface that captured what was left of this battle scene.

Numair bent over a blackened lump and pulled it apart. Daine looked at a mass of bone close to her, and saw it was a pony's skeleton. Metal pieces from the dead mount's tack had fallen in among the bones. Looking around, she counted other dead mounts. The smaller bone heaps belonged to human beings.

Grimly Numair faced her and held up his find. Blackened, half-burned, in tatters, it was a piece of cloth with a red horse rearing on a gold-brown field. "Now we know what happened to the Ninth Rider Group."

Daine's hand trembled with fury. She had a great many ties to the Queen's Riders, and the sight of that charred flag was enough to break her heart. "And you stopped me from shooting those Stormwings."

"They don't kill with blasting fire like this," Numair replied. "This is battle magic. I have yet to hear of a Stormwing being a war mage."

"I bet they knew about this, though."

Numair put a hand on her shoulder. "You're too young to be so closed-minded," he told her. "A little tolerance wouldn't come amiss." Folding the remains of the flag, he climbed back up to the trail.

TWO

THE VALLEY OF THE LONG LAKE

Three days after leaving the cave, the wolf pack led the humans and their ponies through a gap in the mountains. At its deepest point they found a spring, where they ate lunch; from there they followed a stream downhill, until Brokefang stopped.

You must look at something, he told Daine. Leave the horses by that rock—they will be safe there, with the rest of the pack to guard them.

Daine, with Kitten on her back in a sling, and Numair followed them up a long tumble of rock slabs. When they came to the top, they could see for miles. Far below was the Long Lake. Daine noticed a village where a small river—part of the stream they had followed—met the lake. Not far offshore, linked to the village by a bridge, was an island capped by a large, well-built castle.

Numair drew his spyglass from its case. Stretching it to full length, he put it to his eye and surveyed the valley.

What is that? asked the wolf, watching him. "It's a glass in a tube," Daine replied. "It makes things that are far away seem closer."

"This is Fief Dunlath, without a doubt." Numair offered the spyglass to Daine. "I can't see the northern reaches of the lake from here. Is that where the damage is being done? The holes and the tree cutting?"

Most of it, Brokefang replied. That and dens for the soldiers, like those they have at the south gate.

"Soldiers at the northern *and* southern ends of the valley?" asked Daine. "Then why not here, if they want to put watchdogs at the passes?"

Most two-leggers follow the river in and out, answered Brokefang. Few come here as we did. When they do, usually the harriers catch them outside, as they did those Riders you spoke of.

Numair listened as Daine translated. "This is not good," he muttered, squinting at Dunlath Castle. "There is no reason for this fief to be heavily guarded. Under law they're only entitled to a force of forty men-at-arms. . . . May I see that again?" He held out a hand, and Daine returned the glass.

They continued to examine the valley until Brokefang said, Come. We have a way to go still. Let us find the meeting place, and my mate.

Daine and Numair followed the wolf back to the spot where they had left the horses. A strange wolf had joined the others, a gray-and-white female with a boldly marked face. Brokefang raced to meet her, tail erect and wagging gaily.

"Well, he's glad to see this one," Numair remarked as they followed more slowly. "Who's the stranger?"

"His mate, Frostfur. The boss female."

Where were you? Frostfur was demanding of Brokefang. What took so long? You said you were going only to the other side of the mountain and you have been gone four nights.

Daine sighed. She'd forgotten how much she disliked Frostfur. During her time with the pack, Rattail had been Brokefang's mate. A sweeter, gentler wolf Daine had never met. After her death, Brokefang had chosen her sister. The new female pack leader was a cross, fidgety animal who had never accepted Daine.

We were traveling with two-leggers and horses, Brokefang told his mate. They can't run as fast as we can.

The only two-legger we need is *her*. Why didn't you leave those others behind? We can hunt if we are hungry. We don't need food brought to us, like the humans' dogs.

At this, Cloud, who stood between Frostfur and the horses, laid back her ears. Kitten reared up in her sling, bracing her forepaws on Daine's shoulder, and screeched at the she-wolf. Daine was shocked to hear her friend voice something that sounded so rude. Frostfur looked at them and bared her teeth.

"Enough!" the girl ordered. "We're friends. That means you, Frostfur, and these horses. If you disobey, you'll be sorry."

Frostfur met her eyes, then looked away. You are different, the wolf said. You and the pony both. I suppose you don't even realize it. The pack never was the same after you left it. How much will you change us this time?

Brokefang nuzzled his mate. It will be good, he told Frostfur. You'll see. Take us to the pups. You'll feel better when the pack is one again.

Without reply, Frostfur ran down a trail that led north. The wolves and their guests followed. The path took them on a line that ran parallel to the lake. For a game trail it was wide and, if the tracks and marks on the trees and shrubs were to be believed, used by many animals, not only wolves.

"Mountain sheep," Daine commented, showing Numair a tuft of white fur that had caught on a bramble. "A wolverine, too—keep an eye out for that one. They're nasty when they're crossed." Looking up the trail, she saw each of the wolves stop to lift a leg on a pile of meat. Even the females did so, which was odd. Marking territory was normally done only by males. "Graveyard Hag, what are they doing?" she asked, naming one of Numair's gods. She trotted to the head of the line. "What is this?" she asked. "What's wrong with the meat?"

Brokefang replied, One of the two-leggers is a hunter of wolves. He leaves poisoned meat on our trails. We are telling him what we think of this. When he comes to check the meat, he will curse and throw things. It is fun to watch.

Daine laughed, and went to explain it to Numair.

They made several stops to express such opinions: twice at snares, once at a trap, and once at a pit covered with leaves and branches. Each time the wolves marked the spot with urine and dung, leaving a smelly mess for the hunter. At the last two stops, the horses and Cloud also left tokens of contempt.

"That should *really* confuse him," Daine told Numair and Kitten. "He'll never figure out how horses came to mark a wolf scent post."

A lesser trail split from the one they walked; the wolves followed it into a cuplike valley set deep in the mountainside, hidden by tangles of rock. There the woods opened onto a clearing around a pond. At the water's edge trails crossed and recrossed, and large, flattened areas in the brush marked wolf beds.

A challenge-bark came from a bunch of reeds, and five half-grown wolves, their colors ranging from brown to frosted gray, tumbled out. They still bore remnants of soft baby fur, and were in the process of trading milk teeth for meat teeth. Eyeing the strangers, they whined and growled nervously, until the pack surrounded them and shut the newcomers off from view.

Another grown wolf, a black, gray, and brown male, pranced over to say hello. "He's Longwind," Daine informed Numair. "He was baby-sitting." To the wolf she said, "Say hello to my friends. Cloud you know." As Longwind obeyed, the girl walked up to the pack. The moment the pups noticed her they backed away.

Frostfur said with grim satisfaction, I knew bringing strangers was a mistake. Brokefang nuzzled his mate, trying to sweeten her temper.

Fleetfoot stuck her nose under the belly of one of the male pups and scooted him forward. We know this isn't what you're used to, she told him, but you may as well learn now as later.

Russet gripped a female pup by the scruff of the neck and dragged her to the girl, adding, Daine is Pack, and if she is Pack, so are these others.

The female was the one to walk forward,

still clumsy on her feet, to sniff Daine's palm. She is Leaper, Russet said, and Leaper wagged her tail. The male pup trotted over. He is Chaser, commented Russet. These others are too silly to have names. At that the remaining three pups approached timidly, whining.

Daine introduced the young wolves to her friends. The pups came to accept Numair, the horses, and Cloud, but nothing could make them like the young dragon. When she went near them, they would run to hide behind an adult wolf. At last Kitten turned gray, the color that meant she was sulking, and waddled over to the pond. There she played with stones, pretending to ignore everyone.

Why is she sad? asked Russet. They are pups. They don't know any better.

"She's no more than a pup herself," Daine replied. "I can't even talk to her as I could to her ma. She looks big, but as dragons go she's a baby."

I see. Getting up, the red-coated wolf trotted over to the dragon and began to paw at her rocks. Soon they were playing, and Kitten's scales regained their normal, gold-tinged blue color.

Daine was wrestling a stick out of the jaws of a pup she had decided to call Silly when Brokefang came to say, We hunt. Since the pups accept you and Numair and the horses, will you guard them?

"We'll be honored to guard your pups," Daine told him.

The pack left, and Numair began to cook as Daine groomed the horses. The smell of frying bacon called the pups to the fire, their noses twitching. The new scent canceled some of their fear of Kitten: as long as she kept to one side of the fire and they to the other, the young wolves didn't object. When the first pan of bacon was done, Numair gave in to the pleading in five pairs of brown eyes and one pair of slit-pupiled blue, and doled it out to his audience.

After Numair, the pups, and the horses went to bed, Daine lay awake, listening to the chatter of owls and bats. At the fringe of her magic she felt immortals pass overhead. They weren't Stormwings, or griffins, or any of the others she had met before. She sensed she would not like these if they did meet. There was a nasty undertone to them in her mind, like the taint of old blood.

The pack returned not long after the creatures' presence faded in her mind. Was it good hunting? she asked Brokefang silently, so she wouldn't disturb Numair.

He came to sit with her. An old and stringy elk. He gave us a good run, though, he replied. Cloud says you are trying to fit into her skull. It sounds like an interesting thing.

I tried it once, said Daine. Cloud thinks I might do better with wolves. I would have asked before, but I needed to rest first.

Are you rested now? he wanted to know. I would like you to try it with me.

She smiled and said, All right. And thank you. Must I do anything in particular?

No. Just wait.

She closed her eyes, took a breath, let it out. Sounds pressed on her: Numair's snore, Short Snout's moan as he dreamed of rabbits, the pups chewing, Battle washing a paw. Beyond those noises she heard others belonging to the forest and air around them.

She concentrated on Brokefang until she heard fleas moving in his pelt. He yawned, so close that it felt as if he yawned inside her ears. She listened for his thoughts and found them: the odor of blood from his kill, the drip of water from the trees overhead, the joy of being one with the pack. Brokefang sighed—

Daine was sleepy; her belly was overly full and rumbling as it broke the elk meat down. She could see young Silly from where she lay; he was asleep on his back with his paws in the air. She crinkled her whiskers in a silent laugh.

The *smells,* the *sounds.* She had never been so aware of them in her life. There was the wind through pine needles, singing of rocks and open sky. Below, a mole was digging. Her nostrils flared. Here was wolf musk, the perfume of her packmates. There was the hay-and-hide scent of the horses-who-are-*not*-prey, enticing but untouchable. A whiff of flowers, animal musk, and cotton was the girl-who-is-Pack. She looked at the girl, and realized she looked at herself.

It was a jolt to see her own face from the outside, one that sent her back into herself. Daine opened her eyes. "I did it!"

Numair stirred as the pack got up. "You did what?" he asked sleepily.

Brokefang washed Daine's ear as she explained. "I was Brokefang. I mean, we were both in Brokefang's mind. We were wolves—*I* was a wolf. It was only for a few minutes, but it happened!"

The man sat up, hugging his knees. "Good. Next time you can do it longer." He looked at Brokefang. "Did it hurt you the way it hurt Cloud?"

No, the wolf replied as Daine translated. We will do it again.

The girl yawned and nodded. At last she was sleepy. "Tomorrow," she promised, wriggling down into her bedroll.

Brokefang yawned when she did. Tomorrow, he agreed, as sleepy as she was.

When she woke, it was well past dawn. Numair crouched beside the pond, with Kitten and the pack behind him, watching what he did with interest. Faint black fire dotted with white sparks spilled from his hands to the water's surface, forming a circle there. At last he sighed. The fire vanished.

"What was that?" Daine asked, dressing under the cover of her blankets.

"There's an occult net over the valley,"

he said, grimacing as he got to his feet. "It's subtle—I doubt many would even sense it—and it serves to detect the use of magic. It also would block all messages I might send to the king. To anyone, for that matter. And since this valley is hidden beneath the aura cast by the City of the Gods, no one outside can even tell the net is here."

"Wonderful," she said dryly. "So Dunlath is a secret within a secret."

Numair beamed at her. "Precisely. I couldn't have put it better."

"And this net—will it pick up *any* magic?" she asked, putting her bed to rights. "Will them that set it know you just looked at it?"

"No. A scrying spell is passive, not active. It shows what exists without influencing it."

"What's here that's so important?" Daine asked. "Stormwing patrols, two forts, a magical net—what has Fief Dunlath got that needs so much protecting?"

"We need to find out," Numair said. "As soon as you've had breakfast, I think we should see the northern part of the valley."

She ate as Numair set the camp in order and

saddled Cloud and Spots. Mangle agreed to stay with the pack after Daine convinced them—and him—that he was to be left alone. The girl then offered the carry-sling to Kitten. The young dragon looked at it, then at the still-nervous Mangle. She shook her head and trotted over to the packhorse, clearly choosing to stay and keep him company. With the small dragon by his feet, Mangle relaxed. Daine, who knew Kitten was well able to protect herself, relaxed as well, and mounted Cloud. Brokefang, Fleetfoot, and Short Snout led the way as she and Numair followed.

The group used a trail high on the mountainside, one that was broad enough for the horses, and kept moving all morning, headed north. Daine listened hard for immortals, and called a halt twice as Stormwings passed overhead.

Stop, Brokefang ordered at last. We must leave the trail here.

We will hide, Cloud told her, with Spots's agreement. Don't worry about us.

Afoot, Daine and Numair trailed the wolves through a cut in the ground that led up into tumbled rock. Brokefang crawled up to the edge of a cliff, Fleetfoot and Short Snout behind. The two humans kept low and joined them. Lying on their bellies next to their guides, they looked over the edge of the cliff.

Few trees stood in the upper ten miles of the lake's western edge: most lay in a wood between the fort structure and the river that flowed into the north end of the lake. Much of the ground between that fort and their vantage point was heaped into mounds of dirt and rock, some of them small hills in their own right. The only greenery to speak of was patches of scraggly weed.

Roads were cut into the dirt, leading down to deep pits that lay between the mounds. Men and ogres alike toiled here, dressed in loincloths and little else. Some pulled dirt-filled carts out of the pits. When they returned with empty carts, they vanished into the black, yawning holes of the mines.

Wherever she looked she saw ogres, aquaskinned beings that varied in size from her own height to ten or twelve feet. Their usually straggly hair was chopped to a rough stubble that went as low as their necks and shoulders.

They had pointed ears that swiveled to catch any sound, bulging eyes, and yellowing, peg-like teeth. She was no stranger to their kind, but most of her meetings with them had been fights of one sort or another. This was the first time she had seen any used as beasts of burden, or as slaves. All of them appeared to be at the mercy of the armed humans who patrolled the entire area. One ogre, a sad and skinny creature, slumped to his knees. Three humans came after him, their whips raised.

Daine looked away. On her right was the lake. Barracklike buildings, some big enough to house ogres, had been erected of raw wood on the near shore. Between them, human and ogre children played under the watchful eye of an ogre female. The fort on the town's north side was well built and, to judge from the many tiny human figures that came and went, well manned. Boats lay at docks on the lake between town and fort, guarded by men.

She closed her eyes, listening for animals. In the pits she heard only a few rats and mice. Every other animal had fled the zone of destruction, and its fringes were loud with battles fought over every bit of food. In the lake she heard death. Filth lay in the water: garbage from the town and fort, waste dirt from the mines. The fish gasped for air in the lake's northern waters. Their kinfolk in cleaner water went hungry as food sources died.

Brokefang stuck his cold nose into the girl's ear. *I told you*, he said.

"Those are mines," Numair commented, his voice low. He unhooked his spyglass from his belt, opened it, and put it to his eye. "But what are they for? The opal mines around here were emptied nearly half a century ago."

"What are opals?" asked Daine.

"They are used in magic, like other gemstones. Mages will do anything to get opals, particularly black opals."

Daine was puzzled. Since her arrival in Tortall she had seen all kinds of precious stones, but not those. "What do they look like?"

Numair lifted a chain that lay around his neck, under his shirt. From it hung a single oval gem that shimmered with blue, green, orange, and gold fires. "Opals are power stones. Black ones like this are the best. They store magic, or you may use the stone to increase the strength of a spell. I saved for *years* to purchase this.

Emperor Ozorne has a collar made of them—six rows, threaded on gold wire. He has a mine somewhere, but he guards the location even more carefully than he guards his power." He glared at the mines. "Surely we would know if opal dirt were found here once more. Dunlath *is* a Tortallan fief."

The ground shook last fall, Brokefang said. See the raw earth on the mountains, behind the fort? Cliffs fell there. In spring, when the pups were new and still blind, a mage came and exploded holes where the pits are now.

"Let us speculate," Numair said when Daine finished translating. "Something of value—opal dirt, for example, or even gold—was seen in the fallen cliffs, after the earthquake. The lord of Dunlath sent for a mage with blasting expertise, doubtless a war mage, on the chance he would uncover more—and he did. It may be the same mage who destroyed the Ninth Riders. But who buys what is taken from the land? It isn't the king, or he would have told us."

Daine looked back at the mines. The ogre who had fallen was on his feet again, blue liquid—his blood—coursing down his back in stripes. "I don't care if they *are* ogres," she said quietly. "That's slavery down there, and we aren't a slave country."

"It appears they are expanding, too." Numair pointed over Daine's shoulder. Here, in a direction she had not looked before, humans and ogres with axes were hard at work, cutting down trees and dragging the stumps from the ground.

Now you see why we need you, Brokefang said, baring his teeth as he watched the tree cutting. This must stop. It *will* stop. Soon there will be no game, and everyone here will starve, even the ones who ordered this.

"We need to learn more," Numair replied. "We need to speak with those in charge, in the fief village and the castle. Then I want to get word to King Jonathan. Something is badly amiss." He inched back into the cover of the trees, Daine, Fleetfoot, and Short Snout following.

Realizing Brokefang had not come with them, Daine looked back. The chief wolf stood on the cliff, his fur bristling, his ears forward and his tail up as he growled defiance at the ruin below.

On their return to the campsite, Daine let the others go ahead as she took her crossbow and went hunting. She was in luck, finding and bagging two plump rabbits soon after leaving the trail.

Human friends often exclaimed to see her hunt. They seemed to think, because she shared a bond with animals, that she ought to go meatless.

"That's fair daft," she had said when Princess Kalasin mentioned it. "Some of my best friends are hunters. *I'm* a hunter. You eat what you're made to eat. I just make sure I don't use my power to bring game to me, and I stop listening for animal voices with my magic. I close it all off."

"You can *do* that?" Kally had asked, eyes wide.

"I must," Daine had replied. "Otherwise my hunting would be—dirty. Vile. When I go, I hunt like any other two-legger, looking for tracks and following trails. And I'll tell you something else. I kill fast and clean, so my game doesn't suffer. You know I can, too. I almost never miss a shot."

"I suppose, if that's how you do it, it's all

right," the girl had said, though she still looked puzzled.

Daine had snorted. "Fairer than them that kill an animal for its horns or skin, so they can tack it on their wall. I hunt to eat, and *only* to eat."

When she reached the camp, it was nearly dark. The pack had gone, leaving Russet, Numair, and Kitten with the pups and horses. Once Daine appeared, Russet left to hunt for himself. Numair, who had started a pot of rice, smiled when he saw her, but he looked preoccupied. From experience she knew it did no good to talk when something was on his mind, so she let him be.

Once her rabbits were cleaned, spitted, and cooking, she groomed the horses and Cloud, oiled rough patches on Kitten's hide, and wrestled with the pups. She ate quickly when supper was done, and cleaned up without bothering Numair. He wandered to the opposite side of the pond, where he stretched out on the ground and lay staring at the trees overhead.

Russet came back, grinning. All that was left of a pheasant who had not seen him in the brush was a handful of bright feathers in his fur. He panted as Daine pulled them out, then licked her face.

"Would you help me do something?" Daine asked, and explained the badger's lesson.

It sounds interesting, the young wolf answered. What must I do?

"Nothing," the girl said. "I have to come into you." Closing her eyes, she took a deep breath and let it go. All around she heard familiar noises. Numair had gone to sleep. Cloud drowsed where she stood, dreaming of galloping along an endless plain. Kitten sorted through a collection of pebbles, muttering to herself. Daine closed out everything but Russet's sounds: his powerful lungs taking air in and letting it go, the twitch of an ear, the pulse of his heart.

She drew closer and closer until his thoughts crept into her mind. On the surface were simple things, like the shred of pheasant caught on a back tooth, the coolness of the packed earth under his body, his enjoyment of being with her. Below that was the powerful sense of Pack that was part of any wolf, the feeling of being one with a group where everything was shared.

The change from her mind to his was gradual this time. It felt as if she were water sinking into earth, becoming part of him in slow bits. When he blinked, vision came in blacks, whites, and grays, and she knew she saw through his eyes. Her ears picked up the tiniest movement, from the scratch of Kitten's claws on her pebbles to the grubbing of a mouse in the reeds. He inhaled, and a rich bouquet of odors came to her: the individual scents of everyone in the clearing, wet earth, pines, the fire, moss, traces of cooked rabbit and plants.

He sniffed again, and caught a whiff of scent from the trench Daine and Numair used as a privy. The girl was amazed. She disliked that smell, and had dug the trench far from the clearing where they ate and slept on purpose. She certainly couldn't detect it with her own nose. Not only could Russet smell it clearly, but he didn't think the trench odor was bad—just interesting.

Silly galloped over to leap on Russet's back, and Daine was back within her own mind. "Thank you," she told Russet in a whisper.

Thank *you*, he replied, and trotted off to romp with the pups.

She stretched, not quite comfortable yet in her skin. The change to her own senses was a letdown. As good as her ears were, they were not nearly as sharp as the wolf's, and her nose was a poor substitute for his. While she was glad not to be able to smell the trench once more, there had been plenty of good scents available to Russet.

"At least I see colors," she told Kitten. "That's *something*."

The pack returned with full bellies as she was banking the fire. They had fed on a sheep that had strayed from its flock, reducing it to little more than a handful of well-gnawed bones.

Daine frowned when she heard this. "But that's one of the things that make two-leggers hunt you, when you eat their animals."

They will not find out, Brokefang said calmly. When you ran with the pack before, you warned us about human herds. We cannot stop eating them. They are slow, and soft, without hard feet or sharp horns to protect them. What we *can* do is hide signs of the kill. We sank what was left in a marsh, and we dragged leafy branches over the place where we killed, to hide the blood.

Instead of reassuring her, his answer made her uneasy. Here was more unwolflike behavior, a result of the pack's involvement with her. Where would it end? She couldn't even say the change was only in Brokefang, because the rest of the pack helped him. She had to think of a way to protect them, or to change them back to normal beasts, before humans decided the Long Lake Pack was too unusual—too dangerous—to live.

That plan would have to wait. The badger's lesson had tired her again. She went to bed, and dreamed of men slaughtering wolves.

In the morning Daine and Numair rode to the town of Fief Dunlath, leaving the wolves behind. Reaching the village at noon, they entered the stable yard of the town's small, tidy inn. Hostlers came to take their horses. Dismounting from Cloud, Daine took the pack in which Kitten was hidden and slung it over her shoulder, then followed Numair indoors. They stood inside, blinking as their eyes adjusted from the sunny yard to the dark common room. In the back someone was yelling, "Master Parlan! We've guests!"

The innkeeper came out and bowed to Numair. "Good day to you, sir. Ye require service?" he asked with a brisk mountain accent.

"Yes, please. I'd like adjoining rooms for my student and me."

"Forgive me, mistress," Parlan said, bowing to Daine. "I dinna see ye." He looked her over, then asked Numair, "Ye said—adjoinin' rooms, sir?"

"Yes," Numair replied. "If there's a connecting door, it must be locked."

The innkeeper bowed, but his eyes were on Daine. "Forgive me, sir—*locked*?"

Daine blushed, and Numair looked down his nose at the man. "People have sordid minds, Master Parlan." Despite his travel-worn clothes, he spoke like a man used to the obedience of servants. "I would like my student to be spared idle gossip, if you please."

Parlan bowed low. "We've two very nice rooms, sir, overlooking the kitchen garden. Very quiet—not that we've much excitement in these parts."

"Excellent. We will take hot baths, as soon as you are able to manage, please." A gold coin appeared in Numair's hand and disappeared in Parlan's. "And lunch, I think, after the baths," added the mage.

"Very good, sir," the man said. "Follow me." He led the way upstairs.

Kitten wriggled in the pack, and chirped. "Hush," Daine whispered as Parlan opened their rooms. "I'll let you out in a moment."

The room was a small one, but clean and neatly kept, and the bath was all Daine could hope for after weeks of river and stream bathing. The food brought by the maid was plain and good. Daine felt renewed afterward, enough so that she took a short nap. She was awakened by a scratching noise. When she opened her eyes, the dragon was picking at the lock on the door between the two rooms.

"Leave it be, Kit," Daine ordered, yawning. "You've seen locks back home."

The young immortal sat on her haunches, stretching so that her eye was on a level with the keyhole, and gave a soft trill. The door swung open to reveal Numair in a clean shirt and breeches. He was holding a piece of paper.

"Did I know she could do that?" he asked with a frown.

"No more did I," retorted Daine.

Numair glared at the dragon, who was investigating his room as thoroughly as she had her own. "That door was locked for a *reason*," he told her sternly. To Daine he added, "Though actually I *do* need to speak with you. We've been invited to dine tonight at the castle."

"Why?" the girl asked, rubbing her eyes.

"It's typical of nobles who live out of the way. A newcomer is worth some attention—it's how they get news. I don't suppose you packed a dress."

Since her arrival in Tortall, when her Rider friends had introduced her to breeches, she had worn skirts rarely, and always under protest. When the village seamstress showed her the only gown that would be ready in time, Daine balked. The dress was pink muslin, with lace at collar and cuffs—a lady's garment, in a color she hated. She announced she would go in breeches or not at all.

Numair, usually easygoing, sometimes showed an obstinate streak to rival Cloud's. By the time their escort came, Daine wore lace-trimmed petticoats, leather shoes, and the pink dress under a wool cloak to ward off the nighttime chill. A maid had done up her stubborn curls, pinning them into a knot at the back of her neck. Kitten's mood was no better than Daine's: told she could *not* go with them, the dragon turned gray and hid under the bed.

Their escort came after dark to guide them across the causeway to the island and its castle. Hostlers took charge of Spots and Cloud, and servants took their cloaks, all in well-trained silence. A footman led them across the entrance hall to a pair of half-open doors.

Behind those doors a man was saying, " . . . know wolves like th' back of m'hand. I tell ye, these have *got* to be werewolves or sommat from th' Divine Realms. They don't act as wolves should act. See this? An' *this*? *Laughin'* at me, that's what they're doin'!"

"My lord, my ladies," the footman said, breaking in, "your guests are here." He bowed to Numair and Daine and ushered them in ahead of him. "I present Master Numair Salmalín, of Corus, and his student, called Daine."

They were in an elegant sitting room, being

looked over by its occupants. The footman announced, "My lord Belden, master of Fief Dunlath. My lady Yolane of Dunlath, Lord Belden's wife and heiress of Dunlath. Lady Maura of Dunlath, my lady's sister."

Numair bowed; Daine attempted a curtsy. Yolane, in her thirties, and Maura, a girl of ten, were seated by the hearth fire. Though introduced as sisters, there was little resemblance between them. Yolane was beautiful, with ivory-and-rose skin, large brown eyes, a tumble of reddish brown curls, and a soft mouth. Her crimson silk gown hugged a trim body and narrow waist; deep falls of lace at her wrists drew the eye to long, elegant hands. Diamonds glittered around her neck and at her earlobes. Maura was painfully plain, a stocky child with straight brown hair, attired in a blue dress that fit badly.

Lord Belden was of an age with his wife, a lean, bearded man who showed more interest in his wineglass than in his guests. His brown hair and beard were clipped short. His clothing was equally businesslike, though his maroon brocade tunic and white silk shirt and hose were of the finest quality.

Before the nobles stood a man in rough leather. He bristled with weapons, and held a pair of wolf traps. Yolane fanned herself, trying to disperse the aroma that came from the traps; Maura held her nose. The wolfhounds that sat or sprawled at the hunter's feet rose when they saw Daine. Slowly they went to her, their wire-haired faces eager. She offered her hands for them to sniff.

"Here!" barked the hunter. "Them ain't ladies' dogs! They're fierce hunters, and no' t' be cosseted!"

Daine snickered as the hunters crowded around her, tails wagging.

"Yes, you're fine dogs," she whispered, returning their welcome. "You're *lovely* dogs, even if you do hunt wolves."

We *try* to hunt them, the chief of the wolfhounds said. The man would like us to succeed, but how can we, when wolves do such strange things?

"Tait, take those brutes away," commanded Yolane. "This is a civilized gathering."

The huntsman stalked out, whistling to his dogs. They followed obediently, with an apology to Daine.

As they went, they brushed past another man who entered, smiling wryly. He was broad-shouldered and handsome, dressed neatly in a white shirt, brown silk tunic and hose, and polished boots. His brown-blond hair was clipped short over a clean and open face. Coming up behind Numair, he said, "I hope you forgive my—"

Numair turned to look at him, and the stranger's jaw dropped. His hazel eyes opened wide in shock. "Mithros, Mynoss, and Shakith," he whispered.

Daine frowned. Until now, the only one she'd ever heard use that particular oath was Numair himself.

"Arram?" the man asked in a melodic voice. "Is that Arram *Draper*?"

Numair gaped at him. "Tristan Staghorn? They told me you were still in Carthak, with Ozorne."

THREE
FUGITIVES

"Oh, Ozorne," the newcomer scoffed. "No, I felt too—restricted, serving him. I'm my own man now—have been for a year." He and Numair shook hands.

"Tristan, you know our guest?" The lady rose from her chair and walked toward Numair, as graceful as a dancer.

"*Know* him?" replied Tristan. "My lady, this is Master Numair Salmalín, once of the university at Carthak, now resident at the court of Tortall."

Yolane offered Numair a hand, which he kissed. "How wonderful to find such beauty in an out-of-the-way place," he said gallantly. "Does King Jonathan know the finest jewel in Tortall does not adorn his court?"

The lady smiled. "Only a man who lives at court could turn a compliment so well, Master Salmalín."

"But Tristan didn't call you that," Lord Belden said coolly. "He called you Arram something."

"I was known as Arram Draper in my boyhood," explained Numair.

Tristan grinned. "Oh, yes—you wanted a majestic, *sorcerous* name when you got Master status. Then you *had* to change it, when Ozorne ordered your arrest."

Yolane and Belden looked sharply at Numair. "Wanted by the emperor of Carthak?" the woman asked. "You must have done something serious."

Numair blushed. "The emperor is very proprietary, Lady Yolane. He feels that if a mage studies at his university, the mage belongs to him." He looked at Tristan. "I'm rather surprised to see *you* here. You were the best war mage in your class."

War mage, Daine thought, startled. That's who Numair said blasted the mines and killed the Riders.

"I brought the emperor to see reason," Tristan replied, looking at Daine. "I'm sorry, little one—I didn't mean to be rude. Who might you be?"

"May I present my student?" Numair asked. "Master Tristan Staghorn, this is Daine—Veralidaine Sarrasri, once of Galla."

Yolane's lips twisted in a smirk. "*Sarra*sri?"

Daine turned beet red. The lady knew it meant "Sarra's daughter," and that only children born out of wedlock used a mother's name. She lifted her head. She was *proud* she was named after Ma.

"Are you a wizard?"

Maura's question startled Daine; she'd forgotten the girl was even in the room. "No," she replied. "Not exactly."

A manservant entered and bowed. "Ladies and lords, if it pleases you, your meal awaits."

Numair offered his arm to Yolane. She accepted it and guided him toward a door in the back of the room. "Would you explain something? We heard you were at the attack on Pirate's Swoop last year. Wasn't it from an imperial fleet? I was surprised His Majesty didn't declare war on Carthak."

"He nearly did," replied Numair. "They used Carthaki war barges, but the emperor claimed they were sold to pirates. As the king was unable to prove we were attacked by anyone other than pirates, he was forced to drop it."

Tristan offered Maura his arm with a mocking bow. The younger girl sniffed and took it. Belden, who appeared to spend much of his time in a brown study, followed them and left Daine to bring up the rear alone. For the first time in many, many months, she felt like a complete outsider. She did not like the feeling.

The dining hall was large enough to seat a household. Daine had been in many homes in the last year where servants and lords ate together, but tonight, at least, Dunlath's nobles dined alone. Four other guests were already seated at a table placed lower and at an angle to the main board. They rose and bowed when the nobles entered. Daine saw Numair halt, dark brows knit in surprise.

Tristan said, "Numair, I think you know Alamid Mokhlos, and perhaps Gissa of Rachne?" A man in a silk robe and a dark, striking woman bowed to Numair, who hesitated, then bowed in return. "They were on their way to the City of Gods and stopped to pay me a visit."

"My lord's hospitality is so good, we fear we shall be here forever," the woman said in a heavily accented voice. "It is good to see you again, Arram."

"Not Arram anymore," Tristan corrected her. "Numair Salmalín."

"That's right." Alamid had a high, cutting voice. "We'd heard you were the Tortallan king's pet mage."

Tristan introduced the remaining two men in plain tunics as Hasse Redfern and Tolon Gardiner, merchants. Yolane and Belden had taken their places at the main board, and waited with polite impatience for the introductions to end. A maid gave Daine a seat beside Maura, at a table across the room and opposite the four less important guests. Tristan steered Numair to a place next to Yolane. Daine was interested to see that Numair's seat was so far from Alamid, Gissa, and the others that he wouldn't be able to talk to them during the meal.

Her own place beside Maura was entirely out of the stream of conversation. If they strained, they could just hear what was said by the adults on the dais.

"If you're waiting for them to talk to us, you have a long wait," Maura informed her at last.

Daine came to herself with a jerk. It occurred to her that she was being rude. "I'm sorry," she apologized, and tasted her soup. It was cold.

Maura correctly interpreted the face she made. "My sister doesn't want servants eating here, as they did when our father was alive. She says the king doesn't eat with his servants, so we won't, either. That made the servants angry, so they take their time bringing meals."

A mouse was exploring Daine's shoe. She broke off a scrap of bread and fed it to him. When he finished, he whisked out of sight. "Why should the way the king eats decide how you take your meals here?"

"We're his closest relatives—third cousins

or something like that," replied Maura, eating her soup. "Yolane says if he hadn't married and had children, she might be queen today. If you're from Galla, why do you live here? And what was your name again?"

Daine looked at her dinner companion, *really* looked at her, and smiled. The girl's brown eyes were large and frank under limp bangs, and freckles adorned her cheeks and pug nose. Perhaps to preserve her ivory skin Lady Yolane never went into the sun, but her sister was a different kind of female.

"I'm called Daine, for short," she replied. "And it's a fair long story, how I came to Tortall."

"It's to be a fair long meal," said Maura. "*She* insists on having all the courses, just like at court."

The mouse had returned, with friends. The feel of their cold noses on her stockinged legs made Daine smother a giggle.

"I keep telling her, if she likes court so much, why doesn't she live there all year, like some nobles. She doesn't take the hint. Uh— Daine, don't jump or screech or anything, but there's a mouse in your sleeve."

Daine looked. A pair of black button eyes peered up at her. "That's hardly a safe place," she commented.

The mouse replied he liked it there.

"Who are you talking to?" asked Maura.

Daine blushed. "The mouse," she explained. "I understand what animals say, and they understand me. Oftentimes I forget that we aren't speaking as humans do, and I talk to them as I might to you or Numair." To the mouse she added, "Well, if a cat sees you, there will be all sorts of trouble."

"No cats in the dining hall," interrupted Maura. "Yolane hates 'em."

"I knew there was something about her I didn't like," muttered Daine.

Servants took the soup bowls, replacing them with plates laden with meat and vegetables. Daine was glad to see steam rise from her food, although none came from those that went to the head table. She mentioned it to Maura as she coaxed her mouse friend to sit beside her, rather than in her sleeve.

"The servants like me, so they try to keep my food hot. It's just hard with soup—it cools fast."

Daine hesitated, trying to decide how to ask her next question. While she thought, she continued to feed bread to the mice. "You two don't seem like sisters," she commented at last.

"Half sisters," Maura said. "Her mother came from one of the oldest families in the realm. She died a long time ago, and Father remarried when Yolane got engaged to Belden. She tells everyone my mother was a country nobody."

Daine frowned. "Forgive my saying so, Lady Maura, but your sister doesn't sound like a nice person."

"She isn't," was the matter-of-fact reply. "She cares about how old our family is and how close to the throne we are, not about taking care of Dunlath and looking after our people. And Belden's as bad as she is. Father said he's just a younger son, so he has a lot to prove."

Daine shook her head, thinking you could never tell with nobles. Sometimes they were normal humans, and sometimes they worried about the silliest things.

Maura watched the mice for a moment. "I

don't understand. Do they all come up to you that way?"

"Yes. They like me," Daine replied. "I like them."

Maura sighed. "I wish they liked *me*. I get lonesome. *She* won't let me play with commoners. All my friends in the village think I'm stuck-up now."

"Why should it matter who you play with?" asked Daine. Go sit with her, she urged the mice silently, so Maura wouldn't think Daine felt sorry for her. She's perfectly nice, you'll see.

"I don't think it should matter to anyone, but *she* says I have to think of our house and our honor." The girl turned a dangerous shade of pink. "I care more than *she* does. *She* thinks it's a big secret, but I know what's going on with her and Tristan. Oh!" She stared at her lap. A mouse stood there on his hind feet, looking her over. "Can I pet him? Will he mind?"

"Gently," Daine said. She felt sorry for Maura. From the look of things, no one seemed to care what happened to her or what she wanted. "They're shy. If you feed him, he should stay with you." Won't you? she asked the mouse.

If she feeds me, he replied. Please tell her I am partial to fruit. Humans seem to think all we eat is cheese. That's boring after a while.

Hiding a smile, Daine relayed his words to Maura, who proceeded to stuff him, and his friends. They had gone to sleep in her lap by the time the servants cleared the plates and a bard came in, carrying a lap harp. Taking a seat in front of the nobles, he tuned his instrument as the servants returned to find places around the walls. The bard played traditional songs for an hour or more. Long before he was done, Maura had gone to sleep.

Daine barely listened. Watching the adults at the main table, she realized that here was the opportunity to do what Brokefang expected her to do, deliver his request for a halt to the mining and lumber efforts. She cringed at the thought of giving such a message to these polished, self-assured humans. She also knew Brokefang wouldn't understand if she held back. Mockery and shame meant nothing to wolves.

I wish they meant nothing to me, either, she thought, making up her mind as the bard ended his last song and left the room. Forcing herself to get up, she walked out into the open space in front of the dais.

Numair looked at her, clearly puzzled. Then he guessed why she was there. He shook his head, trying to signal for her to return to her seat, but Daine fixed her eyes on Dunlath's lord and lady and ignored him.

Yolane and Belden were deep in conversation. It was Tristan who saw Daine first. Breaking off his talk with Alamid and Gissa, he looked at Daine with a raised eyebrow, then smirked. Gently he tapped Belden on the shoulder. Numair was now pointing at Daine's seat, giving her a clear order, but she shook her head. He did not have to answer to the pack; she did.

Belden called his wife's attention to the girl in pink before them. Yolane's brows snapped together. "What is it?" she asked impatiently.

Daine clenched her hands in the folds of her skirt. "Excuse me, my lord. My lady. I've been asked to speak to you by the wolves of this valley."

"*Wolves?*" asked Belden, looking haughty. "What can they say to anything?"

"Plenty," the girl said. "They live here, too, you see. They take food out of these forests, and they drink from the streams. They told me when they came, this place was near perfect." She knew her face was red by now. The huge room had gone completely silent. She'd never felt so small, or so alone, in her life. "Then *you* began digging and cutting down trees. Mine trash has started to poison the northern end of the Long Lake, did you know that? And the digging and the lumbering is scaring the game out of the valley."

To her surprise, a rough voice in the rear of the hall called, "She's right, about th' game, at least. I tried to tell ye m'self, three weeks back."

Daine looked over her shoulder. She had forgotten that the huntsman, Tait, had come to hear the bard. She ventured a smile, and he winked. Drawing her breath, feeling better, she went on. "The Long Lake Pack asked me to tell you they want you to stop. If you don't, they'll do something drastic."

"How do you know this?" Tristan's voice was too even and sincere. His eyes danced with amusement. "Did the wolves come to you in a dream, perhaps, or—"

"She has wild magic, Tristan." Numair came to stand with Daine, resting a hand on her shoulder and squeezing gently. She smiled up at him in gratitude.

"Surely you do not yet insist 'wild magic' is real," scoffed Gissa. "You are too old to pursue fables."

"It is no fable," Numair replied. "You and the Carthaki university people are like the blind man who claims sight cannot exist, because he lacks it."

"We lost sight of the point of Mistress *Sarrasri's* argument." There was a strangled note in Yolane's voice. "A pack of four-legged beasts wants us to stop mining. And cutting down trees."

"That's right," Daine said, bracing herself for what she knew was coming.

"And—if we don't"—the choked sound was thicker than ever in the woman's throat— "they'll do something—drastic. Do you know what? No, of course you don't. Perhaps— perhaps"—the strangling began to escape her now, as giggles—"they will piddle on the castle walls, or—or—"

"Howl at the sentries," Tristan suggested, grinning.

"Has she been mad for long?" Yolane asked Numair.

"You laugh at your peril," Numair warned. "This is a very different breed of wolf you're dealing with, Lady Yolane."

Yolane began to laugh, and laugh hard. Briefly she fought to get herself under control. "Maybe they'll bury their bones in my wardrobe!" she said, and began to laugh again.

Tristan smirked. "Suppose for a moment— just a moment—that you are right. Do you think we can't deal with a pack of wolves? Brute creation is in this world to serve man— not the other way around. This valley is ruled by humans."

Daine couldn't believe what she had heard. "Is that what you *really* think animals are here for?"

"No. That's what I *know* they are for. Men do not shape their concerns for the benefit of wild beasts, my dear."

Yolane had gotten herself in hand. "You are

a foolish child. Master Salmalín has indulged you too much. Why, in Mithros's name, should I care in the least about the tender feelings of a pack of mangy, flea-bitten curs?"

"Think selfishly," Daine said, trying to make these arrogant two-leggers see what she meant. "You can't go on this way. Soon you will have no forests to get wood from or to hunt game in. You poison water you drink and bathe and fish in. Even if you keep the farms, they won't be enough to feed you if the rest of the valley's laid waste. You'll starve. Your people will starve—unless you buy from outside the valley, and that's fair expensive. You'll ruin Dunlath."

Yolane's eyes glittered. "Who are you to judge me in my own castle?"

"Daine," Numair said quietly.

Daine looked at Yolane, Belden, and Tristan. They stared back at her, sure of themselves and their right to do as they wished. "Well, I tried," she muttered.

Numair bowed. "My lord, my lady—with your good will, we take our leave."

As they walked out, Daine glanced at Maura. The girl had awakened and now watched Daine with a worried frown. Daine smiled, but her lips trembled a little. She hoped Maura wouldn't think she was crazy.

Servants left the dining hall ahead of them to fetch their cloaks and to bring their horses. Within minutes they were trotting across the causeway.

"I'm sorry I didn't keep my mouth shut when you wanted," she said, trying to keep a pleading note out of her voice. "I had to speak. Brokefang wouldn't understand if we came back and said we didn't say anything to them."

He reached over to pat her back. "I know. Please calm down. You aren't the kind of girl who plunges without thinking. I wish I were more like you."

She was glad the darkness covered her blush. It was the highest compliment he had ever paid her. "But you don't plunge without thinking," she protested.

"You mean you haven't *seen* me do so. What, pray, was entering that castle tonight? If I were more cautious— Enough. What's done is done." Reaching the innyard, they gave their mounts to the only hostler still up, then went to their rooms. "Good night," he said cheerfully. "I'll see you in the morning."

Her door closed behind her, Daine used a glowstone from her belt-purse to find her candle, which she lit. Kitten, sprawled on the bed, peeped drowsily.

"You prob'ly would've hated it," Daine told her, shedding her clothes. Hanging them up instead of leaving them on the floor, a habit she'd learned in months of living in the Riders' barracks, she then slipped into her nightshirt. "The little girl is nice—Maura. But the grown-ups—" Daine shook her head as she climbed under the blanket.

Kitten, listening, chirped a question. Though she was too young to hear or to answer in mind-speech as older immortals did, talking to her was never a problem. Kitten understood Common better than some humans they had met. Daine was glad this was so, since from all she had learned in months of study, Kitten would be an infant for thirty years.

"Well, they look nice, but they're cold and proud. And something's wrong. Maura says the mage from Carthak is canoodling with her sister—Lady Yolane, she is." Daine yawned. "If Lord Belden knows, he doesn't seem to care. Put out the light, Kit, there's a girl."

Kitten whistled, and the candle went out. Muttering softly, she curled up with her back against Daine. Within seconds they were asleep.

She was dreaming that she ran with the pack, the scent of elk full and savory in her nostrils, when a voice boomed in her skull. "Daine. Daine."

Wolf body whirling, jaws ready to snap, she realized she was in bed, waking up. A gentle hand on her shoulder tugged her upright. For a brief moment she saw as a wolf saw, with grays and blacks and white the sole colors of her vision. The shadowy figure over her, lit by pale fire, doubled, then steadied back into one form. It was Numair. He had lit no candles; instead, the shimmer of his magic filled the room with a dim glow.

She felt as if she hadn't slept. "What's the hour?" she asked, yawning.

"Just after midnight watch." His voice was so quiet it wasn't even a whisper, but she heard it clearly. "Pack. We're leaving."

She blinked, wondering if she still dreamed. "*Leaving?* But—"

"Not here," he ordered. "I'll explain on the road. Pack."

She tumbled out of bed and did as she was told. Within minutes her saddlebags were ready and she was dressed. Numair poked his head through the inner door, which stood open once more, and beckoned for her and Kitten to follow.

He left the saddling of Spots, Mangle, and Cloud to her. She did it quietly, not wanting to rouse the hostlers. Kitten went into her carrypack, an open saddlebag on Mangle that allowed her to see everything as she rode. At the last minute Numair gave Daine a handful of rags, and motioned for her to cover their mounts' feet to muffle the sound of their shoes on the streets. "Did you leave money for our host?" she asked as she held Spots for Numair to mount.

"With a good tip over that, and a note of apology." He got himself into the saddle, a process she could never watch without gritting her teeth, and motioned for her to mount up. She did so without effort.

Go, she told Spots. He wants silence over speed, I think.

It is just as well, the patient gelding replied, passing the inn's gate with Daine and Cloud close behind. He is so tense, I think if I trotted, he would fall off. What's the matter?

He'll tell us, the girl promised. Do what you can to make him less tense.

I am a riding horse, not a god, was Spots's answer.

When they reached the trees where the road along the lakeshore crossed the river that flowed down from the western pass, Numair dismounted. Kneeling on the northern side of the crossing, he scratched a hole in the road, put something in it, and covered it over, patting the earth down firmly. Walking to the southern branch of the road, he performed the same curious rite.

"If you're leaving an offering to the cross-road god, his shrine is over there." Daine pointed to the little niche where the god's statue rested.

"I'm not," he replied, dusting his hands. He bowed to the small shrine. "No offense meant." Remounting, he guided Spots onto the track that led west, and beckoned for Daine to ride beside him.

"What's all this?" she asked. "Usually you give warning if we have to skip out in the middle of the night."

"I wanted things to seem normal when we got back to the inn, in case someone was listening. We have to get out of here and warn King Jonathan, but I can't send a message from under this shield. Even if I were to succeed, Tristan and his friends would know of it."

"And I guess you don't want them running off before we can get help."

"Exactly. Whatever is going on in Dunlath is big. Anything in which Tristan Staghorn is involved is a danger to the kingdom."

"But he said he didn't work for the emperor anymore."

"In addition to his other talents, he is an accomplished liar."

Hearing iron control in his voice, Daine shivered. It took a great deal to anger Numair Salmalín. She would not give a half copper for the well-being of someone who *did* make him angry. "Then why let us go? Surely he knew when he saw you that there'd be trouble."

"He let us go because he dumped enough

nightbloom powder in my wine to keep me asleep for a century. As far as he knows, I drank it."

"Did you?"

He smiled mockingly. "Of course not. Those years of working sleight-of-hand tricks in every common room and village square between Carthak and Corus weren't wasted. The wine ended up on the floor, under the table."

"He should've known you'd see the potion."

"Not particularly. When we were students, I had no skill in the detection of drugs or poisons. I knew *nothing* practical. People are impressed that I am a black robe mage from the Imperial University, but black robe studies cover esoterica and not much else. Yes, I can change a stone to a loaf of bread, *if* I want to be ill for days and *if* I don't care that there will be a corresponding upheaval elsewhere in the world. Much of the practical magic I have learned I acquired here, in Tortall. From the king, in fact."

"But if it's just Tristan shielding this place, can't you break through? Oh, wait—you think those other two wizards are helping him."

He smiled. "There were *five* mages in that banquet hall. Tristan called Masters Redfern and Gardiner merchants, but if they are, it is only as a cover occupation. They have the Gift, too."

Daine guessed, "Another thing Tristan doesn't know you can tell?"

The man nodded. "From the way the others defer to him, he is in charge of what is transpiring here. That means this affair is the emperor's business. Tristan has been his dog for years—only Ozorne can tell him where to bite."

"Nice," growled Daine. "Then Tristan did for the Ninth Riders?"

"I'm afraid so, magelet. It is probable those missing soldiers met the same fate as well."

"He's got a lot to answer for," she snapped. "*And* that emperor. But why here? Why take an interest in Dunlath, of all places?"

"That's an excellent question. I would like to have it answered. Ozorne does *nothing* unless there is something in it for him. What could Dunlath offer the Emperor Mage?"

A half-familiar whisper made Daine look around, then up. Suddenly she felt exposed on the riverbank. "Where can we get under cover?"

"I see trees over there—"

Mangle, Spots, the trees, she ordered silently. Fast!

The horses leaped forward. Numair almost fell before he grabbed his saddle horn. I thought we broke him of not holding onto the reins when he rides, Daine said to his mount as their group hid under the trees.

I thought so too, replied Spots.

Dismounting, the girl went forward until she could see the sky. A pair of odd shapes reeled overhead, outlined by moonlight, their presence an unpleasant shadow in her mind. It took a moment to identify what she saw: bat wings, spread wide to lift a body not made for flight. Long, wedge-shaped heads craned, searching the ground below. Only when the great creatures gave up and flew north did she see them clearly against the just-past-full moon. They were horses, and something was wrong with their feet.

She had met winged horses. They were shy creatures who tended to keep out of human sight. She sensed them as she could other immortals, and their presence in her mind was never unpleasant.

Returning to Numair and the horses, she

asked softly, "If a winged horse is an evil immortal—if something's *wrong* with one—would it have a special name?"

"Hurrok," Numair said. "The name is a slurring of 'horse-hawk.' They have a carnivore's fangs, and claws, not hooves. Their eyes are set forward in their skulls, as a predator's are."

"Goddess bless," she whispered, her skin prickling. "That's *awful*."

"Is that what you sensed? Hurroks?"

"Yes," she said, remounting Cloud. "And I did once before, too. I think it was the first night we were at the wolves' meeting place." Listening to the animal voices all around, she heard familiar ones. She called to them, and they agreed to come. "Let's wait a moment," she suggested. "The pack's near."

"Daine, I want to be out of this valley by dawn."

"Don't worry," she told him. "I said they're close, didn't I? We can ride a little more if it will make you happy."

"It—stop." He held up a hand, as if he listened for something. "They know we're gone," he said at last. "They're searching along the net."

A lump formed in her throat. "What do we do?"

He smiled. "Unveil our insurance." He raised his hands. Black fire that sparkled with points of white spilled out of his palms, arching up and around him and Spots, who shook his head.

I wish he wouldn't do this when he's on me, the gelding said nervously. *It's really very upsetting.*

Daine could see his point, but told him, *If you're a wizard's horse, you should be used to it. And you are a wonderful mount for him—patient, willing, gentle. I know he couldn't manage without you.*

Spots blew through his nose, pleased by the compliments.

Wrapped in a shroud of glittering fire, Numair pointed to the northern road below. Black fire shot from his finger like a lightning bolt, crackling as it flew downhill. Shifting his aim to the south, he loosed a second bolt.

"What was that?" Daine asked, startled.

"Those things I buried at the crossroads? Once activated, as I just did, they release simulacra of a man shrouded in my Gift, riding hard on the road. Now Tristan has three of me to chase, and the ones that ride north and south will appear much more like the real me than I do."

But they will see Daine with only one of you, Cloud pointed out. The girl passed it on.

The look on Numair's face was one of smug satisfaction. "The magical cloak on my simulacra is very large, and very sloppy, enough to cover more than one person. *Just* the thing a sheltered academic like me would have for concealment, since I'm unused to fieldwork."

"But they *know* you," Daine argued. "They know you handle immortals for the king. Wouldn't they see you *must* have learned something practical by now?"

"Magelet, one thing I have learned is that humans cling to their first knowledge of you, particularly if they have no experience of you once you've changed. Tristan, Alamid, and Gissa knew me in Carthak, where I was a book-bound idiot."

Daine shook her head. She thought her friend placed too much trust in the enemy mage's stupidity.

There was a yip nearby, and the pack streamed out of the trees, Brokefang in the lead. They gathered around the horses, tails wagging. Kitten stuck her head out of the pack and chirped to Russet. Mangle held still unhappily as the wolf braced himself against the cob's withers to lick Kitten's nose.

Where are you going? Brokefang asked. Why are the horses' feet covered?

"The humans are up to no good," Daine told her friend, speaking aloud for Numair's benefit. "We have to warn the king, and for that we must get out from under the magic they put over the valley."

Brokefang backed up so he could see both Daine and Numair. You are leaving?

"To alert the king," Daine reassured him. "He will stop the mining and tree cutting."

I do not know your king. I know only you. You said that you would help us.

"But I *am* helping," Daine protested. The other wolves, looking worried, sat down to listen. "We're going to get help."

That is help for two-leggers. You are needed here.

"Daine, we have to go," said the man quietly.

She hesitated. There was something odd in Brokefang's eyes. Dismounting, she knelt before the chief wolf, tangling her hands in his ruff. Eyes closed, she opened up her mind to his, and his alone, listening hard to the tumble of ideas and images in his skull.

Brokefang was afraid. New thoughts came thick and fast now, more every day, and he did not understand them all. It had taken him this way before, after the girl-who-is-Pack left, in the time when men drove them from their home. Then he had no one to turn to, no one in the pack who would understand and explain these thoughts. He had borne them alone for months, until they slowed to a trickle. The trickle he could bear. Then the girl had come again, and new thoughts roared through his brain like a flash flood.

"Poor Brokefang," she whispered, rubbing her friend's ears. "I don't s'pose wolves get headaches, but if they did, you'd have a grand one."

"Daine, those simulacra won't last after dawn!" hissed Numair.

She looked at him. He was keeping an eye on the road to the village and trying not to grip Spots's reins too tightly. She had to make a decision, and make it fast. He didn't need her to do what was necessary—she would only distract him. On the other hand, she was the only one who could help this wolf.

Going to Mangle, she undid Kitten's pack and the pack that held her things. "I can't go with you," she said as she worked. "Brokefang needs me."

"This is no time for sentiment! Here you're in *danger* until help comes!"

"And they aren't?" she asked, indicating the pack. "They're changed because of *me,* Numair. Me. I didn't even know I *had* magic when this pack saved my life, but my head must have been wide open, and all the magic spilled out. Now they need help to deal with what happened to them when I didn't know anything. I can't let them down, Numair. I'm sorry."

"So you'll let *me* down?" He was so worked up that Spots was shifting position nervously. "What if something delays my return?"

She smiled at him. "You know I can fend for myself in the woods better'n most anybody. I've my crossbow. I'll be fine."

He drew a deep breath. "I could *make* you come with me."

She knew only grave concern for her would make him voice a threat, so she bore him no grudge. "Maybe you could and maybe you couldn't, but while we found out, Tristan would see you doing something your whatchumacallems weren't."

"Simulacra," he corrected automatically.

"Whatever."

He stared down at her, eyes shadowed. "You are too stubborn for your own good," he said at last.

"That's what Ma told me, all the time." Smiling, she added, "If it was you in my shoes, you'd say the same."

He sighed. "Very well. Stay on the mountainsides. Keep moving. Leave the forts alone, the castle, the village—*everything,* understand? Otherwise I will chain you in the worst dungeon I can find when I get my hands on you again"

"Yes, yes," she told him. "Now scoot. The sooner you leave, the sooner you can return." Mangle, go with him, she added. It will get you away from the wolves for a day or two.

Thank you, the cob said gratefully. He trotted off, heading for the western pass, and Spots turned to follow.

"Wait," Numair said. "How *will* I find you, when I return?"

"Spots will know. Please leave. You still have a ride to the pass."

The man reached a hand down, and she gave him hers. He squeezed it gently. "Be careful. Stay out of sight."

"I'll be fine," she assured him.

Spots trotted quickly after Mangle, muffled hooves thudding on the ground. Daine watched them go, feeling a bit forlorn.

FOUR

BROKEFANG ACTS

He mustn't worry, Brokefang said. The pack will keep you safe.

"I know," she whispered. "Besides, who needs humans?" she added more cheerfully, looking at the wolves' faces. "All they do is slow me down and screech when they see my friends. Most humans, anyway."

I like the stork-man, protested Brokefang.

So do I, added Short Snout. Fleetfoot, Russet, and Battle yipped agreement.

He is a good pack leader for you, Brokefang went on. Humans are like wolves. We all need a pack. He looked at Cloud, and added, Or a herd.

"Not me," the girl said, fastening her things to Cloud's saddle. "I can hunt alone."

No, Brokefang said. It is not just for food that you need a pack. It is for warmth, and the pack song. The wolf who sings alone is not happy.

We could chat all night, Cloud put in tartly. Or we can get away from here. The first thing the humans will do when they cannot find Numair is send hunters.

We will move faster if you ride, Russet said. Kitten can ride on me, if she promises not to scratch.

The young dragon chirped and tried to climb out of her carry-sack. Daine helped her, and placed her on Russet. Gently Kitten gripped his fur in all four paws, balancing herself comfortably. Daine looked at the odd picture they made, shook her head, and mounted Cloud. Brokefang trotted to the head of the line. The pack followed in single file, with Daine and Cloud bringing up the rear.

They reached the wolves' meeting place shortly before dawn. Frostfur and the pups were there to greet them. As the wolves celebrated the reunion of the pack, Daine unsaddled Cloud and rubbed her down. The girl noticed that Kitten, still on Russet's back, ended up as part of the ceremony by accident. To her amusement, and Kitten's pleasure, the pups waved their tails slightly at the dragon this time, even if they still would not approach her.

Once Cloud was tended, Daine removed her boots and crawled into her bedroll, though she wasn't drowsy yet. Sharp Nose and Frolic took the pups for a hunt. Most of the others settled around Daine, while Frostfur lay at the pond's edge, within earshot. Kitten stretched out by the girl and went promptly to sleep.

Now, Brokefang said, did you speak to the two-leggers?

"Yes. They won't do anything. They laughed at me. I told you they would."

Why? Longwind wanted to know. What is there about you that is funny?

"They don't see me the same way you do. To them I'm only a girl-child. They think they know all there is to know," Daine told them. "They think they don't have to listen to me. Would you try to tell an eagle how to hunt?"

Did you *try*? inquired Russet. Did you say they are driving off game and killing fish?

"Yes. They don't care. They say they can use the valley as they please."

I didn't think you would be much help, Frostfur said tartly. What are you good for, except to talk to?

That stung. Daine glared at Brokefang's mate. "I'd like to see you do any better, Mistress Know-it-all."

Frostfur bit a flea that was nibbling her backside and did not answer.

"The king will help," Daine said to Brokefang, wanting him to believe and wait for aid, not try something on his own. "The two-leggers are up to something bad here, and he will set it right."

I do not know of kings, the wolf replied. To me they are just two-leggers.

Exactly, Fleetfoot said. We have yet to see two-leggers fix the harm they do. To Daine she added, You are not a two-legger to me— you are People.

Longwind sighed. Brokefang's uncle, he was the oldest of the pack, with gray hairs in the black fur of his muzzle. You were right to act, Brokefang. I questioned you, until you made me submit. I was wrong. At least now we have made a beginning.

Daine sat up, suddenly wary. "What d'you mean, you've made a beginning?"

It was fun. That was Russet, whose eyes shone with delight. You should have been with us. Can I show her? he asked Brokefang. Please?

Short Snout yipped agreement; Longwind stirred the dust with his tail. Frostfur sat up, watching Daine with an odd, smug look in her amber eyes.

Very well, Brokefang consented.

Russet yapped gleefully and trotted into the reeds. He returned dragging something that looked like a big stick.

Do not worry, Brokefang told Daine as Russet approached her bedroll. We did the same thing as with the sheep we ate, the tricks to hide our trail.

Reaching Daine, Russet dropped the "stick" on the ground, tail waving. His trophy was an ax—one of the big ones used by woodsmen to cut down trees. Daine touched the handle, just to confirm it was real. "How—" she croaked, her throat dry. Grabbing the water bag, she drank, then put it aside. "How many of these do you have? Just this?"

Oh, no, Battle replied. We took all the ones we could find in the tree cutters' camp.

It was safe, Fleetfoot assured the girl. Having traveled with Daine and Numair, she knew the odd things these friends insisted be done in the name of safety. The humans don't den where they cut trees. They den with other two-leggers, by the lake. Only the forest People saw us—they wouldn't interfere.

Daine lurched to her feet. "Where's the rest?"

Russet led her to a spot in the reeds. The girl counted, not believing her eyes. Since Numair and she had gone to the castle, the wolves had stolen fourteen big axes, and five two-man saws.

"Goddess bless," she squeaked, and sat down hard. In all the years she had associated with animals, before and after she got control of her wild magic, she had never seen an animal do something like this. This was thinking about the future. This was knowing tools were separate from the men who wielded them.

We stopped the cutting, Brokefang said.

Without these, humans won't destroy more trees. They won't make the noise that frightens deer and elk.

"You don't understand. They'll come after you, just as they did back home."

Only the hunter, the one with the dog pack, can track wolves, Longwind said.

"Tait," mumbled Daine. "His name is Tait."

None of the others can track us, Longwind went on. And Brokefang has a plan for Tait.

Short Snout grinned. I *like* the plan, he said.

Suddenly the night caught up with Daine. It was dawn; she was exhausted. Getting to her feet, she dusted her bottom and went to her bedroll. "Don't do *anything* until I wake," she ordered as she crawled into it. "Not one thing, understand? We'll talk later."

Don't be upset, Fleetfoot advised, curling up on the girl's free side. Brokefang knows what to do.

"That's what frightens me," Daine muttered, and her eyes closed.

As she slept, she dreamed. Ma tended flowers, golden hair pinned up, out of the way. A man with antlers rooted in his curly brown hair watched. Leaning on the garden wall, he was a handsome, muscular creature dressed in a loincloth and nothing else. When he moved, hints of green showed in his tan skin. Her mother looked at him, shading her eyes against the sun as her lips moved. The man laughed silently, white teeth flashing. Except for the lack of sound, she could have been someplace real, watching from the garden gate.

A bluejay screamed, *Thief, thief!* The dream ended and Daine opened her eyes, feeling *very* confused. A year before she'd had a similar vision of her mother and the stranger. What did it mean? Were the vision, and this dream, Ma's way of saying she was at peace in the Realms of the Dead? What part did the horned man play? From all Daine had heard, the Black God's domain was reserved for humans, and he was no human. For that matter, what she had just experienced was too vivid for a dream—her dreams were bits and pieces of tales that seldom made sense and never felt real.

I say she ought to do it, if she is Pack. The snarling voice was Frostfur's. Why leave the pups to search and fail to bring down game four times out of five when *she* is here?

Daine sat up. The pack stood around the chief wolves, in the middle of the lead-the-hunt ceremony.

Call the game to us, Frostfur ordered, coming over to Daine, ears forward and tail up, to force the girl to submit to her as other females of the pack did. Bring us a nice, fat buck. Why must we take chances when you are here, getting your smell all over our camp? Either you are Pack, and that means you obey me, or you are not. *Obey!*

"No," Daine said, meeting the female's eyes squarely.

Frostfur's hackles rose. She drew her upper lip back, baring strong teeth.

Daine crouched. "Do I tell you how to deal with the pack females?" she demanded. "I let you rule your way, and *you* do not tell *me* how to handle other People. If you weren't a wicked, nasty vixen, you never would've mentioned it."

Frostfur growled, a low, grating noise that started at the bottom of her deep chest and forced its way through her throat.

"Don't make me show you what else I learned while I was away," Daine warned. "You won't like it." Her eyes locked onto the wolf's, and held them.

The moment stretched out like the tension on a bowstring. Frostfur broke the staring contest first. She wheeled and plunged into the reeds. Hidden, she called to Brokefang. *She will turn on us!*

The pups whined, looking from Brokefang to the plants that hid their mother. *It's all right,* the pack leader said. *Go on. We will bring you meat.*

Leaper yipped in apology/agreement, and followed her mother. The other pups and the pack females did the same. Fleetfoot was last. She turned in front of the reeds, looked at Daine, and whined.

The girl smiled. "It's all right," she told the brown-and-gray female. "We've just never gotten along." Fleetfoot yipped in sad agreement, and vanished into the reeds. "I'm sorry, Brokefang."

He came over and licked her cheek. *Will you hunt with us?*

Daine smiled. "No, thanks. I have provisions."

Is there cheese? Short Snout wanted to know. Russet says it tastes good.

"I'll give you some when you return," Daine promised. "And you'll get round and fat, like a sheep." Short Snout bared his teeth in a silent wolf laugh.

We hunt, Brokfang said, and trotted off, the other males behind him. Soon the adult females, with the exception of Frostfur and Battle, left the reeds and followed. They had been gone only a moment when Frostfur went after them. Daine smiled. It seemed that a new skill, like sulking, couldn't stand up to the demands of Frostfur's stomach.

Kitten tugged at Daine's belt-pouch. The girl kept flint and steel there, and this was Kitten's way to say it was breakfast time. "I s'pose you're right," she told the dragon. "We'd all feel better for some food."

Working quickly, she built a mound of tinder and wood in the fire pit and set it to blazing. Looking up, she saw that the pups, Battle, Cloud, and Kitten had each brought a good-sized branch for her fire.

"You're learning new things too quick for me," she said. "Thank you. I think there's a sausage in my packs that might feed us."

You don't have to give me any, Cloud said with a shudder. I don't know what meat eaters see in that stuff.

Once she had fed everyone, Daine went to clean up. Not wanting to bathe in the pond, where soap would linger in water drunk by the wolves, she used a stream nearby. On her return to the clearing she found the pups, Cloud, and Kitten fast asleep. It was warm for autumn. Battle was cooling off, lying belly-down on the damp earth by the pond.

"You know the thing I've been trying?" she asked the tawny-pelted female. "I did it with Brokefang and Russet."

When you ride inside them, Battle answered. Russet said it was fun. Do you want to try it with me?

"If you don't mind," the girl said.

Very well. Battle closed her eyes and rested her chin on her feet. All I ask is that we not run around. It is too hot.

Daine grinned. "Fair enough." Sitting next to Battle, she first listened around her, checking for any sense that enemies were close. All she heard was the normal chatter of forest dwellers: squirrels, birds, and the like. Feeling safe, she focused on Battle. The joining happened faster than ever. Settling into the female's mind, she felt as if she belonged there. Perhaps Cloud had been right, and she was practically a wolf.

Battle checked the pups with one drowsy eye. They were hardly pups anymore. Soon they would hunt with the pack. She was sorry they had grown so fast. Watching over them was more fun when they were small and fuzzy.

Gazing at each of the young ones through Battle's eyes, Daine realized that even in daylight the wolf had no color vision. On the other hand, she hardly needed it. The marks on each pup's face and body were clearer to Battle's eyes than Daine's, and she could tell each pup's scent from the others with the wolf's vivid sense of smell. Battle inhaled and identified the scents that came into her nose for Daine. She inhaled again, enjoying Daine's fascination with odors as if she too smelled them for the first time.

Eventually the girl returned to her own

body. Heavy-eyed, she crawled on all fours to her bedroll, turned three times against her rumpled blankets, and went to sleep curled up in a tight knot. When she woke, the late sun shone through treetops as shadows collected below. She had slept through the wolves' return. Brokefang was sprawled beside her, gorged on deer meat and fast asleep.

She touched him to ask, May I join with you?

Brokefang opened one sleepy eye. Do I have to wake up?

I don't think so.

The eye closed. Then go ahead.

She was learning how to listen, to bring herself speedily into his mind. Now, as with Battle, she made the changeover quickly. With Battle fresh in her memory, she saw how different the pack leader's mind was, not in terms of size, but of space. Numair had said, in an anatomy lesson, that humans used little of their brains. She knew that animals were the same, though they used more of what lay between their ears than humans did. For Brokefang the difference was that each nook and cranny in his skull was packed with information and ideas. He knew he would die, as would his packmates and children. He saw humans not as simple threats, but as creatures in their own right, living in packs, with thoughts and plans and reasons for what they did. He understood the animals he preyed on had lives and customs of their own, different from wolves' but with meaning for the creatures involved. It was a rushing-in of knowledge that he frantically tried to keep up with in his waking hours, with only limited degrees of success.

She withdrew hastily, and found her cheeks were damp with tears. Sitting up—wincing because she had gone stiff—she wiped her eyes on her sleeve. For a moment she thought there was something longer and hairier where her nose should be, but when she touched her face, it was gone, if it had even existed.

What's wrong? asked Cloud. Why were you crying?

Daine jumped. She hadn't known the pony was watching. I feel *terrible,* she confessed to her oldest friend. I feel as if I took something from him. As if I ruined his innocence, and yours, and it looks as if I'm ruining the rest of the pack, too. Maybe they won't be as bad as you or Brokefang, but none of you will be happy doing normal People things anymore.

So you picked up that stupid human habit of blaming yourself for things you didn't or couldn't control, retorted Cloud dryly. You did not force Brokefang to care for your wounds that night, any more than you forced me to bite you and get your blood on my teeth all those times. Just be careful who you bleed on in future. Now, come and get these burrs out of my tail. That will give you something *useful* to do.

Daine blew her nose. Cloud's horse sense spoke to her own common sense, as it always had. You aren't a god, she told herself sternly, rubbing the tip of her itchy nose until it was pink. Coarse, dark hairs fell off it into her lap. Where had they come from?

She looked at her pony and smiled. If you're so smart, then you don't need me, she told the mare.

Cloud glared and stamped. Biting back a groan, Daine lurched to her feet. "I'm coming, I'm coming," she said, picking her way through the slumbering wolves. Kitten, with a chortle, came to help as well.

Daine hunted in the gathering twilight,

bringing down a pair of pheasants. As she cooked them, the pack, including the pups, revisited the carcass of the deer they had slain to finish it off. When they returned, they slept again. After a few games of stone, paper, knife with Kitten, Daine joined them.

It was a bad night. She tossed and turned, dreaming she heard a low, nasty hum in the sky overhead. When she woke and listened she heard nothing, and her clothes were sweat-soaked. The hum began once more when she went back to sleep.

Fireballs exploded without warning inside her eyelids, startling her awake. Once her eyes were open, she saw nothing. If hurroks or Stormwings passed overhead in the dark, she couldn't sense them.

She wasn't alone. Kitten woke several times, cheeping plaintively. After the third wake-up, she crawled in with Daine, something she hadn't done for months. She slept better after-ward, but the girl could feel her shiver all night long. The wolves moaned and twitched with disagreeable dreams. Twice they woke Daine with their growling and snapping at invisible enemies.

Daine gave up at dawn and went to bathe and dress. When she came back, the wolves were assembling for another hunt. They ate often when they could, and a single deer was not enough for nine adults and five rapidly growing youngsters.

We do not need to leave one of the pack behind, Brokefang was telling his mate. Daine can look after the pups. She is not a wolf, but her weapons serve her as claws and fangs do us. And you know yourself that Cloud will fight. Let all the adults hunt today.

Frostfur's head drooped. She was tired and didn't want to argue with him. To Daine she said, Old White help you if any harm comes to my pups.

"Old White?" she asked, trying to remember if she'd heard the name.

Old White and Night Black are the first wolf and his mate, Brokefang said. They lead the First Pack. And it is unwise to threaten Daine with Old White, he told his mate. If he comes, he will nip you for using his name lightly.

Frostfur bared a fang in wolf disdain, and the pack left the clearing. The pups whined. They were too big to enjoy being left behind.

"You'll get your chance," Daine told them. "You have to build up your strength and your wind before you can keep up with the pack."

Her listeners were not cheered. They remained edgy, constantly fighting with one another. They teased Cloud, nipping at her flanks, until she placed a gentle, but still firm, kick on Silly's ribs. Chaser bit Kitten a little too hard, and got a scratch on the nose as his reward.

"If I have to tell you to stop it once more—" Daine warned.

Leaper yapped crossly and raced through a trail that led east, out of the clearing. The other pups followed.

"Goddess bless!" Daine went after them, tracking them down the path and planning dreadful things to do when she caught them. "I should have known any pups of Frostfur's would be a pain," she muttered, coming to open ground. Here the rocks that hid the wolf camp ended. Between them and the forest below was a meadow with grass so tall that any young wolves could play hide and pounce.

The stream where Daine bathed was near: she went to it and scrubbed her cheeks. As she did, she heard a sour note among the animal voices around her: someone nearby was dying.

Looking around, she found her patient in a tree on the far edge of the open grass. He sat in a knothole, shivering. Walking down the gentle slope of the meadow, she sent love and reassurance ahead until she stood below him. "Come, tree brother," she called, holding up her hands. "Let me look at you."

The squirrel opened runny eyes. He was too sick to talk. The source of his illness was plain: deep gashes on his back oozed fluid. He was far gone in fever, and his breathing was wet and difficult. As he ventured from his perch he missed his grip, his claws too weak to hang on. Daine caught him as he fell.

She sat, cradling the animal against her shirt. "You pups stay right here," she called. "And play quiet for a minute or two. Poor little man," she whispered.

She leaned back, using the squirrel's tree as support, and closed her eyes. With her magic she looked deep into the body cradled in her arms. The copper light that was the squirrel's life force flickered. Goddess, don't let me fail, she thought, and went to work.

The lungs were first. She made her power into liquid fire and poured it in to dry them. The animal's breathing cleared. Next she tended his blood, scorching out illness as she wove through his veins. Turning to his wounds, she burned off all the infection. The flesh was laid open down to the bone, the edges as clean as if cut by a knife.

Stormwing? she asked the squirrel, picturing one for him.

Yes, he replied. One landed on my branch, without any warning at all.

She nodded, unsurprised. Why would a being that fed on human misery care if it hurt an animal? Just a little more, she told her patient, and concentrated, knitting sliced muscle together. Next came the fat layer, dangerously thin in this squirrel because fever had burned much of it off. Coaxing and pushing with her power, she built it up until it covered the newly healed muscle. Last came new skin to seal his body again.

Finished, she relaxed, enjoying the fresh air and the sun on her face. When she opened her eyes, the squirrel was searching her pockets for edibles. I'm *hungry,* he explained.

Sunflower seeds in my jacket pocket, she told him. The squirrel thrust his head in and began to eat. Looking for her charges, Daine found them seated nearby, watching her and the squirrel with interest.

"Where's Kit?" she asked.

The pups looked past her, and the girl craned around the edge of the tree that supported her back. Several yards away Kitten sat on her hindquarters, staring down the slope of the ground under the trees. Her skin was changing from pale blue to a brilliant, hard-edged silver. It brightened until she actually began to glow. Opening her mouth, she *shrieked*.

Terrified, the squirrel raced up into the safety of his tree. Daine lurched to her feet. Never had she heard Kitten make such a sound, and she was afraid she knew why the dragon did so now. Ignored during her concentration on healing, a warning drone balanced against a high, singing note in her magical ear. The deep sound was so ugly it made her teeth ache.

"Back to the meadow!" she yelled at the pups. *"Hide!"* She ran for Kitten, who had yet to stop screeching. Stooping to grab the dragon, she saw what Kitten was looking at, and froze.

Over a dip in the ground appeared one clawed hand. Another hand followed. The claws were bright silver, the mark of an immortal. They groped for a hold on the flat of the ground; finding one, they gripped, digging into the earth.

The creature's head topped the rise. It was reptilian, pointed, with slits for nostrils and deep-set, shadowed eyes. It swung to the right, quite slowly, then to the left. At last it returned to the center of its field of vision: Daine and Kitten.

Daine was cold—very cold. Her breath, and Kitten's, formed small clouds in the air. Neither of them could move. Frost grew everywhere between them and the stranger, as if an entire winter night had been crushed into a few moments.

The monster dragged its long, heavy body over the ridge, taking its time. Its skin was beaded in colors that ranged from emerald to fiery gold, passing through bronze and jade green on the way. Daine shuddered: in mortal animals, such bright markings usually meant the wearer was poisonous.

Slowly it advanced, moving right fore and left hind foot, then left fore and right hind, in a gait that was half skip, half waddle. The tail that dragged behind it bore a knobbed bone rattle, like that of certain desert snakes.

When it had crossed nearly half the distance between them, the creature opened its mouth and hissed. Its teeth were silver, curved and sharp, predator teeth. Worse, when it hissed, two fangs dropped down on bone hinges. At the tip of one a small drop of silvery liquid formed, grew large, fell.

A shaggy body flew out of the brush to fasten on the green creature's wrist, but jaws that could make quick work of elk bone barely dimpled the green creature's flesh. The pup she'd named Runt snarled defiance as he hung on. Leaper grabbed the creature's other forepaw. Chaser and the pup named Berry darted at the immortal's sides, yapping furiously, while Silly went for the rattle on its tail.

Silly went flying, the rattle broken off in his mouth. Now the immortal used its tail for balance as it rose onto its hind legs. Upright it was barely taller than Daine, though powerfully built. With quick, efficient blows of its head it knocked away the four who attacked from the front.

Kitten darted forward when the creature's eyes left hers. When it swung at her, she seized its paw and bit down, hard. The wolves' jaws had not marked the thing, but the bite of another immortal had more effect. Dark blood welled up to drip on the leaves, hissing where it struck the ground. With a snarl, the thing hurled Kitten into a clump of mountain laurel ten yards away.

That gave Daine the angry strength to break its hold on her mind. She flung herself to one side and yanked a large rock from the earth. "Pick on someone your own size!" she yelled, and threw.

The stone hit the creature's muzzle and shattered. Daine rolled, scrabbling for another rock, but the immortal was on her. Seizing her by the back of her shirt, it lifted her clear of the ground. She had no way to avoid its eyes. Its power caught and held her again. Details fixed themselves in her mind as her captor opened its jaws: dark blood welling from the cut left by her rock, the greens-and-spice scent of its breath, the high, singing note that cut through the harsh jangle in her mind.

Then she heard a sound such as she had

never before heard in her life, a rumbling, ear-bursting shriek that made her think of rocky avalanches. Her captor released her; she crashed to the ground. Free, she scrambled away without understanding *any* of what was taking place.

The jangling sound of the fierce immortal was gone, leaving only high singing in her mind. Gasping, she turned to find the enemy. It hadn't moved from where it had dropped her, and it was no longer green. It had turned gray and dull, looking for all the world like a statue. It was not breathing.

"Horse Lords," she whispered in awe.

Seeing movement in the corner of her eye, she spun. A new immortal walked by, intent on the statue. Taking him in, the girl decided she must be dreaming. She had seen many strange creatures since coming to Tortall— ogres, trolls, winged horses, unicorns, griffins, and more—but the green thing and this one were entirely outside her experience.

Like her attacker, this immortal was similar to a lizard. Walking on its hind legs, it held its long tail off the ground, reminding her of ladies raising their little fingers as they sipped tea. It was taller than Daine's sixty-five inches, taller even than Numair's six and a half feet. Slender and graceful, it had long, delicate paws, fragile-looking bones, and silver talons. Its beaded hide was the pearly dark gray of a thunderhead, with paler gray belly scales.

Stopping at the newly made statue, the stranger broke off a finger, sniffed it, then nibbled. The finger crunched like gravel in its jaws. —*Too raw.*— The voice sounded like a whisper of flutes. —*They really must weather for a decade or so before they lose that acrid aftertaste.*—

Kitten had recovered from her unexpected flight. Chattering frantically, she galloped to the newcomer on all fours and halted by its knee.

"Kit, *no!*" Daine called, but her voice emerged only as a squeak.

The immortal cocked its head. —*Little one, you are far from home.*— Something about that sounded male, and fatherly. —*Where is your mother?*—

Kitten rose onto her haunches, gripping the stranger's leg as she peered up into his eyes. From her throat spilled a variety of sounds Daine had never heard her voice before, in tones that rose and fell like genuine speech.

The immortal looked at Daine. His eyes were deep gray with slit pupils, impossible to read. Neither was there any emotion in the voice that spoke in her mind: —*The little one says you are her mother. You have not the appearance of a dragon. Did an experiment go wrong, to trap you in a mortal shape?*—

Daine knelt to cuddle Berry, who had crept to her with ears down, whining. "You're a brave wolf," she told the pup. To the immortal she said, "Kit's real ma was killed defending my friends and me soon after she gave birth. I've been looking after Kitten—Skysong, her name is really—ever since."

The immortal looked at Kitten as the remaining pups joined Daine. —*What did you take from the humans, Skysong? Or is it this mortal who stole?*—

Kitten squawked indignantly; Daine's fading blush returned in full strength. "We didn't steal anything!"

—*Then you were foolish to stand between a Coldfang and thieves.*— The immortal's tone was one of cool interest, not anger or scorn.

Hearing that, Daine calmed down. She pointed to the statue. "What did you call it again?"

—Coldfang. *They track thieves in all realms, divine, mortal, or dead, and will guard a thing until the end of time. Men brought this one to the camp where they cut trees, last night. I followed her to see what is going on. She picked up a trail there and kept to it since dawn.*—

Daine was about to protest the new hint of theft when she remembered the pack's way to put a stop to lumbering. She took a deep breath and said, "You saved our lives. Thank you."

—*I did not act for you, but for my young cousin.*— The creature reached down to tickle Kitten's nose. She rubbed it against his paw.

"You're family?" Daine asked, alarmed. The thought of losing Kitten was scarier than the Coldfang.

This time she felt a patient sigh behind the response. —*Only in a remote sense are basilisks and dragons kindred, yet both acknowledge a bond.*—

She gulped. While Coldfangs were new, she had heard of basilisks, immortals who turned their enemies to stone.

A whine made Daine look for her charges. The pups were huddled together nearby, anxiously watching the basilisk. "Are you going to attack us?"

Kitten shook her head vigorously. A wrinkle in the basilisk's face might have been a frown. —*I am a traveler and an observer, not a killer.*—

Daine looked at the Coldfang statue: it seemed dead enough to her. Still, she knew she could trust Kitten's judgment. She went to check the pups. Silly was worst hurt, his head cut to the bone and one eye out of focus. Runt limped on a sprained paw, and several back molars were loose. Leaper, Berry, and Chaser had only bruises to show for their tussle with the Coldfang.

Daine knelt in front of Silly. "No more tail grabbing," she ordered, calling up her magic. "He almost knocked you sillier, if that's possible." The young wolf whined and licked her face. "Enough," she told him as she cupped his head in her hands. "We'll have you fixed in no time."

This was quicker work than the squirrel had been. Infection barely had touched the open wound. She seared it in an eye-blink, and brushed through his brain to heal the inner bruises that had put his eye out of focus. The knitting of cut muscle and skin took less than a deep breath, and she was done. She touched the new scar. "I'll let you keep this," she teased. "The young lady wolves will think you're dashing. C'mere, Runt."

The sprained paw was easy, the loose molars less so. She had never rerooted teeth before, so she worked slowly and carefully to avoid mistakes.

—Is this a new thing, this relationship of humans and wolves?— the basilisk inquired when she was done. *—I would not have expected men's dealings with the People to improve.—*

Daine smiled. In many ways he sounded like Numair. "No, sir. I've just had a fair knack with animals since I was a pup myself, and then it turned to magic. Well, my teacher says it was magic all along, but I only learned to use it just a little while ago."

—I have heard of wild magic.— The basilisk looked down at Leaper, who had crept around until she was a few yards downwind. Her nose was up, nostrils flaring as she

breathed the immortal's scent. Her tail waved. —*Except for bird-folk, most of the People fear me. Your wolf friends are unusual.*—

Daine smiled wryly. "You should meet their folks."

—*I would like to do so, if you will permit it,*— was his reply. —*I would enjoy meeting the parents of such brave offspring, if they will not run away.*—

"They won't," the girl assured him. "They're fair unusual themselves."

—*Have you a name, wolf-girl?*—

"Daine. My full one's Veralidaine Sarrasri, but that's too much of a mouthful for everyday use."

The basilisk looked at her, large eyes cool and unblinking. Not for the first time and not, she was sure, for the last, Daine wished she could read an immortal's thoughts as she could an animal's. —*My full name you could not pronounce, either. You may call me Tkaa.*—

Silly raced off, followed by three of the other wolves, as Leaper continued to watch the basilisk. Her litter mates soon returned. Silly, ears and tail proudly erect, bore the Coldfang's rattle, broken off when the monster sent him flying. He dropped it in front of Daine and barked.

"For me?" she asked, picking up the rattle. "You shouldn't have." She wiped it on her breeches. It was silvery and cold, shaped in knobs like the rattle of a mortal snake. She gave it a shake and jumped when the thing buzzed. "Tkaa, you say these things hunt thieves? How much of a trail do they need?"

—*None. They know where a thief has passed, and follow that awareness.*—

Daine shuddered. "We'd best return to camp, then. I must warn the pack."

The wolves raced through the trees and over the meadow, playfully nipping at each other's hindquarters. Kitten followed at a swift, ground-eating gallop on all fours, while Daine and Tkaa brought up the rear.

FIVE
THE TRAP

In the clearing by the pond, the girl introduced Tkaa to Cloud. As the pups took a nap, she groomed the mare and packed. Tkaa occupied himself with Kitten, speaking in the chattering tongue she used to address him, and listening gravely to her replies. The girl fought to understand what was said, with no success.

—*Is something wrong?*— Tkaa wanted to know. —*You are frowning.*—

"I just don't see how Kit can have a language, and actually talk in it, but I can't understand. I almost never have trouble talking to immortals."

—*Your magic permits you to speak mind to*

mind. Skysong is not old enough for that. On the other hand, the spoken *dragon language is one they are born knowing. My people are renowned for knowledge of all languages, mortal and immortal. Before humans forced us into the Divine Realms, we walked everywhere and spoke to all.*— He looked around. —*Now I wander the mortal realm again, the first basilisk to do so in four centuries, thanks to that yellow mage.*—

"What yellow mage?"

—*The one who brought me here. He did not mean to bring me, of course, I sneaked through in the wake of the Stormwings he had summoned.*—

Daine stared at him. "Where was this?"

—*Here. He lives on the castle island. I can see the aura of his power there, brighter than that of the other mages who live inside those walls.*—

More than ever, Daine wished Numair had not left so abruptly. Goddess, let him return soon, she thought. He needs to hear what Tkaa can tell us. She also wanted Brokefang to come, so they could leave the area of the pond. The thought of another Coldfang making its slow, relentless way up from the lumber camp made her skin prickle and her stomach knot.

—*Calm yourself,*— advised Tkaa when she cut her palm slicing cheese for lunch. —*I doubt that the mortals who sent the Coldfang to hunt even know that that one is dead.*—

"But the men who sent him have scrying crystals," she protested. "They'll look for him in those—"

—*They may try.*— The thought was reassuringly firm. —*Did I not say Coldfangs are thief catchers? Too many thieves rely on magic. A Coldfang cannot be seen by magic, nor can one be stopped by it. They may be slain by human weapons, but—as you know—that can be difficult.*—

She made a note of that as, in the distance, she felt the pack's approach. "The wolves are here. They may be upset when they see you. Be patient, please."

Kitten added a chirp, and the basilisk tickled her behind the ears. —*I am always patient,*— he said.

The wolves trotted out of the rocks and stopped, looking from Daine to Tkaa. Ears went flat; hackles came up. "No!" she cried.

"He saved the pups! There was a monster coming, and he saved all our lives!" Quickly she explained the morning's events. Tkaa held still as Brokefang gave him a cautious sniff.

The Long Lake Pack thanks you, the chief wolf said at last. We thank you for the lives of our young, and the lives of our friends Daine and Kitten. Looking at Daine, he said, It sounds as if it is time for the pack to move.

"Please," she said, thinking of immortals who could trace thieves. "I would feel *so* much better if we did."

—*I told you they would not soon place another Coldfang on your trail,*— Tkaa reminded her.

"No, but them that sent it might come looking for the beastie," replied Daine, forgetting months of grammar lessons. "If they find that statue, they might be smart enough to keep looking uphill."

I know a place we may live in for a time, Brokefang announced. There are caves by the western pass where we can den. You will like it. There are plenty of bats for you to talk with. We will go now, if you are ready. The big wolf hesitated, then added, looking at

Tkaa, You are welcome to come there, too.

—*I look forward to seeing your caves.*—

Then let us go, Cloud said. I will feel better when we leave here.

Wait, Brokefang commanded. The tools. The saws and the axes. If we leave them here, and men come, they will find them and go back to cutting trees.

—You *are the thieves?*— There was surprise in Tkaa's cool voice. —*You stole men's tools?*—

They were scaring the game, Brokefang replied calmly. We made them stop.

Tkaa looked at Daine. His tone was coldly stern when he said, —*This was a bad thing you told them to do. Men will hunt them and kill them for this.*—

Stung by the unfairness of it, she cried, "It wasn't *my* fault!"

It was Brokefang's plan, Fleetfoot explained.

Short Snout yipped in approval.

Battle said, Brokefang makes *good* plans.

—*Show me,*— ordered the immortal. Russet led him into the reeds. Daine shook her head and loaded her things onto Cloud. She had finished when she heard that noise again, a screech with a deeper sound of tumbling rock underneath. It lasted for only a breath. When it stopped, Tkaa emerged from the reeds. Russet danced around the basilisk, leaping like a pup for joy.

He did a good thing, the wolf said. He made the tools into rock. Now *no* one can lift them or use them to cut trees!

Kitten whistled in glee; Brokefang grinned broadly. The younger adults—Battle, Sharp Nose, Fleetfoot, and Short Snout—yipped happily, tails wagging. Longwind grumbled under his breath, not liking this newest change in his world.

Frostfur sneezed in irritation. If everyone is happy, may we please *leave*? she demanded. I would like to be far from here before men come!

Brokefang led the way through the rocks. The pack followed in single file, as Tkaa, Daine, and Cloud brought up the rear. Kitten viewed the line of march from her seat atop Cloud's saddle, talking nonstop to Tkaa.

They had gone nearly half a mile when Daine sensed immortals. *Stormwings!* she cried silently to the pack as Cloud bolted for the nearby trees. Hide!

Longwind looked back at Daine. Wolves have nothing to fear from harriers, he said in his dignified way. They have no interest in the People.

Daine, joining Cloud and Kitten under branches that hid them from fliers overhead, yanked out her crossbow, and fitted a bolt into the notch. She thrust extra arrows point-first into the ground by her knee, ready to be fired.

The wolves continued their leisurely trot down the trail. Tkaa dropped back so the Stormwings wouldn't think he was with them, but he stayed in the open. When the four winged immortals saw him, they circled overhead.

"Basilisk! We seek two-leggers," called a filthy-haired brunette. What looked like old blood was streaked across her bare breasts. "A man, tall for a human, with lots of magic, and a young female with dark hair. Seen 'em?"

Tkaa walked on, pretending not to hear.

One Stormwing, whose human parts were the almond-shaped black eyes, black hair, and golden brown skin of a K'miri tribesman, dropped until he could hover a few feet away from Tkaa. His back was to Daine as the girl raised her bow. If he saw her, she would kill him before he could take word of her to Tristan.

Cloud gently clamped her teeth on the elbow supporting the bow stock. Don't, the mare warned. He hasn't done anything to you.

Yet, Daine replied silently. They're evil, Cloud. You *know* they're evil.

There's no such thing as a being who's pure evil, retorted the mare. Just as no creature is all good. They live according to their natures, just like you.

And their natures are *evil*, insisted the girl.

No. Their natures are opposed to yours, that's all. A wolf's nature is opposed to mine, but that does not make wolves evil. Until these creatures do you harm, leave them be. It is as the stork-man told you—learn tolerance!

Unaware of his danger, the K'miri Stormwing spoke to Tkaa. "You want to watch that girl, gravel-guts. She kills immortals. She *likes* it. She stole an infant dragon, you know, and sent the dragon mother to her death." Daine went cold with rage, hearing this version of Kitten's adoption. "You see her, make her stone before she puts an arrow in one of those sheep's eyes of yours."

—*Flapper,*— replied Tkaa with gentle patience, —*your cawing begins to vex me. I am interested in neither your affairs nor those of mortals.*—

"Remember what I said." With a surge of his wings, the Stormwing rejoined his fellows. They circled one last time, jeering, then flew off.

Only when they were gone did Cloud release Daine. Trembling in anger, the girl collected her arrows and put all but the one already loaded back in the quiver. The bow remained in her hand as she and Cloud rejoined Tkaa.

Twice more on the walk to the western pass, Daine and Cloud were forced to take cover to avoid Stormwing searchers. Watching them, the girl realized there was something funny about the sky. She kept glimpsing odd sparkles of colored light winking against the clouds. At least it wasn't in her own mind: Tkaa admitted to seeing it when she asked him, and the wolves, though they were unable to see color, said they noticed light-sparks overhead.

They were about to cross the stream that flowed down from the gap in the mountains when Brokefang halted, nostrils flaring. The wind had brought some odd scent to his nose. Abruptly he turned right, heading along the stream bank, following the path Numair had taken the day before out of the valley.

"Now what?" Daine asked tiredly as the pack followed him. "There aren't any caves that way!" she called. She could hear the distant bat colony in her mind. To reach them her group would have to cross the stream and follow the path Brokefang had taken to show her and Numair the view of the Long Lake.

The wolves disappeared from view. "Maybe they smell game or something," she grumbled, sitting on a boulder to rest her tired feet.

A scream—a human scream, high and terrified—split the air. Seizing bow and quiver, Daine went after the wolves at a dead run. A horse galloped by, white showing around his eyes as he raced toward the distant lake. Daine was reaching with her magic to stop him when she heard another scream. She let the horse go, and ran in the direction from which he had come. The horse would be all right. She could tell he wouldn't stop until he reached his stable.

Rounding a bend in the rocky pass, she

found the wolves in a clearing. They were in a circle, attention fixed on the small human at the center.

"It's all right," Daine called. "They won't hurt you!"

The human whirled. Huge brown eyes stared at Daine from a face so white its freckles stood out like ink marks. The mouth dropped open in shock. "*Daine?*"

It was Maura of Dunlath.

"Horse Lords," Daine said prayerfully. She didn't think those K'miri gods could help at a time like this, but all the same, it couldn't hurt to ask.

Maura gulped. "If they're going to eat me, can they get it over with?"

Daine sighed. She could feel a headache coming on. How was she to keep out of sight, as Numair had commanded, when trouble dropped into her lap? "They won't eat you, Maura. That's just stories. Wolves never eat humans."

They taste bad, Short Snout added. You know by the way they smell.

"*Everyone* says wolves eat people!" The girl wiped her eyes on her sleeve.

Daine walked through the circle of wolves, pausing to scratch Battle's ears and Fleetfoot's ruff as she passed. "*Everyone* is wrong. They say wolves kill to be cruel, and no wolf kills unless he's hungry." She put a hand on the ten-year-old's shoulder. "Do I look eaten to you?"

Maura stared up at her. "Well—no."

"These wolves are friends of mine, just like the castle mice."

Maura looked at the pack; they looked up at her. "They're a lot bigger than mice," she said fretfully.

Who is she? asked Brokefang. Why is she here?

"Good question," replied Daine. "Maura, what *are* you doing here?"

The girl's face went from scared to scared and mulish. "It's personal."

Daine looked around. The ground nearby was trampled, as if Maura had let her horse graze for a while before it smelled wolves and fled. Saddlebags and a bedroll lay under a nearby tree. The bags showed every sign of hasty packing: they bulged with lumps, and a doll's arm stuck out from under a flap, as if the doll pleaded to be set free. Maura's eyes were red and puffy. Her clothes—a plain white blouse, faded blue skirt, and collection of petticoats—looked as if they had been put on in the dark.

"You ran away."

Maura clenched her fists. "I'm not going back. You can't make me."

A starling flew by on her way through the pass. She called to Daine, who smiled and waved back. Returning her attention to Maura, she asked sternly, "Just how did you think you were going to live, miss? Where would you go?"

"My aunt, Lady Anys of the Minch, said I can visit anytime." Obviously making it up, the girl went on, "I even got a letter from her a week ago—"

"Lady Maura," Daine began, "I may be human, but I am *not* stupid. That is the most—" Agony flared nearby; a life went out. It felt like the starling. Frowning, she went to investigate.

Fifty yards away, the bird's crumpled form lay in the road. She picked the body up, smoothing feathers with a hand that shook. The head hung at a loose angle. When she had first visited Numair's tower, she had seen that birds couldn't tell that the windows on top of the building were made of clear glass. Many killed themselves flying into the panes before Daine warned them of the danger. The starling looked as if she had met the same end, but there was no glass here.

Instead Daine saw something else. The sparkles she had glimpsed against the sky were thick ahead of her. Near the ground, they formed a visible wall of yellow air flecked with pink, brown, orange, and red fire.

Gently she put the dead bird on a rock, trying not to cry. Starlings died all the time, but this one need not have died here and now.

Be careful, Brokefang warned as she approached the wall.

She put her hand out. The yellowish air was stone hard. It also stung a bit, like the shocks she got from the rugs in Numair's room on dry winter days. When she pulled her hand back, her palm went numb. She looked north. The colored air stretched as far as she could see, forming an unnaturally straight line along the spine of the mountains. Toward the south, her view was the same.

Behind her, Maura screamed. Daine turned to see what was wrong. The rest of her company had arrived, Tkaa bearing a sleepy Kitten in his arms, Cloud walking behind the basilisk.

"Stop it," Daine ordered Maura crossly. "Those are my friends. If you don't quit yelling when you get upset, you'll bring the Stormwings down on us."

"I don't see giant lizards every day," complained Maura.

—*I am no lizard.*— Tkaa's voice was frosty.

"He's no lizard," Daine said, looking at the barrier again. "He's a basilisk. His name's Tkaa." With her back to the girl, she didn't see Maura gather her nerve and curtsy, wobbling, to Tkaa. Brokefang did, and approved.

The little one has courage, he said, showing Daine an image of what Maura had done. You could be nicer to her. She *is* your own kind, after all.

Daine bent, picked up a rock, and hurled it at the barrier. She had to duck to save herself from a braining when the rock bounced back. Picking up her bow, she checked that an arrow was secured in the notch. "Everyone get back," she warned. She sighted and loosed. The arrow shattered.

"It's no good." The gloomy voice was Maura's. "You can't get through it. Nothing can. I would've ridden right into it, but my horse saw it and balked."

"But where did it come from? *When* did it come? Was it here when Numair tried to leave the valley, or did it appear after?"

—*It was done last night,*— Tkaa said. —*You must have felt something going on. The little one did; she told me so.*— Kitten chirped her agreement.

Brokefang trotted up to sniff the barrier. He jerked back with a snarl when the air stung his nose.

"Shh," Daine whispered, kneeling to wrap an arm around his shoulders. She looked up at the basilisk. "Tkaa? Can you pass it?"

—*Yes,*— he replied. He thrust a paw through the barrier. It moved slowly, as if in syrup, but it went. —*It is only human magic.*— He withdrew the paw.

"Could you carry me through?"

The immortal shook his head. —*I would not advise you even to try.*—

Daine stared at the barrier. Would Numair be able to cross it on his return? He was a powerful mage, but even *his* Gift had limits.

On a nearby bush, a sparrow peeped a greeting, and took off in flight. *"No!"* Daine cried with both her voice and magic. Stunned without striking the barrier, the little bird dropped. She picked him up. She touched him with a bit of her fire, to bring him around and to erase that ache that would result from her overreaction. "I'm sorry," she explained as he roused. "But keep away from the colored stuff, all right?"

Puzzled but obedient, the sparrow cheeped agreement and flew away. The girl turned to her oddly assorted audience. "First things first. I have to warn the birds about this, before any more are killed. Then we'd best get under cover. Maura, we can talk then. Cloud, will you carry Her Ladyship's packs?"

The mare nodded. "Load her," Daine told the younger girl. "This won't take but a moment." Sitting, she closed her eyes. Her studies had included shields to keep her from distraction by animal voices: now she let her shields fall. The common talk of every vertebrate creature within range poured into her mind, then quieted when she asked for their attention. Daine showed them the barrier's image, the many-colored lights within it, and its terrible solidity. To that she added the image of the dead starling.

The People acknowledged her warning: they would know the barrier when they saw it and would avoid it. They would pass her warning on to those outside her ten-mile range, and keep sending it along, until all Dunlath knew the danger.

Finished, Daine rose. "Let's find those caves."

The wolves led the way from the pass until they descended into a fold of rock. It was an entrance to a small cave, which in turn opened up onto a much larger one. A pond inside provided water, though it was bone-chillingly cold and tasted strongly of stone. Passages in the rear led to other caves: escape routes, if the pack ever need them.

The company settled in. Daine relieved Cloud of her burdens and groomed her. Maura built a fire pit around a dip in the stone floor. The pack adults explored or napped; the pups were nowhere to be seen. Tkaa wandered about with Kitten in tow, gouging chunks from different stones with his talons. He tasted each sample carefully, discarding most and stowing the rest near Daine's packs.

"What are they for?" she asked.

—*Supper,*— replied the basilisk.

"Weapons?" suggested Maura, who couldn't hear Tkaa speak.

"He eats them, he says," replied Daine, thinking, This could be complicated, if I'm forever translating when I should listen to animals. She conveniently forgot that she often did such translations for the king's staff and the Riders. A full day and a restless night had combined to make her grumpy.

Maura yelped. Daine spun to glare at her, and the younger girl clapped her hands over her mouth, looking guilty. The cause of her yelp had been the pups, who had come to the fire pit, each carrying a good-sized piece of dead wood. They dropped their finds and went racing outside for more.

"I don't need help," Maura called after them, voice shaking. Avoiding Daine's eyes, she knelt to arrange tinder and kindling in the pit.

"I guess they're chewing on logs because they can't eat me." She frowned: a fuchsia-colored puff of sparks flew up from the tinder. Within seconds a small fire burned in the kindling, and she was feeding it larger pieces of wood.

"I didn't know you had the Gift," commented Daine, getting supplies and pans from her gear.

"Not much of a one," replied the ten-year-old. She built up the fire as the pups returned with more wood. This time she actually took a branch from Leaper, though her hand trembled as she did so. "I can light fires and candles and torches. Yolane hates it when I do that. We get the magic from the Conté side of the family, same as the king, but she doesn't have any. It's no good telling her lots of people from Gifted families don't have the Gift themselves. She thinks she'd look like a queen if she could light the candles with magic."

Daine found a cloth ball and smiled. It was a basic soup mixture of dried barley, noodles, mushrooms, and herbs. With the addition of water and salt pork, it would make a good meal for two humans. Taking a pot to the spring, she filled it and brought it to the fire to heat.

As she cut open the ball and poured its contents into the water, she said, "It seems daft, your sister worrying about what a queen looks like. Tortall *has* a queen, after all, a young, strong, healthy one. Unless Thayet catches an arrow or a dagger somewhere, she's going to be queen a long time."

Maura looked away. "It's just one of those things people worry about, even if it doesn't make sense. Don't mind me. I talk too much; Yolane says so all the time. Tell me how you got your dragon. Did you catch her in a net, or with magic, or how?"

Daine was so upset at the suggestion of trickery that she launched into the tale of Kitten's mother dying to defend the queen at Pirate's Swoop. It wasn't until she was dishing up the soup that she realized Maura had changed the subject, and quite effectively, too.

Tkaa read this in her thoughts. —*She is no fool, the little one. There is something quite serious on her mind.*—

She's only *ten*, Daine pointed out silently. How serious can it be?

—And how old are you, Grandmother?—

She blushed and replied, Fourteen.

—Ah. A vast difference of years and experience. Certainly no one could believe her affairs are as vital as yours.—

"How's the soup?" she asked Maura hastily, before the tall immortal could make her feel even younger and sillier than she did just then.

"Ungerfoll." Maura swallowed her mouthful of noodles, coughed, and said, "It's really good. And clever, how you had most if it in that cloth ball."

"The Riders use them for trail rations," Daine said, hearing voices in search of her. She put her bowl aside and got up facing the rear entrances to the cave. The wolves gathered near her, ears pointed in the same direction.

The bats streamed in from the lower caves to whirl around Daine in a dance of welcome. She laughed as the leaders came to rest on her clothes and hair, landing with the precision they used to find roosting spots among hundreds of comrades. These were little brown bats, an inch and a half to two inches from crown to paw, with a wingspan of three to four inches. Clinging to her, they looked like brown cotton bolls. Though the whole colony, nearly three thousand animals, had come to greet her, most hung overhead rather than chance a welcome from Daine's other companions.

They greeted her in high, chittering voices, introducing themselves as the Song Hollow Colony of bats. She asked if they minded that she and her friends were in their home.

They didn't mind at all, they replied. All they asked was that her friends not try to make a meal of them.

"I think I can promise that," she assured them with a smile.

But what if they taste good? asked Short Snout wistfully. It's true, one wouldn't be more than a mouthful, but there are plenty of them here—

"He's *joking*," Daine said when the bats screeched in alarm, their voices sending jolts of pain through her teeth.

Not about food, retorted Short Snout. Meals aren't funny.

Daine pointed to the entrance. "Out," she commanded.

I probably wouldn't eat *many,* he said as he obeyed. It would be too much like work to catch them, anyway.

Brokefang stretched. We go to hunt, he told Daine. Tonight, the pups come too. It is time, he added as the young wolves, deliriously happy, frolicked around him. Whatever we see, we will tell you.

"Good hunting," Daine called.

—*Good hunting,*— added Tkaa.

Startled by the basilisk's remark, Brokefang asked, Do you wish to come?

—*I thank you, but no,*— Tkaa replied. Daine heard pleasure at the offer in his voice. —*I will remain with Skysong and the small two-legger.*—

If Tkaa was willing to keep an eye on Maura, that left her free to try something. "Would you do me a favor?" Daine asked the bats. "You prob'ly know, from my sending before, that the pass is cut off by some kind of barrier."

We had heard, one of the leaders replied.

"As you hunt, would you explore the barrier and find its limits? You're the best ones to do it. You won't hit it, and if you all go, you can map the whole thing before dawn. And may I ride along with one of you?"

After a short conference, the bats agreed. One of the leaders clambered from her perch on Daine's boot top to her collar. I am Wisewing, she said, tiny black eyes sparkling. You may try this magic with me.

"Give me a moment," she said, tickling the bat's chin with a fingertip. "I have to sit." The other bats clinging to her took flight. Daine went to Maura, who was covering her head with her hands. "I need to go with them," she told the younger girl. "Why are you doing that?"

"They'll get in my hair."

Daine planted her fists on her hips. "Odd's bobs," she said crossly. The brown eyes that looked pleadingly at her filled. She sighed. "Don't cry. I'm sorry. But Maura—they got in *my* hair because I *invited* them. Bats don't fly into hair. They never bump into anything they don't want to."

"But everybody says—"

"*Everybody's* wrong. See, they squeak at things, and listen to the squeak." She pointed to Wisewing's ears. The long, sensitive flaps wriggled to and fro, hearing every bit of sound in the air. "If the noise comes funny into their ears, they know something's there, and they fly around it. They don't smash into glass, or even that barrier, like birds do. Nothing's invisible to bats."

Maura's hands left her hair. "How can you go with them? You can't fly. Can you?"

Daine shook her head. "Just with my magic, inside this lady." She patted Wisewing. Going to where her packs rested against the wall, she sat, using them as a cushion for her back. "Don't leave this cave," she cautioned Maura. "And you'd best go to bed soon. I have a feeling tomorrow's going to be a long day." Closing her eyes, she fitted herself into Wisewing instantly.

Sounds poured into her ears, echoes from the cavern walls, each scratch of Tkaa's or Kitten's talons, Cloud's munching, wind blowing through the caves. Wisewing leaped into the air, reaching forward with her leathery wings and scooping air back with easy grace. They were in flight.

The voices of the Song Hollow bats rippled ahead of them, a river of sound that Wisewing followed eagerly. Cooler air brushed her face, and they were in the open. Daine could hear the rest of the colony flying along the barrier, heading north, south, and east in waves. Wisewing flew straight ahead, soaring until she skimmed the underside of the barrier's highest arch.

Please stop trying to see it, she protested. You're making my eyes hurt. I don't use them that much. *Listen* for it. You can hear it everywhere.

She was right. The barrier was a constant soft crackle of sound, reflecting the voices of the bats. Wisewing herself struck it constantly with her voice, and the returning echoes not only told her how far off it was, but that its underside was unnaturally smooth, like the inside of a bowl.

Daine just had time to register a different, softer echo when Wisewing scooped the moth that had caused it into her waiting jaws. The taste reminded Daine of roasted, honey-glazed duck. The bat's next vicitm was a tangy mosquito, followed by a moth that tasted more like fish. She'd always known that bats ate insects by the pound on their hunts, but it was one thing to know this in her mind, another to taste flavor after flavor on her tongue.

I don't want to slow you down by eating, but the Big Cold is soon, said Wisewing. I must be as fat as possible by then, or I won't wake up.

I know, Daine replied. You don't have to apologize.

On they flew, the barrier solidly above them. From all around, other bats sang out information, comparing notes about the magic, the insect supply, and the weather. The crispness of the air made Daine feel giddy and silly.

Then she heard something unpleasant in the distance. The bats' voices came to their ears from something big, something with leathery wings and claws. Her bat darted at the giant, squeaking at it from all angles, building a picture of the great creature in her mind. She had filled in little more than the huge wings and four sets of talons when Daine guessed what it was.

Hurrok, she said nervously. We don't need to hear more. Please let's go!

—*Little squeaker, get away from me.*— The immortal's voice was much deeper than the chorus of bat voices surrounding him. —*I don't* like *squeakers.*—

Wisewing dove in, settling between the hurrok's wings. Chittering across the immortal's withers, mane, and ears, she picked up the sound of metal. It hummed with a sound the bat recognized as that of human magic. Interested in this new object, Wisewing fluttered across the immortal's chest, to find that a metal band or collar went all the way around the hurrok's throat.

I would have to pick a nosy bat, Daine thought, sick with nerves.

—*It's a slave collar, squeaker,*— the hurrok said. —*It means I must obey a human, a mortal wizard whose power makes it burn into my flesh with only a word. And do you know what that pain, and that knowing, and this collar, do to me? They make me feel like tearing up* every *living creature I see.*—

She heard a roar of air as something large snapped right over her head: the hurrok had tried to catch them in its teeth. Please Goddess, prayed Daine, let me get through this without losing my life and I will be good forever.

Scolding, Wisewing dropped down, letting

the hurrok go its way. Don't let it scare you, she told Daine. It's much too big and slow to catch us. An *owl*, now—an owl is dangerous. You want to stay away from them, particularly barn owls.

I shall keep that in mind, Daine replied.

See that you do, the bat said firmly, and scooped up a fly.

She didn't know how long she flew with the bats, but it must have been for hours. When she opened her own, human eyes and lurched to the cave's entrance, false dawn had turned the eastern horizon pearly gray. She still heard the Song Hollow bats as the returned to their home, greeting her as they flew by. Her mind full of Wisewing's memories, she identified each by his or her particular squeak: Singwing, Chitter, Eatsmoths, Whistle, Flutter. Reunited in the cave where they roosted, they sang their news. From their combined voices Daine built a picture of the barrier's shape. By true dawn her worst fears were confirmed. The wizards' barrier sealed off the entire valley, with no crack or cranny left for a determined girl to wriggle through.

Mission done and bellies full, the bats went

to sleep. Daine stayed at the entrance, listening to the shift of hooves on stone as Cloud changed position in her sleep, a soft munch that was Tkaa as he nibbled on a piece of rock, the bustle of voles in the grass. Her ears were tired and sore, the muscles around them cramped from use. Reaching up to rub them, Daine touched a long flap of leathery skin that flicked to and fro, catching each quiver of sound in the air.

Her hand shook. Slowly, praying to the Goddess, the Horse Lords, Mithros, and any other god who might be listening, she felt the other ear. It too was long, and twitching independently of its mate, gathering every sound from that side of her head. She knew without looking that the stone of the cave entrance was six and a half inches behind her, that Kitten lapped water from the spring, and that a raccoon on the mountainside twelve feet and eight inches above her head was finishing a late-night supper of something crunchy, probably acorns.

What *is* this? she thought, her skin prickling. Why is my body changing? It's staying right where I left it. *I* don't change when I do this, I just send my mind someplace else. So how could I have bats' ears?

Unless I'm just imagining that part of me changes. If I am, it means I'm going mad after all, she thought, strangely calm. Surely someone would have told me that it's possible to change part of yourself into something else.

If I ignore these ears, they'll go away, or my mind will let go of them, or whatever. Maybe if I sleep, I'll wake up and be normal again.

That seemed like a good idea. Returning to the large cave, she found her bedroll. When I wake up, the ears will be gone, and I won't be crazy, she told herself firmly as she slid into her blankets. She pulled the covers over her head, just in case. If the ears were still there, she didn't want Maura to wake her with a scream.

SIX

REBELLION

She awoke slowly, leaving dreams in which she clung to the cavern with the other Song Hollow bats, becoming her normal self in the cave that she shared with her motley group of friends. For a moment she thought she was deaf, the sounds she heard were so few and so dim. She clapped a hand to one ear and found a small, curved shell where the long, ribbed flap had been. Feeling relief mixed with sadness, she knew she was not deaf. Her ears were human once more.

"You're up," said Maura. "I wanted to wake you for breakfast—I was afraid you'd sleep all day—but Tkaa said leave you be."

She came over with a steaming mug and set it on the ground as Daine sat up. "I hope you don't mind me'n Kitten getting in your things. I didn't bring any food, and we were *starving*. I found your tea, and the wolves found a beehive, so me'n Kitten had honey for our porridge, and I made tea with honey for you."

"Thanks." Half-awake, Daine asked the first question that came to mind, the one she ought to have asked more firmly the day before. "Why'd you run off?"

The younger girl looked down. "I can't say."

Daine sniffed her tea: it smelled wonderful. "You must. If you had a spat with Yolane, or if you think it's fun to live out in the woods like me, that's no good. You'll have to go home."

"What if she wants to send me to school to be a lady, and I want to go to court to be a knight?"

Under Daine's sharp look the girl reddened. "You've heard too many tales about the King's Champion. I'm not here for fun, Maura, and it's wrong to run off for fun. Leaving home's serious." Remembering the wreck of her own home, she added, "You're lucky to have a place that's yours. You don't

167

just throw that away." She grinned. "And I doubt you'd have any luck as a knight. You screech whenever you see something odd."

Maura smiled, then looked at her hands. "I *have* to see the king. I can't say why. I know girls my age aren't supposed to know important stuff, but I do, and he has to know."

"If it's that Tristan is making trouble for Tortall, you're behind the fair," Daine replied. "We know he's in the Carthaki emperor's service. Numair went out of the valley so he could report to the king and get help. As soon as he does, he'll be back."

Maura looked at Daine with a frown. "Is that all you know? About Tristan?"

"I know for a fact he brought Tkaa here."

"For which I am grateful," a whispery voice said from the entrance.

Daine squeaked and lunged for her crossbow. Maura rescued the endangered mug of tea. When Daine brought the cocked and loaded bow to bear on the entrance, she saw only Tkaa and Kitten. "Who said that?" she demanded.

The basilisk stared at her. "I *told* you my people speak all tongues." The whispery voice did come from his mouth. "The only reason I did not address Lady Maura in this wise from the first was that my skills were rusty. In the Divine Realms and with you it is easier to speak mind-to-mind."

"Mithros, Mynoss, and Shakith," Daine breathed. "I don't know what to say."

"Then say nothing," advised Tkaa as he put Kitten down. "That is best."

Still unnerved by hearing him speak human, Daine got clothing out of her packs and took it into her bedroll to dress. As she did, wriggling under the covers, she heard Maura tell the basilisk, "We need to think about laundry and supplies. I can't eat all Daine's food."

If Tkaa answered, his voice was drowned out by a sound. Once Daine had heard a great bell, its sides as thick as her hand, clang as it was struck with a mallet. This noise was similar, but so loud it made her teeth and ears ache. Hundreds of yards away, cushioned from the outer air by tons of rock, the Song Hollow bats heard it and were startled into flight. Cloud neighed in protest outside; Kitten dived into Daine's blankets, pulling them over her tender ears. Tkaa clapped his forepaws over his earholes and shut his eyes in pain.

"What was that?" cried Maura.

It came again, so loud it pressed on Daine's eardrums. Where? she asked the bats, knowing they could pinpoint it. Confused and frightened, they sent an image of the western pass as it would appear to them, painted in sound at night.

She grabbed her crossbow and quiver. Barefoot, shirt half-tucked into her breeches, she ran outside. Cloud followed at a gallop, and when she drew alongside, Daine leaped onto the pony's back in a trick learned from the Riders. As the mare raced for the barrier, Daine counted the bolts in her quiver with her fingers: ten. She hoped that would be enough if Stormwings caught her in the open.

When they reached the barrier, they saw no one. Daine could hear a marmot scolding on the other side of the magical wall. "If you see danger, nip me or something," she ordered her mare, and sat down. Closing her eyes, she listened for the marmot.

She found her quarry instantly. The marmot, a female, was on the sloping ground that was the southern wall of the pass, guarding the entrance to the burrow she shared with her large family. Shocked, frightened, and irate, she was calling the man below names that Daine hadn't thought a marmot would use.

You must have learned that from squirrels, she commented. None of the marmots *I* know ever said such things.

They weren't scared out of their wits, retorted the chubby rodent. I was minding my own business, standing watch, and the two-legger made that noise. He scared me out of a month's fat! I'll have to eat *twice* as much now to be ready for the Big Cold and—Look at him! He's going to do it again!

If you do I will bite you! she screamed at the man. I don't care if you kill me, I will take a big chunk out of you before I'm dead!

May I? asked Daine, and slipped into the marmot so she could see with her hostess's eyes. At the spot where the barrier closed the way into the pass stood two horses and a tall, lanky human. He was raising his hands again. Sweat trickled down his palms. He shouted something and hurled the fire at the barricade.

The noise was so loud that Daine was jolted back into her own body. "Tkaa!" she called.

—*I am here.*— The basilisk had caught up

with her while Daine was speaking with the marmot. He looked a bit odd: someone, probably Maura, had wrapped cloth around his head to protect his earholes.

"It's Numair—my teacher."

—*A mortal is doing that?*—

"Would you cross and tell him to stop? Oh, wait—perhaps he's doing it to break down the barrier. If he is, would you ask him how long it will take, so I can warn my friends? I suppose he'll want to know about the Coldfang, and you should tell him Maura's with us."

—*Let me go,*— said Tkaa, sounding faintly amused. —*You may think of other things for me to tell him while I am gone.*— He walked over to the barrier and was halfway through when Daine remembered something else.

"Tkaa, wait!"

He looked at her. —*Quickly, if you please. This is not comfortable.*—

"If you can go through, Stormwings can go through. Warn him, please. They might be on their way now, if Tristan heard all this racket."

The basilisk walked through the barrier. Daine looked at Cloud. "I need my writing kit. Tkaa doesn't know all I've learned, and Numair has to be warned." She stopped. In her mind she heard approaching Stormwings. "We've got trouble," she said, and mounted the pony. "What did Tkaa call them? Flappers?"

Just what we need, replied the mare.

In the distance she heard Maura say pleadingly, "Go away! *Please!*"

Cloud picked up her pace, and they rounded a bend. Maura stood where the trail to the caves met the pass road. Above her was a flock of Stormwings.

"Maura, get *down*!" shouted Daine. Cloud stopped as she brought the crossbow to bear on one of the monsters.

"*No!*" Maura lunged at Daine, grabbing for the bow. Her weight dragged Daine's arm down. For one perilous moment the crossbow was aimed point-blank at the ten-year-old's chest. Cloud reared. Maura lost her grip on the bow, and Daine swung it away from her. She was trembling in fear and anger.

"Dont *ever* do that again!" she cried. "I could have *killed* you!"

"I'm sorry," Maura said, looking down. "But I couldn't let you hurt them."

Stormwings were landing on the ground in

front of them. Three moved out of Daine's sight. Turning, she saw them settle on the road behind her, cutting off any escape. Coldly she leveled her weapon at the nearest Stormwing, a male who wore a collection of bones braided into his long blond hair.

He stared back at her, contempt in his eyes, then looked at the younger girl. "Tell her we mean you no harm, Lady Maura."

"You're on speaking terms with *them*?" Daine asked.

Maura shrugged. "They visit Yolane and Belden a lot. He is Lord Rikash."

"And she is a Stormwing killer," barked the snarl-haired brunette who had spoken to Tkaa the day before. "She slew one of our queens last year!"

"She tried to kill me," Daine snapped. "It was a fair fight—a lot fairer than she deserved."

Riskash hopped around Maura and stopped near Cloud, looking her and her rider over with chilly green eyes. The mare had seen his kind before. While their scent of rotten meat and bad death hurt her nose, she had learned to stand fast when they were near. She eyed Rikash, small ears flat against her skull. Daine knew what was in the pony's mind: one more hop and he'd be in range for a bite.

Don't hit the feathers, warned Daine silently. They'll cut your mouth.

Don't teach your dam to nurse a foal, Cloud retorted.

"You are quick to judge us, Stormwing killer," Rikash snarled. "Too quick, for a *human*. You come from a race that spends more time murdering your *own* kind than do all the immortals put together, yet you insist you are better than us." He spat on the ground, and looked at Maura. "You cannot leave Dunlath, and you must not stay here. Come home. Yolane doesn't need to know you were away."

"You mean she hasn't noticed I'm gone," Maura said bitterly. "Has anyone?"

"That is unjust," the Stormwing replied, firmly and gently. "You know very well that the cook and your nurse are frantic that you've vanished."

"I left them notes. I told them not to worry."

There was something odd between these two, Daine realized. The immortal spoke to Maura with affection. That was impossible. Stormwings were cruel, heartless: she had enough experience of them to know that. Worse, Maura addressed Rikash as she might an older brother or an uncle.

Watching the immortals, Daine saw that she needed help. Starlings gathered with the coming of fall, to gossip and to migrate. Nearby she found three such flocks, each with over fifty birds, and called them to the trees and rocks around her before she looked again at Maura and Rikash. "Do you know what *his* sort do?" she asked the younger girl. "They befoul the dead who fall in battle. They live on human fear and anger. They're monsters!"

Maura shrugged thin shoulders. "They can't help how they're *made,* Daine."

"Maura"—Rikash shook his head—"you can't just run away from home. And *you* shouldn't encourage her," he told Daine. "You're old enough to know better."

"I already know better," retorted Maura.

Daine glared at the Stormwing. "I *haven't* been encouraging her. I *tried* to make her go back. *You're* the one with the wings—*you* take her."

Maura sat on the ground, chin sticking out. "I won't go back, and you can't make me.

They're traitors. I won't stay under the same roof with them. My father would haunt me all my life if I did."

"Let us talk of this away from prying ears," Rikash said, an eye on Daine.

"We can speak of it now. Daine can't tell anyone. She's stuck here too!"

"Quiet!" ordered the Stormwing. "You're a *child*. You do not understand what is taking place, and you must not speak of matters you cannot comprehend."

Her sense of humor overpowering her hatred of Stormwings, Daine looked down so Rikash wouldn't see her smile. Obviously he liked Maura, or he would have bullied rather than debated her. She also could see debate was useless. Maura had the bit between her teeth and would not obey orders. "Go on," she urged the fuming immortal. "Shut her up. I never thought to see you stinkers balked by anyone, let alone a ten-year-old."

Rikash turned red under his dirt, and a few of his own flock cackled. "It is hard for us to bear young," he said, a hint of gritted teeth in his voice. "That being the case, we value others' young, particularly when they are neglected.

Affection has led me to indulge Lady Maura more than is wise."

Maura sighed. "All right, Lord Rikash. I'll hush. Only, I'm not coming back with you. You don't have to tell them you saw me."

Rikash shook his head. "If you were mine, I would beat you," he said with grim resignation. He looked up at Daine, eyes sharp. "As for *you*—"

Daine grinned, and made a silent request of the starlings. They set up a clamor, flapping their wings and voicing painfully shrill, *loud* whistles. "Go on," she told Rikash, raising her voice to be heard. "Take me in. You might last two or three minutes in the air with my friends going for your eyes."

The Stormwings looked at the birds with alarm. Starlings, cowards and clowns alone or in small groups, were bullies in a flock. Their whistles alone made the immortals try unsuccessfully to cover their ears.

"The gods help you if I catch you in the open," Rikash snarled, flapping his wings. "Maura, you had better rethink your choice of friends!" The Stormwings took to the air as the starlings jeered and insulted them. Wheeling, the immortals flew straight at the barrier and passed through.

"But what about your friend?" Maura cried, grabbing Daine's arm. "It was him making the noise, wasn't it? They might hurt him!"

"I don't think so," said Daine, watching the barrier. There was a sound like a thunderclap. The Stormwings returned, covered with soot from claws to crown and reeking of onions. "They *hate* onions," Daine told Maura as they flew by, tears running down their faces as they sneezed frantically. "We found out last fall, when we helped mop up after pirates raided Port Legann."

"Goddess bless," the younger girl breathed, watching the retreat until the Stormwings were no longer in view.

Dismounting from Cloud, Daine let the pony go ahead of them on the trail to the caverns. "I can't believe you *like* them," she muttered.

Maura glared at her. "Well, *I* can't believe you like wolves."

There was little Daine could say to that. She

didn't try, knowing Maura would disagree with whatever arguments she made.

When they entered the caves, Kitten greeted her with joyful chirps and whistles. Smiling, Daine held and petted her for a little while. "Sorry, Kit," she said at last, and put her friend down. "I have plenty to do." Locating her writing tools, she stowed them in a pack.

"You're going back there?" Maura asked.

"I must. There's things Numair has to know."

The younger girl took a deep breath. "Then you'd better tell him Belden and Yolane are going to rebel against the king, and soon."

Daine, stunned, let the pack slip to the floor. "A *rebellion*?"

Maura nodded, red with shame. Kitten, chirping in concern, rubbed her head against the girl's knee. "I didn't know anything for sure until the day after you left," Maura explained. "It was after lunch sometime, because my nurse wanted to put me on the backboard, and I didn't want her to catch me."

"A backboard?" asked Daine.

"It's so old-fashioned. Nobody uses it any-more. You're strapped with your shoulders against it for *hours*—it's supposed to teach girls to sit up straight. Nurse says I'm round-shouldered, and she puts me on it whenever she can."

Daine shuddered. "It sounds horrible. I've never heard Kally—Princess Kalasin—mention such a thing."

"Good. If we get out of all this, please tell my nurse the princess doesn't have one. Anyway, I left through the secret passage in the family wing. I was behind Yolane's study when I heard Belden yell, 'What do you mean, he's *gone*?' I heard Tristan and Yolane say be quiet, and I stopped. There's spy holes in all the rooms, so I could see and hear everything. It was them and the others, Alamid and Gissa and Redfern and Gardiner. Tristan lied, you know. They weren't going to the City of the Gods. He wrote and invited them."

Daine's stomach growled. She dug out cheese and a sausage, cutting off portions for herself and for Maura. "So what did you hear?"

"Tristan told Belden it's all under control. And Belden said Tristan told him Master Numair would pass out from the nightbloom in his wine and when *that* didn't work, Tristan said there was no way Master Numair could leave the valley. Yolane said they're in trouble if Numair warns the king, and Tristan said he only knows Tristan and Alamid and Gissa are here. He said they'll warn the other con— conspirators, and speed up the rebellion. They'll strike with the next full moon, not at Midwinter like they planned."

Daine dug her brushes, paper, and ink out of the pack. "Wait—let me write this down." Shaking the bottle of ready-made ink, she unstoppered it and wet her brush. Swiftly, using Rider code symbols to speed up note taking, she wrote the main points of what Maura had said thus far. "Go on."

Maura drank some water. "Belden said he didn't like how this is going, and Tristan told the mages to show Belden how they'd ward the valley, and they left. After that Yolane said she hoped this would work. Tristan said as long as she keeps up her end, she'll be queen by the first snows. And Yolane said how can she keep her bargain when the next shipment is sealed in with us? Tristan said they'll handle that when the shipment's ready. Then he started kissing her and saying what a fine queen she'd make, and I left. I snuck out of the castle that night—I hoped I could get out of Dunlath before they closed it off."

"Can you remember anything else?"

Maura shook her head. "I told you everything. I kept going over it in my head so I could tell the king without leaving anything important out."

"What's this shipment they talked about?"

"Whatever they mine up in the north part of the valley. They've been sending that out of Dunlath all summer."

Daine put her things away and tucked her notes into the waistband of her breeches. "Numair has to know all this. He can warn the king."

"He can speak over distances with his Gift?" The younger girl sighed. "I wish I could do that. It would make things a lot easier."

"Is there anyone in the valley who can?"

Maura shook her head. "Just Tristan and his friends. Some villagers have the Gift, but it's like mine. Just good for a couple of things, and nobody can far-speak. Anyone who has a strong Gift leaves to get better training."

Daine sighed. "That's typical. One last thing—

didn't you sort of promise Rikash you wouldn't tell me any of this?"

"I know he probably thinks I did, but I didn't. Maybe Yolane forgot her duty to the Crown, but I haven't." She rubbed her sleeve over her eyes.

Touched, Daine gave her friend a quick hug. "All right. I have to take this to Numair. Look after Kitten while I'm gone, won't you?"

Cloud also stayed behind as Daine returned to the barrier. On a slope nearby, the girl found a tumble of rock, one huge slab of which formed a lean-to against its fellows. She hid there, out of the open, and began to write, using the notes she had taken from Maura. To that she added the news that the barrier enclosed the entire valley. She was finishing when she heard the high, singing note that was Tkaa's presence in her mind. Peering out of her shelter, she saw the basilisk step through the barrier, and waved him up to her hiding place.

—*He says he cannot break this spell,*— the immortal told her. —*He says he must summon more help.*—

Daine rewet her brush and added a further

note to her letter: "Can't you use one of those words of power on it?"

—*He is unusual,*— Tkaa remarked as Daine waited for her ink to dry. —*When I crossed the barrier, he thought I meant to attack. He threw fire at me. I sang the rock spell without blinking—I am not at my best when I am rushed.*— A note that might have been amusement entered his soft mental voice. —*He became stone, of course. The spell never fails. It lasted for a breath, and then he shattered it, as if all I had done was pour clay on him and bake it. And then he asked me to do it again, to see if he could break the spell twice.*—

Daine rubbed her aching head. "He would," she said dryly. "And did you?"

—*I suggested that the time to conduct experiments will be when all of us have the leisure to enact them properly. If you encounter dragons, you will find the same excuse works with them. More than anything, dragons and mages like to take time with their studies.*—

"Well, thank Mithros for that," replied the girl. "Will you take this to him? It's important."

—*To become a messenger at my age,*— Tkaa remarked, shaking his head.

Daine smiled up at him. "Thank you. I am grateful for your help."

There was affection in his voice when he replied. —*It is I who must thank you. In four hundred years in the Divine Realms, I have not enjoyed myself as much as I have in the last two days. Life is more vivid here, much headier.*— The message in his hand, he returned to the glowing barrier and passed through.

She waited for a moment and then decided she wanted to hear Numair's comments as he read her note. Reaching, she found the marmot and asked again for permission to become part of her. The chubby creature, named Quickmunch, agreed. Daine had the knack of it so well by now that it took only an eye-blink to enter the marmot. It took a bit longer to convince Quickmunch to leave the safety of the burrow and her family, and to approach Numair and Tkaa so Daine could hear them.

If he makes that noise again, I *will* bite him, Quickmunch said as she made her cautious way down the rock slope, with frequent checks overhead for eagles. Humans never stop to think of the People when they are up to their tricks.

He doesn't mean to be rude, Daine said as they stepped onto the road. From here, Spots and Mangle were as big as houses. Quickmunch's first reaction was to run. Daine persuaded her that the horses were peaceful, but Quickmunch still passed them in a wide arc. When she saw Tkaa with Numair, she barked in alarm.

As the immortal bent to examine the rodent, Numair looked up from Daine's note and saw what Tkaa was doing. "Daine, is that you? Can you understand me?"

Nod, Daine told the marmot, and Quickmunch nodded stiffly. This means something to him? she asked.

It means yes, the girl said. It means we understand human speech. Now let me hear what he has to say.

Numair held up Daine's letter. "Your news is serious, but not surprising. Dunlath is too well guarded to be a country backwater. When we're done talking, I'll get under cover and speak to the king again." He shook his head. "As to the barrier—did you notice the mixture of colors? It's hard to break a joined spell like this, in which several mages take part." His mouth tightened. "Also, there is an added dimension to this working. The mages Tristan has are disciplined; Alamid and Gissa are both Masters. I believe Redfern may be, as well. All the same, I should have produced a reflection of some kind, from the power I just threw at the barrier." A blush rose in his dark cheeks. "I shouldn't have done that, of course. I'm afraid I lost my temper.

"The fact remains, the barrier absorbed my Gift and didn't deflect it. That means it is fueled with more power than the combined Gifts of Tristan's group can produce. They must be using gemstones that act as power sources to anchor it. If that's the case, I may have to wait for mages to come from the City of the Gods and the Royal University to break it."

She pointed to the paper in his hand.

"Remember what I told you of the words of power." He rubbed his face. "For each one used properly, there is a reaction elsewhere of similar magnitude. The word that *may* break this spell will cause an earthquake somewhere else. I will not kill untold numbers of people to get through, not when other mages will soon come to aid me. I do have some good news. King Jonathan said that two Rider groups and a company of the King's Own are nearby, on border patrol. They're to be sent here. The Sixth Rider Group will arrive in two days, the Twelfth in four, and the men of the King's Own in three days. The mages may take as long as a week to reach us, but that can't be helped."

Daine shivered. She did *not* like the idea of days passing before Numair got help. True, he could defend himself, but there was no telling what unpleasant surprises were tucked into Tristan's sleeve.

"You said each word of power 'used properly,'" remarked Tkaa in Common. He had been listening intently. "What if a word of power is used improperly?"

Numair grimaced. "The magic backfires. It's one reason there are so few of my rank. The others who tried to reach it are dead." He looked at Daine. "Are you comfortable shifting into your friends' minds? Is it difficult?"

The marmot nodded yes to the first question

and shook her head to the second. For a moment Numair sank deep into thought, pulling his long nose idly.

"Daine, I have a tremendous favor to ask," he said finally, coming out of his brown study. "We need more precise information. Is there a way, *without putting yourself in danger,* that you can enter the northern and southern forts and count the men posted there?"

Daine nodded, through Quickmunch. It *was* the next logical step.

"You can do it from within an animal's mind, and your human self will be at a safe distance?"

Again the marmot nodded.

"And you'll be able to return to your own body without mishap?"

Another nod.

"The sooner you can do it, the better. And be careful, or I will *not* put you in the deepest, darkest dungeon I find, understand? I will take you to the glaciers in northern Scanra and drop you in the deepest crevasse known to man."

Quickmunch turned her back to Numair and flipped her tail up, then faced him again. I like this way of talking, the marmot confided to Daine.

The mage was grinning. "How are you fixed for supplies?" He glanced at the horses' packs. "I can share what I have, particularly since you are feeding Maura as well as yourself."

Quickmunch shook her head and began to climb to her burrow. He's being silly, Daine told her. I'm a lot better able to supply myself than he is.

I know where there are good roots, if you'd like to dig them up, the marmot offered. They're really very nourishing.

That's sweet, Daine replied. But I can find enough food. You eat them. After all, you can't take chances when the Big Cold is on the way.

Now you sound like one of the People, Quickmunch said. Good-bye, and if you want to do this again, please let me know. It was interesting.

Smiling, Daine returned to herself. The opening of the stones that hid her was blocked by a large, dark shape. She nearly panicked before she saw it was Maura and Kitten, peering at her with the strangest expressions on their faces.

"What's the matter?" she asked, and frowned.

Long hairs stuck out on both sides of her nose, and her front teeth felt odd. "And what are you doing here?"

"Why did you do that to your face?" asked the ten-year-old. "You look like a mummer at Midwinter Festival."

"Do what?" No, she was not mistaken. Something was very wrong with her front teeth. "What do you mean, a mummer?"

"You know—they play the parts of the animals, asking Mithros to bring back the sun, so they glue whiskers and furry noses to their faces."

Daine explored with her hands. Her nose had gone flat and—there was no way to get around it—furred, and she had long whiskers curving from either side of her mouth. Her top and bottom incisors were long and extremely sharp, sharp enough to cut her skin. "You can see all this?" It was hard to talk around rodent teeth. Kitten trotted over and touched the new parts with gentle claws.

"Of course," Maura replied scornfully. "It's as plain as the nose—" She stopped just in time. The rest, "on your face," didn't seem tactful.

Daine whooped and stood up, nearly braining herself on the rock overhead. Going outside, she grabbed Maura by the hands and danced her around, laughing.

"I'm not crazy!" she cried. "I'm not mad! It's real! The changes are real!" She skidded to a halt, realizing something. "I think the badger *knew* this would happen. He *said* I'd be surprised." She touched her face, but it was human again. "Odd's bobs. Could I make the whole change? Change entirely into an animal? That would be *wondrous*."

"Don't ask me," replied Maura. "Do you know how it happens?"

"No, but I'll find out." There was a screech overhead. Daine looked up in alarm, but the caller was only a hawk. "And here we are, dancing in the open like idiots. Let's get under cover, and decide how we'll eat tonight." She trotted back toward the caves, Maura and Kitten right behind her.

"I should have brought food and stuff," Maura complained, panting as she ran. "I didn't stop to think about anything like that. I just wanted to get out of there and get word to the king."

"Are you sure you can't go home now?" asked Daine. "You know that help is on the way, and you'll get proper food." She glanced at her friend. Maura's face was set. "I can't be attending you, you know. Numair wants me to count the soldiers in the forts—unless *you* know how many are there."

Maura shook her head. "They never talked about anything like that around me. If they had, I'd've gotten help a long time ago."

"But wouldn't you rather be sleeping on a soft bed under warm blankets? Not to mention your servants being afeared for you." They had reached the entrance cave. Once inside, they slowed to a walk.

"You don't understand," Maura said, catching her breath. "If you're noble and you find treason, and you live with the plotters or go to their parties or marry into their family or *anything*, then you are just as guilty as they are."

"You're only *ten*," Daine argued, taking all of her remaining supplies from her packs. "Surely no one's going to haul a child up before the Lord Provost."

Maura sat by the fire pit. "My father said the laws were written long ago, when times were simpler. They used to hang children for stealing bread, did you know that? Some things have changed, but not chivalry and the nobles' duties. That's what makes me mad. Yolane was raised the same as me. She *knows* what's right and wrong, but she doesn't care. By law Dunlath can be plowed up and sown with salt, and our people made to leave, but does she care? No. She'd rather risk lives and our home so she can wear a crown and order people around."

Daine patted her friend's arm. "She won't get that chance, and nothing's going to happen to Dunlath. You trust Master Numair. He'll fix it."

Maura smiled crookedly. "It isn't him—I don't know him at all. *You're* the one I trust."

Daine hunted and fished until dark, gathering enough food to ensure that Maura would eat properly. Fish would do for that night, with rice from her supplies. The game birds could be baked in clay for Maura to have later. Kitten found mushrooms and blueberries, which would make pleasant additions. When they returned to the caves, Tkaa was there.

"He is under cover, natural and magical, for

the night," the basilisk said as the girls began to cook. "I promised him that I would stay with Lady Maura."

The ten-year-old grinned. "I'd like that." Seeing the pleasure in her face, it was hard to believe that one day ago she had screamed upon seeing him. "The wolves still make me nervous." When Daine glanced at her, she shrugged. "I'm sorry, they just do. Speaking of them, where have they been all day?"

"Hunting, I s'pose," Daine replied. "Some days it takes longer than others." She tried to remember when she last saw the pack, and realized it had been the evening before. "They'll be back when they've fed."

She was dishing up the rice and fish when she saw Tkaa reach into a pouch in the skin of his belly. "Did I know you had that?" she asked, curious.

"One does not expect the very young to know a great deal," he replied. He drew several chunks of rock from the pouch and placed them near the small pile of stones that was to be his own meal. "Dessert," he explained in his soft voice, when he saw that the girls, Kitten, and Cloud watched him intently.

"The birds and the rice and the rest of my supplies will hold you whilst I'm gone," Daine told Maura as they ate, wincing as Tkaa crunched his meal. "You'll be fine here. Tkaa will be with you, and Kitten." The young dragon, wrinkling her muzzle at Tkaa's idea of food, nibbled daintily on a trout.

"Wolves—?" Maura started to ask, voice quivering. "I'm sorry. I don't mean to whine. Only, all my life I was told wolves will eat me. It's hard to forget."

"But you think Stormwings are fine." Daine knew she kept returning to that point, but she couldn't help herself. She had battled them for so long that it was well-nigh impossible to see them as anything but foul.

"Not *all* of them. The one that called you a Stormwing killer and some of the others can be nasty. But Lord Rikash takes me flying sometimes."

Daine gaped. *"Flying?"*

"Yes. They made a rope sling for me, and they carry me in their claws. It's fun! They're a lot stronger than you think."

"Smell?" Daine's voice came out as a strangled squeak.

"Oh, I dab perfume under my nose, and I breathe through my mouth. Once I was getting over a cold, and I couldn't smell a thing. That was the best time. And when you're up in the air over everything, who cares about smells?"

The rest of his meal eaten, Tkaa put a dessert rock in his mouth and hummed his satisfaction. Daine, glad to change the subject, asked, "It is good, then?"

Tkaa nodded. "The best I've ever had. They are well aged, and I am most partial to this dark variant."

Maura shook her head. "Wouldn't you rather have real candy? I have spice drops. You just reminded me." She fished a crumpled paper from a pocket and offered its contents to Daine and Kitten, who accepted with pleasure, then to Tkaa. The basilisk thanked her politely, but it was easy to see he was not tempted to trade his "candy" for hers.

"What is it, the stone you're eating?" Daine asked.

The basilisk chose a rock and made a sound that was half whistle, half croak. The rock flared with a multitude of lights colored blue, violet, and green, with tiny sparks of red and amber. Slowly the lights faded. "Black opals," the immortal announced with pleasure. "The finest I have ever eaten."

Kitten sat up and whistle-croaked. The pile of stones shone with the same rainbow of colors, and went dark. "Very good, Skysong," approved Tkaa.

Daine frowned. Here was the answer to the mines and the emperor's interest. "Yolane ships opals to Carthak," she said. "And Ozorne gives her mages, gold, maybe even soldiers, for when she rebels against King Jon."

"This just gets worse and worse." Maura's voice was tight. "It's illegal to mine precious metals and stones without telling the Crown."

"Prob'ly for just this reason," Daine pointed out. "So folk won't sell them and use the money, or the magic, to make trouble." She put a hand on Maura's shoulder. "We'll stop them, Lady Maura. You'll see."

SEVEN

COUNTING SOLDIERS

Tkaa promised to tell Numair of the opals in the morning, then entertained Maura and Kitten with tales of the Divine Realms. Daine put out the food and made sure Maura knew how to cook it. She was impressed by the girl's camplore: few ten-year-olds could build a fire, let alone cook on it. Maura gave the huntsman Tait the credit.

"You're lucky in your friends," Daine said as she tucked Maura in.

"If not my family," agreed Maura, yawning. "The wolves really won't eat me?"

Daine took a breath and counted to ten, so she wouldn't give an angry reply. It worked, simply because Maura was asleep by the time she finished counting.

"I leave to go south at dawn," she told Kitten, Tkaa, and Cloud later.

Tkaa switched to thought-speech, confiding that so much spoken talk that day had made his jaw muscles ache. —*Have you decided how you will go in?*—

"I'll see who's about," replied Daine. "Oh, listen—the pack's coming."

—*We must take your word for that,*—remarked the basilisk, amused. —*In this, your magic is more powerful than ours.*—Kitten nodded.

Daine went to the cave entrance to greet the wolves. The moment she saw them, she wished she had remained seated. Brokefang, in the lead, bore a ham in his jaws. Frostfur was next with a rope of sausages. Each wolf had something: small bags of grain, meat, sacks of potatoes. Each pup proudly, and gently, bore an egg in his or her mouth. Also, enthroned on Sharp Nose's back, nagging the wolf to trot slower, was the squirrel she had healed two days ago.

Brokefang put the ham at her feet as the rest

of the pack carried their burdens into the cave. The squirrel asked to come, the chief wolf told Daine, panting happily. He wants to help.

"Help with what!" Daine whisper-screamed. Tkaa, Kitten, and Cloud came out to see why she was so excited. "Are you *crazy*? Why did you steal all this food? *Where* did you steal it? Mithros above, *how* did you steal it?"

Easily, Battle replied. We visited the tree cutter den. They had more food than they could use. We ate some ourselves, and we spoiled the rest.

Frolic added, We knew you and the human pup would soon eat all you have. Besides, if the men have no food, they will not have the strength to cut trees.

"I *told* you, the Coldfang was set on your trail because you stole the axes! It'll be a lot easier to track you when you stole hams and onions! They smell!"

If they follow, we are ready, said Brokefang coolly. There is rockfall up the slope. When pushed, it will bury a Coldfang, and we can use other ways out of the cave.

It will do no good to moan, 'What have I done?' as you have been. (Only Frostfur can be that charming, thought Daine.) It is time for us to think this way. Men bully us all our lives. It is time for some revenge.

Only a little, Brokefang cautioned. Avoiding two-leggers is still best.

"What of you?" Daine asked the squirrel, knowing there was nothing she could say to change the wolves' minds. "How did you get pulled into this madness?"

You told me to listen to nonwolves, Brokefang reminded her. Surely listening means speaking, too.

The big fellow here told me they fight tree cutters, the little rodent said. If *anyone* fights them, I will help. Do you know how many of my kind lost homes and feeding grounds this year? The Highbranch family *starved*, in the growing season, because their nesting places were cut down! And the big fellow—

My name is Brokefang, the wolf said, looking up at the squirrel.

I am Flicker, replied the squirrel. My family name is Round Meadow.

—*It is useless to get excited,*— Tkaa said to Daine, not unkindly. —*As you told me, you did not ask them to do this. They thought of it themselves, and perhaps it is not such a bad thing to think.—*

Daine sighed. Tkaa was right. Also, there was nothing she could say to the pack that she had not said before, clearly with little effect. Instead she looked at Flicker. Squirrels had nimble forepaws, as good as hands in their way, and quick reflexes. They had keen eyes and ears, and a great deal of curiosity. Flicker was perfect for her needs.

"How would you like to go for a walk in the morning?" she asked him.

Often during her ride south Daine cursed the need for secrecy that kept her, Cloud, and Flicker high on the mountainsides, rather than on the road by the lakeshore. They stopped often to rest Cloud, although the mare argued that she was not a soft valley pony, to be coddled every step of the way. By the time they reached the woods near the southern fort, the afternoon was half gone.

Daine cared for Cloud before taking a seat under an old willow. Its long branches swept the earth, screening her and her friends from view. With the mare to stand guard, she was as safe here as anywhere in Dunlath. Making herself comfortable against the bole of the tree, she asked Flicker, "Ready?"

The squirrel finished the nut he was eating and launched himself into the willow's branches. Ready! he replied.

Daine closed her eyes. Before she could draw an entire breath, she was in Flicker's mind. Swiftly they climbed high on the bole, then leaped for the next tree. He seized what looked like a clump of leaves and little more, and fell.

Daine opened her eyes. She was in her own body again, shaking. Flicker dropped to the next branch down and scolded. How are we to do *anything* if you go away on the easiest jumps? Come back at once, and don't be such a baby. I thought you went flying with a bat just the other night.

The bat was *flying,* not falling and missing his grip! she retorted silently.

I did *not* miss my grip. That was a controlled drop. Now are you coming?

Just a moment, Daine replied. Finding her water bottle, she had a drink.

Back so soon? asked Cloud, wickedly.

"Very funny. I'd like to see you leap through trees."

But I don't try. That is why *my* kind has horse sense, and yours does not.

Daine made a face at the mare and settled back against the willow. This time all she did was close her eyes, and she was inside Flicker.

You can trust me, he said as he set out once more. I've done this all my life.

The rest of the trip was a blur. Flicker used jumps as she might use large steps over puddles, whipping his tail for balance, then racing to the next leap.

The trees were cut for a hundred yards around the fort, but the grass was tall enough to screen a gray squirrel. The fort's long walls were easy to climb. At the top Daine made Flicker check for guards. The two they saw were distant and not looking their way: she urged him over. He dropped onto the walk and climbed headfirst to the ground as Daine cringed. You won't make a good squirrel at this rate, he informed her when they were safely on the ground.

They checked the inner enclosure: it was nearly empty. Horses were picketed in front of a low wooden building Daine guessed to be the commander's office. A horse-boy dozed near his charges under the single tree allowed to grow inside the wall. He was the only human in view, though they heard others in the buildings.

Everything was fairly new, built from raw wood. As well as the mess and the command post, she identified a stable, a building that had to be a barracks, and the privy. One other building had only a roof, three walls, and a long, low railing. Straw was scattered on the floor; the rail was scarred with what looked like knife cuts.

What's that? asked Flicker. It looks strange.

I *think* it's a Stormwing roost. They're the only creatures big enough to need a rail that large to sit on.

Flicker's teeth chattered angrily. If they have their own perches like this, they had no business landing on *my* branch and almost killing me!

Too right. Now, let's try the command post, she suggested.

The squirrel raced to the closest building, the stable, and ran up the side. One leap: they were on the roof of the Stormwing mews.

Even the wood between them couldn't keep the reek from Flicker's sensitive nose. He sneezed, then jumped onto the command post roof. Trotting to the edge, he swung down under the eaves and saw a broad window.

They climbed in and looked around. On the wall by the door, a large slate was mounted. Written across the top in white chalk was Duty Roster—Troops.

Daine examined it. Thirty privates were listed, as well as three sergeants, three corporals, and a captain, making a total of thirty-seven. She counted twice, to be sure, then noticed papers in a stack on the desk.

Let's have a peek at those, she suggested to the squirrel.

Flicker jumped onto the desk and picked up documents one at a time for Daine to read. The first two were supply orders; the third was not. At its foot was a heavy wax seal that bore an image of a crossed sword and wand, topped by a crown and wrapped in a jagged circle. It was the seal of the emperor of Carthak: she knew it from histories and official papers Numair had shown her. The writing was bold and easy to read.

The criminal Arram Draper, also known as Numair Salmalín, is to be taken alive and transported to Carthak by Stormwings.

Try also to capture the young dragon. If this immortal is shipped to Us live for inclusion in Our menagerie, there will be a reward of 500 gold thaks. As to the dragon's handler, she is not required. Kill her.

The girl was so absorbed in her reading that she didn't notice something had darkened the window. When a wave of stench reached Flicker's nostrils, he sneezed and turned.

Rikash had landed on the rail outside and was looking in. "Well. A tree-rat. I think it's odd, a tree-rat going through papers. It's not the kind of thing you little crawlers usually do, is it?"

Flicker's tail whipped savagely in anger and fear. Come here, he cried. I'll show you what a "crawler" can do!

Rikash slid until he could block the window if he raised his wings. "Only magic would let a tree-rat read." He yelled, "Humans to the command post! *Now,* ground pounders, *now*!" Raising a claw, he pointed at Flicker.

The floor! Daine ordered. Flicker jumped as gold fire smacked into the spot where they had been standing.

What was *that*? asked the squirrel, breath coming fast.

Magic. They don't use it much, but when they do . . . *jump*!

Flicker leaped atop a cabinet as another fire bolt struck his last position. I'm getting angry, Smelly, he scolded. How would you like your nose bit off?

This is *not* the time to insult him, Daine warned, looking for an escape. She heard feet pounding: humans were answering Rikash's summons.

Their location had the Stormwing in a bind. His feathers got in the way as he tried to aim. What's wrong? taunted Flicker. Can't work yourself around to point? But one of you was limber enough when it came to *landing* on me!

Someone banged on the door. "Hello! Is anyone there?"

"Yes, you dolts!" snarled Rikash. "Get in here now!"

"It's locked!" yelled the man outside.

"Out of the way!" the immortal cried. He *could* point at the door, and did, to loose a bolt of fire at the lock. Flicker jumped to the floor and ran over just as the door swung open.

Three men, two of them cooks to judge from their aprons, dashed in.

"*Get that squirrel!*" shrieked Rikash as Flicker bolted past.

The cooks gaped at him. "Get the *what*?"

The exit was open. Flicker darted through and raced for the fort's wall.

"Don't argue with me! *It's getting away!*" Rikash's voice was clear even through the command post walls.

The squirrel didn't even pause. By the time a search party could leave the fort, he had reached the woods and was scrambling through the trees.

Daine returned to herself. She tried to get up, but something was not right with her feet or hands. They were squirrel paws. "Oh, no," she whispered. "Not now." Looking up, she said, "Flicker, are you all right?"

The squirrel climbed down the willow. You should have let me bite the Great Stinky, he snapped. Then *he'd* know what it's like! Looking her over, he remarked in a milder voice, You know, parts of you are almost normal.

"Funny," mumbled Daine. "Cloud, we have to go. I think Rikash will search for us. But—" She looked at her hands and feet. They were still paws. "Please change back," she said wistfully.

Why? asked the squirrel. You don't have claws of your own—keep these.

If they are hunting you, it might be wise to warn the local squirrels, Cloud remarked. They'll just kill anyone they see, hoping it's you.

Daine winced. "You're right." She called to the nearby tree folk, whether they were red, gray, or the shy black breed. When she finished, all were finding places to hide, and her hands were human. Teetering on human-size, clawed feet supported by her boots, she saddled Cloud and mounted, with Flicker on her lap.

They halted some hours south of the western pass when the light had gone. Stormwings had forced them under cover several times on the way: she dared not start a fire they might see. Instead she gnawed on waybread and jerky, trying to ignore a pounding headache.

To complete her happiness, fog rose from the lake to cover the valley in a clammy shroud.

Flicker cleaned out her supply of sunflower seeds, dug up and ate all the nuts other squirrels had cached within sight of their camp, and curled up in one of Daine's packs to sleep. Daine shoved herself under a rock ledge to get out of the damp, and gingerly removed her boots. Her ankles looked human, but the rest looked squirrelish. "When will I get my toes back?" she asked Cloud.

The mare liked fog no better than her rider. I am a pony, she snapped. You have to ask that question of someone who understands magic. I do not.

—So.— Daine jumped, and banged her head on the rock over her. How the badger had crept up on her she could not begin to guess. *—I see you have learned the wider applications of the lesson I mentioned to you.—*

"You could have warned me," she snapped, rubbing her scalp. "I thought I was losing my mind."

—After the man said there was no madness in you? If you cannot trust your own instincts, you could at least trust his.—

"He has no instincts, only things learned from books," she grumbled.

—*Why do you say that?*—

The question brought her to a sudden boil. "He walked us into a mess of traitors." She knew she was being unfair, but couldn't stop. "*And* evil mages. He got stuck on one side of a magic wall with me on the other. He won't use a word of power on it 'cause the word might cause a mess somewhere, which I don't believe it will. *Now* I have to count soldiers at opposite ends of the valley. He thinks I'm safe because I'm inside Flicker. He didn't think of folk who'd see a squirrel looking at papers and know something was amiss!"

Her toes hurt, sending darts of pain up her legs that did nothing to help her thinking. She rubbed them. "I'm saddled with a two-legger who won't go home when she's only in the way. I'm running from Stormwings, hurroks, Coldfangs, and the Horse Lords know what else. I'm cold and hungry and tired and I have squirrel feet!"

The badger breathed on the afflicted parts. His breath was warm and soothing. Hair and claws melted, turned pale and smooth:

Daine's toes were back. They cramped, and she winced. The badger breathed on them again. The cramps eased, and stopped. So did her headache.

—*You have been a foolish kit,*— he informed her. —*To return to your original state, you must do the same thing you did to begin to change, only in reverse. You have to think yourself into your two-legger form.*—

"Oh." She drew on stockings and boots, feeling ridiculous. The badger sighed, and lay beside her. The weight and warmth of his furred body against hers was pleasant, and the heavy badger aroma was comforting. "No matter what I say, the wolves are doing terrible things, things that will get them hurt if they're caught! How can I help when they won't *listen* to me?"

—*You don't grasp why you were brought here. Haven't you seen, in your travels, that you alone speak to all three kindreds: humans, immortals, and beasts?*—

"No. Is that important?"

—*In other places, perhaps not. But here . . . What do you think of this valley?*— he asked, appearing to change the subject.

She blinked. "Dunlath?" He nodded regally. "Well, it's—*nice*. Lots of farmland, the lake for fishing, good forests—or they would be, if Yolane and Belden didn't rip the covering off to get at every drop of what's under it. Except for mountain winters, Dunlath is almost perfect, not only for the Peole, but two-leggers." She remembered the ogre falling at the mines, blood rolling down his back. "Maybe even immortals, too, if they wanted to just live here and raise families."

—*Now you see the shape of our plan. You were brought here to help* all *of Dunlath, not just wolves.*—

"That's twice you've said I was brought, like a cat in a sack. The wolves asked me to come help, but I came on my own two feet, and on Cloud's four."

—*Were you not surprised to get a request for help from Brokefang? Is it the nature of wolves to think to ask for help?*—

"Well, no . . . Maybe—"

—*They do not ask their kinfolk. Packmates already know what is needed. And those beings who are not Pack are unimportant unless they serve as food.*—

"But he changed, because he licked my wound—"

—*He didn't change that much, not in the beginning.*—

"Well, then, why *did* he think to ask for me to come?"

—*Old White suggested it. We thought that if you came for the wolves, you would ease into the true matter, the problem of all Dunlath. I had hoped you would see for yourself what is required by now.*—

Daine blushed, feeling absurdly guilty and stupid. "I'm not a seer or a diviner," she protested. "I need things spelled out. That isn't a crime."

The badger rumbled. —*Then here is the spelling. Fish, fowl, four-leggers, two-leggers, no-leggers, you are to set this whole valley to rights.*—

She listened with dismay. "*How?*" she wailed. "I'm fourteen! *Only* fourteen! How do *I* set everyone to rights? Get someone bigger! Get someone older!"

—*Someone older and bigger will not do.*— His voice was tightly patient. —*You are the* only *one for the task. If you weren't tired and wet and frightened, you would see it for yourself.—*

"No I wouldn't," she muttered rebelliously. "I still don't—"

—Shape a bridge between kindreds.— He pressed his blunt head to her palm. *—Find allies, my kit—not just among the People, but among humans and immortals.—* Idly he added, *—How do you deal with the Stormwings, may I ask?—*

She made a face. "We've had words. You know how they are. They're here in force, and it looks like they're serving the Carthaki emperor once again."

—It may be they have no choice. If hurroks can be bound to the service of humans, so can Stormwings.—

"Why is everyone I meet defending them? You sound like Maura." Remembering her friend's behavior with the immortals, Daine snorted. "Though I'll tell you, yesterday I almost felt sorry for Rikash and his crew. He wanted Maura to go home as bad as I do, but she said no, and he wouldn't make her. It was funny."

—They sound almost like real people, not monsters.— The badger's voice was so bland,

so clean of any emotion, that Daine looked at him suspiciously.

"What's *that* supposed to mean?"

—*Nothing, young kit.*— Rising, he nudged her in the side, hard. —*Get some rest, then go to work. Unless you want to be here for the Big Cold?*—

"Goddess, no!" Smiling, she added, "Thanks, Badger."

—*Stop feeling sorry for yourself, mind. My patience has its limits.*— As if to prove his point, he glared at the wide-eyed Flicker, who had listened to the entire conversation. —*What are you staring at, nibbler?*—

He didn't wait for a reply. Silver fire bloomed around him and he was gone.

Badgers, Flicker remarked wearily. They always have to be wiser and grumpier than anyone else.

The next day dawned gray and wet, a mixed blessing. It meant they didn't need to worry much about Stormwings or hurroks: they had trouble staying aloft with damp wings. However, she and her friends were *also* wet, which did nothing for moods. They were all aware of the long trip to the northern fort.

"At least we can dry off and get some hot food here," Daine told the others as they reached the caves. "We can't stay long, though."

When they entered the big cave, Maura squeaked and ran to hug Daine. "I'm so glad you're back!" she whispered. "Are you done with your counting?"

Daine felt a guilty twinge. Her comments to the badger about a two-legger who got in her way felt as if they were branded on her forehead. "I have to do the northern fort yet," she said. "How is everything here?"

Maura pulled away. "Fine," she said, the tone of her voice falsely bright. "Tkaa's teaching me'n Kitten—"

"Kitten and *me*," Daine corrected automatically.

"About rocks. You know, how you can tell what's what. He teaches Kitten how to change them, too, but I can't make the noise."

—*Some of the wolves frighten her,*— said Tkaa, emerging from one of the rear caverns. Daine looked for the pack. The pups, napping beside the pile of human gear, thumped their tails and dozed off again. —*The gray-and-white female, Frostfur. The older male, Longwind. They do not harm her, but they watch her, and she knows it. The female growls if Maura comes too close.*—

"Oh, dear." Daine looked at the girl. "Tkaa says Frostfur and Longwind are upsetting you."

"Oh, no." Maura's eyes avoided Daine's. "I hardly notice them. Fleetfoot and Russet are nice, and the pups will play with me. Would you like corn cakes? I still have some batter. I made it from the food the pack brought."

Daine tended Cloud, feeding her the last barley and oats. Her pony cared for, she tried the cakes, and praised them. Flicker liked them too, particularly with honey. *It will be a shame to go back to the trees,* he confided to Daine. *I like the variety of food you have.*

You'll get as fat as a marmot, Daine said, oiling rough spots on Kitten's hide.

"Daine?" Maura asked. "I was thinking, don't you need help with your counting? I could write numbers down for you. I wouldn't be in the way."

Dismay warred with pity. "We've only one horse," Daine said, "and I have to move fast.

The only way you could go would be if we had a mount for both of us. I can't call your horse—he's in his own stable by now. And there's nothing else you can ride."

"A deer, maybe, or an elk? No. I guess that's a stupid idea. I'm sorry. I didn't mean to bother you. I know you'd rather I went home."

Daine winced. It was what she thought, but hearing it in that polite, well-bred voice made her feel like a bigger monster than a Stormwing.

"If travel is the only problem, I may be able to help," Tkaa remarked. "I will carry Lady Maura on my back."

Kitten whistled: the basilisk nodded. "You may ride in my pouch, Skysong."

Dumbfounded, Daine stared at the tall immortal. He looked no stronger than a birch sapling. "Impossible."

"You of all people should know better than to use that word," reproved Tkaa.

"Even if you could carry both, which I doubt, you couldn't keep up."

"I do not see how so young a mortal came to believe she knows all there is to be known of immortals. I would not offer if I felt I could not do it."

Daine was a well-mannered girl, but she liked being talked down to no better than any other teenager. "Very well," she said, standing. "If you can fit Kitten in your pouch, carry Maura piggy-back, *and* keep up with me and Cloud—"

"Cloud and *me*," Maura interrupted. She blushed and covered her mouth with her hands when Daine made a face at her.

"—then you're welcome to come," the older girl finished, feeling beset on all sides. "But if you fall behind, I won't linger for you."

Before they had been on the trail more than an hour, Tkaa caught up to Cloud, Daine, and Flicker and passed them. Maura drooped over his shoulder, sound asleep. Kitten sat up in his pouch, watching the trail.

They traveled all day, getting soaked as the damp turned to rain. At midafternoon they passed the cliff where Daine had first seen the mines. She sighed. That spot would have been good to work from if she only had to listen to the fort's animals, but she wanted to be closer before Flicker went there. She wasn't sure how far her new magic would stretch.

So they followed the mountains farther

north, around the fields of heaped and barren dirt. Tkaa found a wooded ridge that overlooked the fort. It was ideal. Large trees nearby would shelter them from the hurroks Daine was sure lived in the northern fort. Also, a line of rock formed a clear path from the base of their ridge to within fifty yards of the palisade.

Flicker agreed. Easy as eating corn, he told her.

Using branches and a fallen log over a pocket in the earth, Daine and Maura built a rough shelter where Tkaa, Kitten, and the girl could sit out of the wet. Daine unsaddled Cloud. As she did so, Maura, Kitten, and Tkaa returned to the ridge, looking not at the fort, but at the mines. The weather might have been damp and miserable, but operations below were in full swing. Human and ogre workers labored in thick mud while overseers cursed those who fell.

When Daine joined them, Maura said quietly, "These poor ogres are *ugly*."

"I don't know," replied Daine. "At least they're of a piece, all one thing. They prob'ly think *we're* funny looking, all pink and hairless."

"You don't hate them? But I hear so many

stories. Outside the valley they fight with humans all the time. It's said the King's Champion lives in the saddle these days because she's always battling them."

Daine shrugged. "It's not so bad. Lady Alanna doesn't *always* fight them. Ogres just don't understand they can't take things that belong to others." Since her talk with the badger, she had done a great deal of thinking. "I wonder—if humans didn't attack and tried to be nice, maybe ogres wouldn't be so nasty." She pointed at the mines. "And I know one thing for certain. This is just plain wrong. Look at their ribs—you could count them. When d'you suppose they had their last meal? And whatever it was, it can't have been much."

Maura stared at the scene below, small face unreadable.

Come *on*, Flicker said. We'll have to do some of this in the dark, and I *hate* the dark. Can we get moving, before we have to do it *all* in the dark?

"I have to go," Daine told the others. "Keep your heads down while you're here, and get under cover soon. No fire, mind, and talk *softly*."

Tkaa looked at her. "We will be fine. I will keep the little ones safe."

Daine smiled. "I know you will."

Seated in a corner of the shelter, Daine shut her eyes and entered Flicker's mind. The squirrel's hide itched with anxiety over the coming of night. He scratched, then clambered down the ridge to the line of rock.

The mine workers were trudging home as Flicker reached the fort. Daine was glad to find a chink where the log palisade met the ground: she had not liked the idea of climbing up when they could be seen by those being herded past. Once inside the wall, Flicker scaled one of the watchtowers, tucking himself in where two of the supports met the platform floor.

What is that building over there, the newish one? he wanted to know. *It has a terrible smell.*

She peered at the structure he meant. It was set apart from the other buildings in the enclosure. Built like a stable, its doors extended from the ground to roof. When the wind blew from its direction, a scent of hay, dead meat, and rage, one she had first smelled as a bat, filled the air.

Hurrok stables, she told Flicker. They

patrol this part of the valley. They're nasty. Lucky for us, I don't think they can fly in weather like this.

She examined the rest of the fort. It was larger than the one in the south, and older—no doubt it had been here before the mining began. There were painted shutters open on the buildings' windows. The men wore the uniform of Maura's house, green tunic over gray shirt and breeches, with a shoulder badge of the Dunlath coat of arms, a green two-headed griffin on a gray field.

Stands to reason that it's fancier, she told Flicker. Most local visitors must come from the north, from the City of the Gods or Fief Aili. Only traders come in from the south.

The sun is *going,* the squirrel replied.

I'm afraid we have to let it go, she said, as kindly as possible. That room with the light in it looks to be the commander's office like the one we visited in the south. We have to wait for him to leave, and that probably won't be till it's time to eat. Look at it this way—at least we're out of the rain.

We're going back to our friends in the *dark*? asked Flicker.

We must.

He sighed. I know you wouldn't ask it of me if it weren't important. I just *hate* the dark.

The meager daylight was gone and torches were lit when the mess call was sounded. The lamp in the commander's office continued to burn, but the commander emerged to join the flow of men to the mess. Daine and Flicker waited until everyone but the guards in the towers had left the yard, then raced to the headquarters. Swiftly they climbed in the window through an open shutter.

Like its counterpart, this fort had slates with the duty roster nicely laid out in white chalk. I love soldiers, Daine confided to Flicker. They always try to do things the same as every other soldier. She read what was on the board, counting forty soldiers, four corporals, four sergeants, one captain.

More soldiers because of the two-leggers entering this way? asked Flicker.

Has to be, she replied. Come on. Let's get out of here.

Their return took longer than the trip out. Flicker was almost as blind in the dark as a human, and more nervous than Daine had ever seen him. Each rustle and squeak was an owl, a bear, a bush dog, or something worse come to eat him. Daine nursed him along as patiently as she knew how. Flicker had done great things for her, things no squirrel would dream of, and that knowledge kept her gentle when he made one of his many stops to hide. She stayed with him up the face of the ridge and over its edge, rather than leaving him to do it alone.

He nearly expired when a huge shadow moved and snorted. Hello, squirrel, said Cloud. Bad night?

Flicker sat down against a tree bole, shuddering. It was *terrible,* he told the pony. How can you stand walking in the dark?

Daine knew Cloud would ease the squirrel's shattered nerves if the two were alone, so she thanked Flicker again and left him, to open her eyes in the shelter.

There was no light anywhere, only noises, the sounds of large bodies moving nearby. Nervous, she looked around, ears twitching. Now she could see a little, but what she saw was *not* reassuring. Two monstrous shapes moved just outside the shelter's door, one tall and thin, the other wide across the shoulders and slumped. Between them was a smaller but still big shape.

A whistle by one of her ears nearly deafened her, and a face thrust itself near hers. It was long and sharp-toothed on the end. Large, faintly glowing eyes with catlike pupils looked her over. She squeaked and tried to back away.

The smaller of the big shapes turned, showing a face like a pale blur in the darkness. Its owner crawled toward Daine on hands and knees.

It was very strange to find Maura so much bigger than she was.

"Oh, dear," the girl said. "Uh—Daine, you, um, you shrank."

Tell me something I don't know, Daine said: it came out as angry squirrel chatter. She looked at her hands and feet. They were still human, but a fine gray fuzz covered them, and the tips of her nails were now black claws.

She closed her eyes and tried to remember who Daine the human was. It was easier to remember her wolf self, or her bat self. Who was she?

An image appeared before her eyes, a pool of

copper fire with a central core of white light. Between core and pool lay a wall of clear power, like glass, flickering with sparks of white and black fire. The white core was her inner self; the sparkling wall was the barrier Numair once put between her self and her magic, to stop her from forgetting her humanity.

Start there, she thought. She found memories of Ma, of Grandda, of the house where she grew up. Next were the Snowsdale humans who tried to kill her for running with wolves. She saw Onua, who gave her work in Galla and a home in Tortall. Here were others who filled important places in her life, a mixed bag of nobles, commoners, warriors, and animals. So *that's* who I am, she thought, pleased to have so much that was good in her human life.

She opened her eyes.

EIGHT
FRIENDS

Maura sat with her back to Daine. "I can't look anymore," she was saying. "Tell me when she's done." The nearby, cat-eyed shape was Kitten, who made a questioning sound. Daine lifted the dragon into her lap, then looked at the bigger shapes at the opening of the shelter. One was unmistakably Tkaa. The other was a stranger.

"I'm done," she announced.

Maura turned and gasped. "You're you! I mean, you were always you, but you were starting to looking kind of—squirrelish."

I'm sorry I missed that, commented Flicker from outside the shelter.

Tkaa said, "It is good you have returned. We have a guest. Iakoju, this is Daine, the human Maura spoke of."

The stranger nodded. She was an ogre, clad only in a short, ragged tunic in spite of the damp. "Are you cold?" Daine asked. "We have a horse blanket somewhere." She found one and offered it to the immortal.

"I *said* Daine would welcome her," Maura informed Tkaa. To Daine she added, "Iakoju's our friend. She wants to help us get rid of Yolane and Tristan."

Iakoju stared at the blanket, pointed ears twitching back and forth. At last she took it. "Thank you," she said quietly, and bowed from the waist.

Maura helped the ogre drape the blanket around her shoulders. "She's running away," the ten-year-old explained.

Placid eyes met Daine's without blinking. Despite skinniness and poor clothes Iakoju was clean, smelled of soap, earth, and something vaguely spicy. Daine sniffed, trying to identify the spice odor. "Are you eating something?"

Iakoju smiled. "Maura gave me candy."

Maura blushed. "Well, she looked so scared

when I found her, and I remembered what you said, about people being mean to them and maybe if somebody was nice . . ."

There's one for your side, Badger, thought Daine.

"Did you succeed at your mission?" asked Tkaa.

Daine nodded and found her water canteen. Politely she offered it first to Iakoju who shook her head and held up a gourd water bottle of her own. As Daine drank, Maura said, "Iakoju thinks some of the ogres will help us."

"Why?" Daine sat by Tkaa, where she could see their guest. Kitten and Flicker joined her, Flicker curling up on one shoulder, Kitten on her lap.

"Stormwings and Tristan lie," Iakoju said flatly. "They say, come through gate, we give you farms to keep, so we come. Only farms here are rock farms, under ground. We say, don't want mines, where are farms? Tristan say, you farm what we say farm." She scowled. "Ogres are angry. They send me from valley to find kin clans. Kin clans come help, bashing lying men on the head."

Flicker yawned and nearly tumbled off

Daine's shoulder. She slid him into the crook of her arm and asked, "Didn't you have farms in the Divine Realms?"

Iakoju shook her head. "Too many ogres. No room. We come here for farms."

Maura frowned. "I don't understand. If you're peaceful—if you really only like to farm—how come you're called 'ogres'? Ogres are monsters, aren't they? And how come your people are always fighting with ours?"

"We are big," replied Iakoju quietly. "Ugly. Our color different from men color. No all ogres are same, either. Some take what they want. Some fight with men. My people, kin clans, we only like farming, not fighting. Some ogres only like fighting. Are all men the same?"

"No," Daine said thoughtfully. "Of course not."

Maura poked the dirt with a stick. "It's a shame the lake's east shore can't be plowed. It's too steep."

Daine sensed what her young friend had in mind. "The fief is Yolane's. I don't think she'll approve of ogre farms on the east shore."

"Under law she forfeits her lands for treason," argued the ten-year-old. "And the fief isn't all hers. Half is mine—Papa willed it to me, and maybe the king would let me keep it. The way it was supposed to be, Yolane would buy my half when it came time for me to marry, so it's my dowry. That's why I got the eastern half. It's mostly uphill, though," she said with a sigh.

Iakoju's eyes lit. "We make farms. Find ridge, dig out cup, pour in growing dirt. Make small valleys up and down, grown corn, beans, flowers. Peas, herbs—we *like* growing. If ogres help you, will you give us farms?"

"Maura cannot promise," Tkaa reminded her. "It may be she will lose the land. Her sister, whose holding this is, plots against the Crown."

"Tkaa's right," Maura told Iakoju, hanging her head. "I guess I can't promise, not if it might not come true."

The ogre looked at her, at the basilisk, then at Daine. Her mouth curved in a smile. "Maybe I don't leave Dunlath. I go with you instead. We will talk."

Daine was about to object, and changed her mind. The badger's words were still very fresh in her memory. In any event, it couldn't hurt. Before she slept, she wrote a report for Numair, using a glowstone from her belt-purse as her light. Once the report was done, she napped uneasily, dreaming of hurroks.

The company awoke at dawn. The clouds had gone, and the day promised to be lovely. Daine's enjoyment of its beauty was soured by the knowledge that winged patrols would be aloft today. Cloud told her, We had best take another route to the pass, one with lots of trees. Iakoju will stand out like a bear in a puddle.

A nearby stag told Daine of trails lower on the slopes, ones that skirted the mines and lumber camp and passed almost entirely under the trees. She led the way to them with a thank-you to the stag. The tip was a good one. The path was wide and much-used, taking advantage of every bit of cover the forest provided, perfect for much-hunted animals like deer.

As the morning ended, the path took them by the round meadow, past Flicker's tree and the Coldfang statue. Daine passed it with a shudder. Twice since meeting the creature she had awakened with a pounding heart, sweat-damp hair, and the feeling that something icy advanced on her, slowly and relentlessly. She would be glad if she *never* saw another live Coldfang, and it pleased her to leave the stone one behind. One other fear, that Flicker might choose to stay, faded when the squirrel made no mention of returning to his home.

An hour later she heard an animal's call and signaled for the others to halt. Where are you? she asked. What do you want?

A dog broke from the pines fifty yards ahead and raced up to her. It was the huntsman's head dog, one of the wolfhounds Daine had met at the castle.

Dismounting, she said, "I'm sorry—I didn't get your name, before."

I am Prettyfoot, the dog replied. Daine covered a smile with her hand. It is the name the man gave me, the wolfhound insisted. It is a good name.

"It's a lovely name," Daine replied soothingly. "How may I help you?"

Please come, the hound begged. The man is hurt. The wolves did it.

Daine looked at her friends. "Something's up. I have to go with this dog." To Prettyfoot she said, Is it complicated? Will it take me awhile to help?

I don't know if you can help at all, Prettyfoot said, dark eyes sad under wiry brows. Our pack could do nothing.

"Tkaa, will you take this to Numair?" Daine asked, pulling the letter she had written from her shirt. "I think the sooner he gets it, the better."

"Very wise," the basilisk said, lifting Kitten from his pouch. "When it is delivered, I will walk back this way to find you again." He took the letter and set off down the trail, long legs carrying him quickly out of sight.

"We go with dog now?" asked Iakoju.

Daine nodded. "His master's in trouble, he says."

"Tait?" Maura said, alarmed. "Then what're we waiting for?"

Prettyfoot led them onto a new trail, explaining that his pack had been calling for help for a day and a night. No matter what they or the man did, there was no way to take him from the hole. In a small, rough clearing crossed by the trail, they found the rest of Tait's dogs beside a pit. They came running to bark greetings to her and Maura.

Going to the rim of the hole, Daine peered

in. Tait, coated in mud, leaves, and filth, sat at the bottom. Suddenly she knew what the wolves' plan for Tait had been. "Huntsman," she said. "You're in a fix."

"Laugh all ye like, girly," he said tiredly, "but get me out of here."

"I don't know," she drawled. "May I ask if this was a wolf pit, to start?"

"It was a lot smaller!" he bellowed. "And the trail marks I put here t' tell me where the damned thing was got moved! If that was your work—"

"I haven't been next or nigh this spot," she retorted, "so don't raise your voice to me!" She was tempted to leave him there. Maura had told her, during the morning's ride, that Tait had killed the last wolf pack to live in Dunlath.

Do not be angry, begged Prettyfoot. He is cold and wet and hungry. And he *smells*.

Daine turned to Iakoju. "I have a rope. Can you pull him out?"

The ogre went to the rim of the hole and leaned over. A sound like a yelp rose from the pit. "It's all right, Tait," called Maura, trotting over to stand next to the large, aqua-skinned immortal. "She's with me."

"Lady Maura?" the captive said. "What kind of company are ye keepin' now?"

The ten-year-old scowled. "Better company than is at home," she snapped.

"And what's that supposed to mean, miss?"

"Never mind. I'll tell you later."

Iakoju looked at Daine and nodded. "Man not too fat. I bring him up."

With a sigh, Daine got the rope and gave it to Iakoju. "I'm not doing this for you, Tait," Daine called. "I'm doing it for your dogs."

"I don't care who ye do it fer, as long as ye do it afore I turn gray!"

Iakoju took several turns of rope around her waist and dropped the free end into the pit. Tait wrapped it around his waist in the same manner, and grabbed the rope between them with both hands. "Haul away!" he yelled.

Iakoju backed up. With some cursing on Tait's part, she dragged the hunter from his prison. The moment he was on solid ground, the wolfhounds surrounded him, yipping their pleasure as they nuzzled him.

Seeing him up close, Daine winced. The pit didn't seem to be the cleanest spot in the forest. Tait now smelled greatly of wolf urine and dung.

"Have ye water?" he asked, petting his dogs. "And food would be fair nice."

Maura gave him Daine's canteen. The first gulp went to rinse his mouth; the rest went into his belly. "Weiryn's Horn," he gasped, "I needed that."

Maura offered him sliced ham and cheese. He shoved the cheese into his mouth as the dogs watched, licking their chops. "Ye shouldn't be here," he said when his mouth was empty. He looked at Daine and Iakoju. "No offense meant."

"Berate her all you like," Daine replied. "If you can make her go home, it's more than I could do, *or* that Stormwing lord."

"Things are crazy here now," the man grumbled. "The lords don't care for land or people, bringin' monsters t' keep their servants in fear . . ." Shaking his head, he tore the ham up and gave it to his dogs. Seeing that Daine watched him, he looked down. "Don't care for more'n cheese just now," he growled.

"M' throat's that sore from bellowin'."

Why, you softy, thought the girl. She got more cheese and two apples, and gave them to him. For the dogs she cut up the rest of the ham.

"Kind of ye," muttered the huntsman.

"They're good dogs," she replied shyly. "They really love you, you know."

"I know. They could've left me, but they didn't. They run off a bear last night, when it wanted t' come a-callin'." He looked at Iakoju. "Give a man a hand up?" he asked. "M' legs went t' sleep, bein' cramped down there."

The ogre held Tait by the elbows and lifted until he got his feet under him. He winced. "I need t' get this stink off me." He looked from Maura to Daine. "Will ye wait so I can wash? I've clothes and such hid by a stream nearby. I came out here with no plans to go back. Don't like what's happenin' in that castle these days."

Daine smiled. With luck, she had another recruit. "Go ahead. We'll wait for you."

With Iakoju to lean on and the dogs frisking around him, Tait hopped off to his bath. As they passed out of sight, Daine heard him tell the ogre, "No peekin' once I'm out of my clothes, mind."

"I want to check something," Daine told Maura. "Don't stray." She leaned against a tree and closed her eyes. Finding an eagle, she got permission to enter his mind. From the spot where he glided in the warm air that rose from the trees she could see glimpses of Tkaa. The basilisk was on all fours and galloping, his long, delicate limbs taking him faster than she would have believed possible. He was close to the western pass already.

Knowing her letter would soon reach Numair, she let the eagle take her where he wished. He flew low to avoid the barrier overhead, but he was still high enough to have a good view of the valley's heart. Not far from Tait's pit Daine glimpsed the lumber camp. The wolves, it seemed, had achieved their aim. All work was at a halt. The camp was nearly empty; the few humans there lay idly about or walked lazily around the area.

The eagle then flew south. Below lay the village and the castle, like toys. Smoke of an ugly green-brown color billowed out of a tower window in the castle. Every flying creature gave the weirdly colored plume a wide berth.

Why? Daine asked the eagle.

I do not need to fly through death to know what it looks like, replied her host. I do not have to bathe in danger when I know what it smells like. There is always something bad going on in that tower.

We're going to stop it soon, Daine assured him. It's almost over.

Good, replied the eagle. Tell me if you need help, and I will give it.

When the bird wheeled north, Daine saw trouble. Three creatures flew in criss-crossing patterns along the slopes where she had been the night before. The eagle squinted, and shapes came into focus: the bodies and heads of horses, batlike wings as big as sails. The hurroks worked their way south, skimming above the treetops. They were hunting for something, and she had an unhappy idea of what it might be.

I have to go, she told the eagle hastily. Thank you!

She opened human eyes. Something huge and brown filled her vision and surprised her into a yelp that came out a keening screech. I wish this would happen when I need it, not when I'm rushed! she thought peevishly, and blinked. The brown thing moved to show a patch of hairy skin.

Trying to rush the change was not going to work. With a sigh she began to remember Daine the human. She thought of nights in the Rider barracks hearing stories, of sword practice with the King's Champion, and of stargazing at Numair's tower. Under her memories now she felt talons become feet, and wings become arms. When she opened her eyes this time, Tait sat beside her, a golden brown feather in his hand. It was his rough tunic and skin that had seemed so close.

"Sorry. Didn't mean t' scare ye, lass." He offered her the feather. "Ye lost one. Actually, ye lost a few. Maura's got one."

Daine looked around and saw only Kitten and Prettyfoot. "Where is she?"

"Iakoju took her fishin'."

Raising her voice a bit, she said, "Kitten, get Maura and Iakoju. Hurroks are searching the valley—they're coming this way." To the man she said, "Is there cover around here?"

"The laurel bushes can hide Maura and the dragon." Tait stood. "There's a willow by the stream for Iakoju and the pony. The dogs can go where they like—I don't think the hunters will care about them."

The ogre and Maura came at a run. All of them listened as Daine explained where to hide. They hid their belongings, too. Daine kept her crossbow and quiver. Tait had a bow of his own, a fine weapon polished and supple with much use. He strung it quickly.

"They hunt me." Iakoju's eyes, the dark green of oak leaves, were sad. "They count us in the morning, before work. My brother supposed to say I am sick."

"I guess they didna believe him, lass," Tait said, patting the ogre's arm. "Not yer fault. Get under cover. We'll sing out when all's clear." Iakoju tramped off toward the stream with Cloud and Tait's dogs behind her.

Daine pointed to a spot where a fallen tree leaned against an oak. Where they met, the dirt underneath had worn away, leaving a hollow. From that spot they would be able to see the clump of laurel and the stream. Tait nodded and followed her to it. Flicker was already there, sunning himself on the log.

Sitting next to the huntsman, Daine put an arrow in the crossbow's notch and secured it, then placed it at her side, ready to fire—just in case. At the limits of her awareness came the first tingling sense that hurroks were near.

Tait had tucked the eagle feather behind his ear. Now he ran it through his fingers thoughtfully. "Can ye change entire?"

"No," the girl replied, fingering the badger's claw around her neck. "I can't even control what changes. I just learned how to turn myself all human again the night before last."

"Aye. Maura said at first ye thought ye were mad." Tait's brown eyes met hers. "She told me why she left home. Do you believe me when I say I'd no idea treason was afoot? I knew things was strange—that's why I left. But treason . . . That's worse than I thought."

Daine studied him. His was a square, stubborn face. He looked as if he would be as bad a liar as she was herself. "Yes," she replied, and smiled.

He smiled back. "Truthfully, I'm as glad she's here and not home. I don't think Tristan has the grip on what's goin' on that he thinks he does."

"What do you mean?"

The man teased Flicker with his feather as

the squirrel tried playfully to grab it. "Two days ago I was in the courtyard when the female mage, Gissa, came out screamin'. She was holdin' her wrist like her hand turned into a serpent, yellin' fer someone t' 'take it off.' I saw a wee drop of red on th' hand. Th' skin was *bubblin'*, like, and red streaks was growin' on the back toward the wrist, like they do when a wound's gone bad. Tristan and Master Gardiner was on the steps, and they just stared at her." Sweat appeared on Tait's forehead. "So she run t' th' woodpile, grabbed th' ax, and chopped her hand off."

Daine stared at him. "She cut off her own *hand*?"

"Weiryn leave me hungry if I lie." He wiped his face on his sleeve. "Praise the Goddess the lass wasn't there. She'd've had nightmares for months, what with the blood and Tristan not carin' about Gissa, but yellin' if she let 'it' boil over they were all dead. He run inside—didn't even try t' help Gardiner make the wrist stop bleedin'. He—"

Daine put a finger to her lips, then pointed up. A large, winged shape passed overhead, its shadow falling on the spot where Flicker had lain. Nearby she felt the other hurroks, their presence tainted, as always, with rage. They remained directly above for some time before moving higher on the mountainsides.

"I think if we're quiet, they won't hear us," she whispered. "They've gone off a ways, but they might come back."

"Ye can tell where they are?"

"When they're in range."

"More witchcraft, then?"

"Yes," she replied, and he shook his head. She knew this attitude too well. Some people were uncomfortable with magic; the more things they heard she could do, the more uncomfortable they became. Rather than argue, she changed the subject. "Who's this 'Weiryn'?" she whispered. "You mention him all the time, and I don't think I ever heard of him."

"A mountain god of the hunt. He's rooted in the forest and rock, kin to all that walks or swims or flies. On Beltane, ye can see him pass in the woods, with his hounds. Got antlers like a deer, he does. All us huntsmen swear by 'im."

Something about that description was familiar, but she couldn't place it. "I never had much to do with huntsmen at home. Well, *they* didn't have much to do with *me*. Have you heard of my village, in Galla? Snowsdale?"

The look he gave her was thoughtful, and very sharp. "So ye're *that* one."

Daine felt herself turning red. "I don't know what you've heard, but it's prob'ly blown way out of proportion."

"Not after what I've seen today," the man said, and grinned.

They waited for a long time. As they waited, Daine filled Tait in on all she knew, from the wolves' summons to the orders she'd seen from Carthak. Just as she thought the hurroks were going, she sensed fresh arrivals: Stormwings. Keeping low, she checked on the others and warned them the danger was not over. As she rejoined Tait, screams and snarls exploded overhead. It seemed hurroks and Stormwings did not get along.

"We could get old here," she whispered to Tait. "What are they looking for?"

"The dragon, perhaps?"

She winced. "Kitten. It figures." She made herself relax, and took a nap. When she woke, the Stormwings and hurroks were gone, and

Tkaa had returned. They all left their hiding places, hungry and stiff. While Maura introduced Tkaa to the huntsman, Daine did some thinking. She did not like the story of Gissa's hand, not after seeing that oddly colored smoke over the castle. What were the mages brewing there—more trouble, like the barrier?

A touch on her arm was the basilisk. —*I am to tell you soldiers are at the southern gate to the valley. Also, the King's Champion and the Knight Commander of the King's Own are there. Master Numair says that should cheer you up.*—

Hope surged in her mind, and she asked silently, Can he break the barrier with Lady Alanna's help? She's a fair powerful mage.

—*He said you would ask. He and the Lioness cannot break this working. It continues to absorb what power they strike it with, not reflect it. No mages can be spared from the City of the Gods. Some are riding here from the south, and will be here in four days.*—

The girl shook her head. With Tristan up to something, she wasn't sure they had four days. She had to know more, and that meant entering the castle.

It took time to convince the others to push on without her. At last they agreed to move on toward the western pass until dark, then camp, while she and Cloud rode to a spot near the village. No one liked that decision, but Daine's growing fear that something bad was brewing made her overrule them. If Tkaa, Iakoju, and Tait could not keep Maura and Kitten safe, no one could, and only she could wander the castle with no one the wiser.

Cloud worked hard to reach a place near the village before sunset. Twilight had fallen when they halted inside the trees on the town's fringe. Murmuring compliments, Daine rubbed her friend down. Stop that, Cloud said when she was dry and clean. Go do what you must.

Daine opened her bedroll and lay down under the trees. I don't know how long this will take, she warned her friend. Cloud was nibbling the grass that grew close by and did not answer.

Daine's magic flowed out readily, reaching the castle before she had taken more than two deep breaths. Inside its walls she found horses, goats, chickens, geese, and pigs, all nice animals in their way (although she detested chickens), but ill-suited to a search in a human dwelling. She was nearly resigned to asking the mice for help, and praying they would not be seen. Then, in the kitchen garden, she found two cats.

She approached the elder, a fat, dignified tom who busily washed the inky black fur of a cat not far out of kittenhood. Since the younger cat objected to the tom's vigorous methods, he kept her in place with a powerful forepaw as he cleaned her white bib. When Daine interrupted, he stopped washing, but kept his grip on the younger cat as Daine politely explained her errand.

The tom—named by men Blueness—listened with interest. When she finished, he inspected his claws. I am not sure I am the cat you need, he told her. There are nooks and crannies where a creature of my noble bulk may not go. He looked at the other cat. You take the Scrap, here. Even for a kitten she is most inquisitive, and she can get into anything.

Say yes, pleaded Scrap. Please!

Daine had to smile. Thank you, Blueness.

Do not get dirty, Blueness warned Scrap, or I will wash you again.

I can wash myself, the young cat retorted.

Not as well as I can, the tom replied. Now sit quietly while Daine does whatever she must to ride with you.

Daine turned her attention to Scrap, hearing the cat's eyes blink, and the soft pound of her heart.

Are you here yet? asked Scrap, breaking Daine's concentration.

No, Daine said. Almost. Hold still, and hush.

She listened. That was the sigh of Scrap's lungs, and her heartbeat. Her stomach growled softly, digesting milk a cook had left unattended.

Scrap yawned. Well? she demanded. Are you ready?

Now you know what I put up with, muttered Blueness.

Daine focused hard, and Scrap gave a squeak. Now the two of them scratched an itch, and looked at Blueness with Scrap's eyes. He was the most handsome tom she knew, his glossy fur a mix of pure white and sable black. She *loved* Blueness. She would follow him anywhere, particularly if she could attack his tail. She pounced. Blueness, with the ease of practice, whipped the tail clear and gave her a solid cuff with his forepaw.

Come on, Daine said, and showed Scrap images of Tristan, Yolane, Belden, and the other mages. I'm looking for them.

I can find them, but the female will screech and throw things if she sees me, Scrap replied.

Then don't let her see you, Blueness ordered. Daine, keep her safe.

I will, and thank you, Daine called as they galloped through the kitchen. Why is he named Blueness? she asked as they trotted up a long flight of stairs.

My mama said when he was my age, he fell into a bowl of color the cook uses on food, and he came out all blue. I can't believe he would be that undignified, but that's what my mama said, and she knows everything. Here we are. The man with the yellow magic lets the others visit him here.

"I can't fit the hand if you won't hold still," a man was saying as Scrap entered. She went under a table and peered out. The room was big, with shelves of books along the walls and silk carpets to cushion feet from the stone floor. Scrap, heedless of the expense or quality of the carpet that extended under the table, kneaded it luxuriously, sharpening her claws.

Daine examined the humans. The mage Redfern sat with Gissa of Rachne on a sofa. He worked on a metal skeleton hand fixed to the stump of the mage's wrist, making tiny adjustments to it with instruments from the table before them. Gardiner leaned against the sofa's back, watching with interest.

"If Gardiner and Master Staghorn had kept their wits about them, this wouldn't be necessary!" snapped the woman. Pain had aged her face ten years.

"Recriminations are due on *your* side of the ledger, Gissa." That smooth, oily tone could only be Tristan, Daine thought, and she was right. He sat in a chair beside the table where she had taken refuge. "You are no greenling, fresh from the country. Letting bloodrain splash as you stirred it was—"

"Tristan!" cried a feminine voice. The door opened and humans entered. Scrap looked out cautiously, and Daine saw Yolane, Belden, and Alamid. "Tristan, Alamid showed us the warriors at the southern pass in his crystal. That's the King's *Champion* out there, and the

Knight Commander of the King's Own!"

"Alamid shouldn't worry you with minutiae." There was more than a hint of poison, and meaning, in Tristan's voice.

"*Minutiae?*" cried Yolane. "The Lioness and Raoul of Goldenlake are *minutiae?*"

Tristan sighed. "My dear Yolane, calm down." He went to a wine table and filled the goblets there, bringing one to her and keeping one. "If I faced Lady Alanna and the Knight Commander with weapons they have mastered, I might feel some concern. I am not such a fool. Believe me, we were prepared for this. In three days they will cease to be even a mild irritation."

Belden went to the wine table, drank the contents of one of the goblets Tristan had filled, and poured himself a second drink. "Why?"

"My colleagues and I have prepared a little something to welcome the king's representatives. It's called 'bloodrain.' You might say Gissa already tested the brew for us, and that was before it reached its full potential."

"She cut off her *own hand*," Yolane said.

"It was my hand or my life," snapped the female mage. "If the poison had gotten into my blood, I would have rotted from the inside out."

"But how will you poison them?" Yolane asked. She finally sat down in the room's biggest chair. "Surely they'll have magical protections on their camp."

Tristan sat on the chair's arm, sipping his wine. "I don't plan to go near them. At sunset the day after tomorrow, I will take the blood-rain to the southern pass, where the river runs through the barrier, and dump it in." Gardiner shivered. "By sunrise of the next day, there won't be a living soul in that camp."

"Or anywhere else for ten miles," Gardiner said.

Yolane looked at him. "What is that supposed to mean?"

"Bloodrain will kill anything that uses moisture from the river." The cold, metallic voice was Alamid's. "Animals, plants—it doesn't matter. The zone of destruction will extend nearly five miles on each side of the river, and ten miles downstream." All the hair on the cat's—Daine's—back stood up.

"For how long?" Belden finished his second cup of wine and poured a third.

"The effects begin to fade after seven years or so," Gissa replied softly.

"It's necessary," Tristan said firmly. "Our departure for the capital is scheduled for a week from today. Nothing can be permitted to interfere."

"What if they're warned?" demanded Yolane. "They might withdraw."

"If they do, they should meet the two companies of mercenaries we have been keeping across the Gallan border," replied Tristan. "I took the liberty of calling them up in your name, and they will be at the southern gate in three days. Gardiner, tell Rikash to warn Captain Blackthorn to bring his own food and supplies."

"And Numair Salmalín?" Belden's drinking hadn't affected his hands or voice as he poured another refill. "He's still in the western pass, isn't he?"

"I have a net I will use to bottle him up. The emperor wants him alive. It is *always* a good idea to give His Imperial Highness what he wants."

"I don't like it." Yolane's face was white under her makeup. "I swore an oath to keep Dunlath safe, when my father gave me his signet. This bloodrain—"

"My dear, you are overscrupulous." Belden's tone was scornful. "It isn't going to kill anything in Dunlath proper, is it? And what will you care, once you sit on Jonathan's throne? Dunlath is a long way from Corus. Besides, you heard Master Staghorn. It will all grow back in less than a decade."

Tristan picked up one of Yolane's hands and kissed it. "Yolane, leave command decisions to your generals. As queen, you must get used to sacrificing the lives of a few for the good of all. Think of this as a masterly stroke, which it is. In one move you deprive the king of his champion and the commander of his most personal guard. Those are tactics you need. You have to convince not only your enemies, but your allies, that you deal promptly with opposition."

"Believe me," Gissa added, accented voice quite dry, "once they see what is left of those who interfered with you here, they will hurt themselves for the chance to be the first to swear to you."

Yolane looked at all the mages, frowning. "Why does it have to wait two whole days? Why can't you kill them now?"

"Bloodrain takes time," Redfern told her.

"Once combined, the ingredients must brew for three full days and three full nights."

Tristan smiled at Yolane in a way Daine thought Belden should object to. "You see, Majesty? Everything is under control. You chose your generals well."

Yolane looked as if she were about to object again, but Tristan put his finger to her lips. She sighed and looked around the room. Her eyes rested on Daine, and her mouth went tight. Picking up her goblet, she hurled it at Scrap, who ducked out the door, soaked in wine. "If I see that cat again, I'll kill it!" Daine heard her snarl as Scrap raced down the stair.

Now Blueness will wash me again, the youngster told Daine with a sigh. *Did you hear what you wanted to?*

I heard too much, replied Daine. *I think I have to go. Thank you. A lot of people will owe their lives to you for this.*

She fled to her body, scrambling to rethink herself human. She succeeded only partly—there were claws on her hands and she appeared to have a tail—but at least she was almost normal size as she entered her skin. Rolling up her bed, she jammed it under some bushes, thinking fast. Could she build wings for herself and fly up to Numair?

You will tire and fall, Cloud informed her. Use common sense. If you are in a hurry to get to Numair, take the way you know best. But don't ride me—I'm not up to a mad dash to the western pass, not after today. Steal one of the big horses from the village. I will follow you as quickly as I can.

Daine nibbled a fingernail and winced as the claw dug into her lip. I hate to steal, she admitted. But I think I must. She sent out an urgent call.

A large, bony horse grazing nearby came racing over. You want the fastest horse in the valley, he told her. I am the one.

Daine heard the other village horses agree: Rebel was the best at running.

You don't look like much to me, Cloud said, looking the stallion over.

Rebel snorted. That is what everyone thinks. That is why my man wins money when he races me against strangers, and that is why I am fed oats every day.

I am not impressed by your oat ration, Cloud retorted. Seeing that Daine was about to mount, she said, Don't forget your pack, or the crossbow.

Daine slung the pack over one shoulder and the bow over the other, after popping a bolt into the crossbow's notch and clipping it in place. Satisfied? she asked the pony.

And don't take any sauce from this jacka-napes. I will follow soon.

Daine had ridden fast horses in the king's service and with the Riders, but none matched Rebel. The ride through the village, past the crossroads, and onto the road to the western pass left her breathless. Once the last farm-house was behind them, Daine began to call for Tkaa, Tait's dogs, and the pack as she hung on for her life. When she felt their reply, she told them what she had learned. They agreed to meet her at the barrier.

No fighting, she ordered dogs and pack. We don't have time, and the stakes are too high. She felt some wolves ignore her, and some dogs. I mean it! she cried. I'll *make* you obey if I have to!

We will not fight, she heard Brokefang say, iron strength in his thoughts.

We will not fight, Prettyfoot said reluctantly. Any dog who wishes to fight may fight *me,* right now.

Daine relaxed. Let the dogs and the wolves concentrate on the *real* enemy: those who planned to dump bloodrain in the Dunlath River in two days' time.

In the pass, Daine halted Rebel under some trees and dismounted. Briskly she rubbed him down. "You need to rest. You'll find grazing over there. And don't mind all the weird folk who are coming here. Nobody will hurt you." He lipped her shirt and wandered off to graze, as Daine walked to the barrier.

Shapes that looked like rocks on the slope under the three-quarter moon rose to their feet and came down to her: the Long Lake Pack. Daine knelt so her eyes would be on a level with theirs. Adults and pups alike, they surrounded her in the greeting ceremony, licking her face and wagging their tails. Brokefang let the girl hug him fiercely about the neck and nuzzled her in reply.

You will stop it? he asked.

We will stop it, she told him. By ourselves if

we must, but I don't think it will come to that. We have friends now.

Two-leggers? That was Longwind, the conservative. They never cared before.

They were not friends before, Daine replied firmly. They are friends now—*strong* friends. They can go places and do things we can't, hunt-brother.

The dogs are *almost* wolves, offered Fleetfoot. If we sing, they listen. They have their own songs.

Two-leggers? Wolf killers? Longwind sneezed. I am too old for such changes.

Brokefang turned on his uncle, teeth bared. You are *not* too old for changes until I say you are, he snarled, advancing. You will change for now because the pack *needs* you to change. When it is done, we will return to the old ways.

If we can. The comment, unusually quiet and thoughtful, came from Frostfur.

I *like* changes! The thin, high voice in Daine's mind was Runt.

Me, too, added Silly. We see new things and do new things.

"I hear them," whispered Daine. "I can hear the pups. It's because of Scrap, maybe. She was a young cat at the castle," she explained. "I was with her when I heard of the bloodrain."

Would we like her? asked Berry. What is a cat?

Thinking of the castle reminded Daine that she had a letter to write. She left the explanation of cats to Fleetfoot and Russet, who had met them in their journey to fetch her. Taking her pack, she entered the stone lean-to where she had hidden to write once before.

With the help of her glowstone and cat eyes that had not changed during her ride, she put down all she had heard. Once the facts were laid out, she added:

> We must do something. I won't let them put bloodrain in the river. I hope you know a smart way to fight them. If you don't, I will think of a stupid way to do it. I was wrong to call Stormwings monsters. The creature that could brew and use this bloodrain is the real monster.

Gently she blew on the wet writing to dry it, then put her tools away.

NINE
WAR IS DECLARED

In the distance she felt the approach of Tkaa, Flicker, Kitten, and Iakoju, which meant that Tait, Maura, and the dogs had come as well. Tkaa immediately took the letter through the barrier, and Iakoju went with him. Flicker muttered a greeting and crawled into Daine's pack to finish his night's sleep.

"It's true, what the basilisk said?" Tait asked, sitting next to Daine. "They've cooked up some infernal broth?"

"Gissa had a drop of it on her hand when she cut it off," Daine replied grimly, tickling Kitten's belly. The dragon, sensing her agitation, voiced a soft run of clicks and chirrups

268

that had always comforted Daine in the past. The girl smiled at her young charge. "I'll be all right, Kit," she whispered.

Tait watched Maura as the girl, yawning, bedded down in the shelter of the rocks. "How can ye speak with Tkaa and not Iakoju? She told us she couldna hear ye, and that's fair strange."

Daine shook her head. "No, it's not. I can't mind-speak with immortals that have some two-legger in them. Only the ones who're made entirely like animals."

The dogs came to lie down with Tait even as the pups, Russet, and Fleetfoot arranged themselves around Maura. For a moment both groups, separated by only a few feet of ground, stared at one another. Then Prettyfoot yawned, and Silly yawned in reply. Daine felt something relax in both clusters of shaggy bodies, and gave an inner sigh of relief.

"I'd like t' ask a favor," Tait said, his voice soft. "If aught's to happen in the castle, let me warn my brother, so he can get the servants out. He'll make sure none of the nobles or their guests are the wiser."

"You don't think someone might warn

Tristan or Yolane?" she asked, examining the silver claw at her throat.

The hunter shook his head. "Nay. We accepted milady—she's Dunlath blood, and Mithros knows ye can't pick your lords—but none will back her in treason. And the outlanders she foisted on us treat us like slaves."

Daine heard a soft whistle from the barrier: it was Tkaa, half in and half out. Getting up, she ran to him, with Tait close behind.

"You may breathe easier," Tkaa informed them quietly. "The Stormwings and hurroks are at the soldiers' camp, harrying those who would sleep. The Lioness says they spend as much time battling one another as they do the mortals."

"How can ye know what goes on more'n a day's ride from here?" asked Tait.

"A speaking spell?" Daine asked. Tkaa nodded. To the man she explained, "It helps mages to speak to other mages, no matter how far off they are. They know about the bloodrain and the mercenaries coming?"

"Yes," the basilisk replied. "Once all may speak without interruption, Master Numair wishes you to cross the barrier. Perhaps the marmot who helped you there before will serve?"

Daine checked the eastern horizon. "She won't be up until dawn."

"It may take that long for the harriers to break off their attack. I will return when all is secure." Tkaa went back to Numair.

They trudged up to the stone cluster, Daine yawning until her jaw ached. "Sleep," Tait ordered. "I'll wake ye when Tkaa says they're ready t' talk."

"We need a plan," Daine mumbled. "And we don't have much time."

"Sleep," Tait repeated. "No one will make a plan without ye."

Cloud had arrived when Tkaa summoned Daine at sunrise. The girl watched her pony join Rebel, then sat back to listen for Quickmunch. The marmot was glad to hear from her, and eager to serve Daine again in communicating with her friends.

As they made their way from Quickmunch's burrow to Numair's camp, Daine felt a crackling tension in the pass. Numair was the source. She never had seen a look on his face like the one that was there now. He radiated fury. Iakoju watched his every movement, dark green eyes wary. Tkaa, as impossible to read as ever, munched quietly on a small pile of rocks.

When he saw Daine, Numair spoke a word. The air near him developed a sparkling blotch the size of a floor-length mirror, then opened to frame two figures Daine knew well. The smaller was a red-headed warrior in chain mail, breeches, and boots—Alanna the Lioness, the King's Champion. She was cleaning a sword. The other was a mammoth a few inches shorter than Numair and much wider. Raoul of Goldenlake, Knight Commander of the King's Own, wore plate armor over a sweat-soaked, quilted tunic. Sipping from a mug, he saw the image of Numair and his cohorts before his companion. "Alanna," he said, and pointed.

The woman looked up, her famous violet eyes grim. "I hope you have a plan—I don't. We could retreat, but that leaves Dunlath secure and you in a bad position. Numair, you told the king Daine's news?"

"Yes, but you know the problem as well as I.

It will be days before more help can reach us."

"And maybe Tristan still put bloodrain in river," Iakoju pointed out.

Sir Raoul made a face. "It goes with what we know of the man."

Alanna's eyes narrowed. "Daine, is that really you inside this animal?"

Quickmunch nodded, but she said to Daine, I'm a *marmot,* not an animal.

Two-leggers, Daine replied with a mental shrug. She made a note to tell her friend Alanna that marmots were touchy, prideful creatures.

Numair sighed. "I'm afraid we must implement the plan we discussed earlier." The other two humans nodded.

"I do not like it," remarked Tkaa. "Is there no other way?"

Alanna shook her head.

Daine chattered with annoyance. Was somebody going to tell her *anything?*

An unhappy look in Numair's eyes silenced her. "Daine, there is one other way to break the barrier."

"It means a lot of risk." Alanna put her sword down. "And it won't work unless your friends can draw the mages out of the castle."

Daine looked at Numair, thinking, So what do *I* do? He was in a brown study, pressing his nose and staring into the distance. She was about to ask Quickmunch to get his attention when she thought, Can Tkaa hear me? He hears mortal animals. It's worth a try, anyway. Reaching with her magic, she called, Tkaa!

The basilisk peered at her. "You can speak to me through this creature?"

The "creature" barked. Daine said, She's a marmot. Her name is Quickmunch.

Tkaa bowed. "Forgive me, Quickmunch. I spoke from ignorance, not contempt."

Numair, Alanna, and Raoul were looking from the marmot to Tkaa. "Daine can speak to you even when she isn't doing it from her own body?" asked Numair.

Tkaa listened to Daine and said, "She has learned she has that ability only now. She asks me to say if you do *not* tell her what she can do once the mages have left the castle, she will ask Quickmunch to bite you."

Raoul snorted; the Lioness covered a smile. Numair sighed. "Patience is a virtue you should cultivate. Daine. Not you—Quickmunch, is it?"

The marmot squeaked her reply.

"Of course," Numair said. "Daine, remember what I told you of image magic?"

Yes, Daine told the basilisk, who translated for her. If you do something magical to an image of a person, it's the same as doing it to the person.

"That is true not only of people," Numair said. "As it is impossible for Tristan and the others to walk around the valley to create the barrier, they must have enclosed a model of the valley itself. You must find that image in the castle. Once you have broken the circle of magic around it, the barrier will evaporate, and we can enter the valley."

"Opals," the champion put in.

Numair cracked his knuckles. "Alanna and I have assaulted the barrier. It continues to absorb, not reflect, our Gifts. This shows power stones are being used to take magic and feed it into the working. Those stones will be embedded in the model of Dunlath Valley. You'll have to break them to break the circle."

Daine said to Tkaa, I understand. Now what about the diversion? Tkaa repeated the question.

The Knight Commander leaned forward.

"We think Tristan will send the other mages to deal with a disturbance at the forts, especially if the trouble is odd in any way. If it's serious, he'll probably go himself. Numair says Tristan never thinks underlings can handle real trouble without him. If both forts are attacked, there's a good chance the castle will be left unguarded."

"That ties up the Stormwings, maybe even the hurroks," Alanna said. "They're the quickest transport for the mages. Iakoju thinks she can raise her people—"

Iakoju nodded. "If I say so, my kin will fight human masters. We make plenty of ruckus in north."

"I can cause trouble in the south," added Tkaa. "But I will need help." He cocked his head to one side. "I am too big a target even for humans to miss."

Quickmunch scratched a flea, and Daine said, Tkaa, will you and Iakoju cross back to talk to everyone with me? Let's see what we can come up with. And tell them that Tait thinks he can get all the local people out of the castle.

"One thing," Numair said after Tkaa was done translating. "Time is vital. To be at the southern barrier by sunset tomorrow, Tristan must leave the castle no later than noon, and there is a chance he will leave earlier. Whatever you do, it must be ready to go by tomorrow morning."

Wait a moment! Daine cried, alarmed. What about the mercenaries who are supposed to come—that Captain Blackthorn and his men?

When Tkaa passed this on, Sir Raoul grinned. "We have two Rider groups here—sixteen irregulars *and* their ponies—plus a company of the Own, a hundred warriors. Yes, Blackthorn has a hundred more men than I do, but if we're in Dunlath when he comes, the game is *ours*—not his. Blackthorn also hates to fight mages even more than he hates to work with them. If he even *hears* that Alanna and Numair are waiting, I think he'll run like a rabbit."

"If that's all the questions, would you get moving?" Numair hinted with awful patience. "It's going to be a long day."

Tristan's crew aren't the only ones who need to fly, Daine thought, resuming her human shape. I will, too. The animals in the fort should be warned, so they can escape somehow. And I can ask local animals to do some damage, like the pack's raids on the lumber camp. I hate to endanger them, but this is too important *not* to involve them.

When Daine, Tkaa, and Iakoju explained the attack plan, their friends in the valley had plenty of ideas. The wolves chose to visit the northern fort, to support the ogres and to attack the hated mines. Maura offered to set the southern fort afire if she got close to it, and promised to leave the gate alone so the horses could run. Tait wanted to go with her, and the dogs followed him. Rebel, who itched to help, agreed to carry the man and girl south.

Kitten whistled a query. Daine smiled. "You're with me, Kit. I need you for locked doors." The dragon chuckled and sharpened her claws on a rock.

Flicker said he would go with Maura and Tait to the southern fort. He also advised Daine to recruit the valley's squirrels. They could free the fort horses. They also could chew ropes, bowstrings, and the like, once the sun was up. "You think squirrels will want to get involved that much?" the girl asked.

Yes, replied Flicker. The walls in the forts are made of logs, aren't they? Plenty of my kindred lost homes and lives when those places were built. And the southerners have family by the river where they want to put bloodrain.

"Then I'll talk to them. What about the castle servants?" Daine asked Tait.

"I'll give ye a note t' my brother Parlan," the huntsman replied. "He's the innkeeper. He'll see it's done, and done quiet."

"If we fight at dawn, I must go," Iakoju commented. "I have to talk to ogres, give them hope for freedom. Talk might run all night."

"Let's take a bit more time," advised Tait. "Gie the squirrels a while with the sun to work in. If the mage hits the barricade hard, we'll all hear it. The ninth hour, say? Then Maura can start burnin', and the ogres can rise."

Iakoju frowned. "Big noise? Like being inside a bell?"

"It is very hard to ignore," Tkaa remarked dryly.

"Ogres hear. Ogres hear good, four-five days ago. That's *good* signal."

The basilisk went to tell the plan to Numair.

While he was gone, Tait wrote his brother. When he was through, Daine summoned a crow and asked if she would carry a note to the inn. The crow, intrigued, accepted it and took flight.

Tkaa returned. "The ninth hour, three hours past dawn," he told them.

"Does everybody know what to do?" asked Maura, hands on hips.

The dogs and wolves yapped; Flicker squeaked. The humans, Kitten, the ogre, and the basilisk nodded. Rebel and Cloud stamped.

"I'm off to the northern squirrels, then," Daine said. "And everybody?" They all looked at her. "Be careful," she cautioned, eyes stinging a little. "Goddess bless us all."

"Goddess bless," whispered Maura and Tait. Silently the animals called on their gods, and perhaps the immortals did the same.

When the others had gone, Daine turned to Cloud. "If I tie myself to you and make sure Kitten's secure in her pack, can you carry us to the place we were last night? I don't want to linger here while I talk with the creatures in the north and south if I can help it." She studied her friend: Cloud *looked* fresh. "If you can't, say so. I'll call another horse from the village, if I must."

And risk thief catchers coming after you? retorted the pony. I think not. I can do this. You forget, I took my time walking here, and I've had plenty of rest and water and grazing. How will you be traveling?

"I thought to try that eagle again."

So much the better. You won't weigh as much as you do now. I noticed the first thing that seems to change is your bones. If you have bird bones, you'll hardly weigh anything, just like *her*. Cloud nodded to Kitten, who was tucking herself into Daine's pack. And make sure you bring that bow.

"Cloud, it'll be too much, me and Kit and a crossbow—"

Don't be a fool, retorted the mare. You need a weapon.

The girl sighed and got the rope. "This is going to be fun."

With the help of some birds and a marmot colony from inside the barrier, Daine tied herself, her crossbow, and Kitten to Cloud's back, with the knots in easy reach. When everything was secure, the pony set off at a walk.

As Kitten chirped soothingly, Daine relaxed and listened for Huntsong, the golden eagle who had taken her so far the day before. She found him nearly a mile away, about to leave his treetop nest. When she explained what she needed, he agreed to help. Quickly she slid into his mind, and they were off.

Word of Flicker's adventures had gone from tree to tree in the days since the making of the Coldfang statue. The eagle too had been gossiping with other birds, and the Song Hollow bats had added their information. Daine was startled to find that the woods and rocky slopes all along the western side of the Long Lake buzzed, not only with her name, but with the names of her companions—humans, immortals, *and* animals. When she called from Huntsong's mind to the squirrels near the north fort, they asked what they could do to help end the destruction. Wood rats, overhearing what she told the squirrels, wanted jobs of their own. Three flocks of starlings reminded her that they had come at her call before, to drive off Stormwings. Did she have more fun for them?

With the wild beasts clamoring for Daine's attention, the domestic animals who lived in the fort were eager to listen to her. The dogs and cats left right away, not waiting for the next sunrise. The horses agreed to flee to the docks, once Daine promised that the wolves and other hunters would leave them alone.

As Huntsong wheeled south, Daine saw the pack running single file down the trails, the steady pace eating up the miles between them and the fort. Iakoju, heavy legs pumping in an equally constant tempo, brought up the rear. When the eagle dropped down to eye level, the ogre realized who it must be and waved, grinning cheerfully.

On their way to the southern fort, they found a trio of Stormwings going from there to the castle. With a shiver, Daine saw Rikash was one of them.

Have they ever bothered you? she asked Huntsong.

The great bird glared at the approaching immortals. Not in a general way, he replied, talons clenching. We had a few misunderstandings when they first came here, until they learned the error of their ways. His wrath faded, and he added, All the same, I shall give them a wide berth. They cut my mate to ribbons when she defended our nest.

He drifted to one side. Two Stormwings flapped past, making rude noises. Only Rikash changed course, to fly around Huntsong in a wide circle. The other two, a blond female and the K'miri male, came back and joined him.

"They soar, don't they?" Rikash asked them. "Wheeling, wheeling, always in the same place?"

"Like toy kites, and twice as wood-skulled," joked the K'mir.

"But now here is this one, flying in a straight line, going somewhere. You don't see prey when you go too fast, am I right?"

Get ready to drop, Daine warned Huntsong.

Rikash spat, not looking to see if anyone was below. "This valley has a disease, one where cute little animals don't *act* like animals. Did I tell you about the squirrel?"

"Only a million times," said the K'miri Stormwing with a groan.

Daine saw muscles bunch in Rikash's neck. Drop! she cried. Huntsong threw up his wings and dropped, hurtling earthward at terrifying speed.

"Go, go, *go*!" screamed Rikash.

The female whooped, and steel-winged bodies followed Huntsong down. Grimly Daine hung on, urging him into the trees that covered the road south. The eagle shot into the clear space between road and branches, scudding down the corridor they made. There was a scream and a crash: a Stormwing had come to grief. Huntsong risked a glance back. The female, scratched and bleeding, was trying to free herself from a chestnut. Seconds later the K'mir came in view, fighting to pull out of his stoop before he slammed into the dirt. He failed.

Relieved, Huntsong looked forward. Rikash awaited them ahead, where the trees fell briefly away from the road. Land, Daine urged.

I look stupid when I walk, complained the eagle as he obeyed. Hopping like a sparrow is not eagle's work.

If you think *you* look stupid, imagine how *he* will look, Daine consoled him.

Rikash cursed and darted forward, flying low, trying to keep his great metal wings from clipping the earth or trees. Called from their nests, the squirrrels leaped on him, biting with very sharp teeth. Rikash screamed, tried to cover his eyes with his wings, and slammed into an elm. Now *run,* Daine told the squirrels; they obeyed. Huntsong liked that advice, too. He took off, flapping lazily past the spot where Rikash fought the elm's entangling branches. The air filled with the Stormwing's curses as Huntsong broke free of the trees.

With battle already joined, Daine had no trouble persuading the southern animals to do what they could to help Tkaa, Maura, Tait, and Flicker. The fort's animals, told what was going on, were as eager to stop the use of the bloodrain as Daine was.

I think we're done, the girl told Huntsong, feeling more tired than ever. Let's go home. I'd return by myself, but I'm prob'ly outside the range of my magic, and I don't know if I would make it.

Would you mind terribly if I left you inside your range, and went back to that fort? the eagle inquired. I could help there. It would be a pleasure.

Daine smiled and replied, Of course.

Flying low over the treetops, keeping away from the road, they passed Tait, Maura, Tkaa, and the others. Daine pointed out the basilisk.

Talk to him, she told Huntsong as they continued to head north. He can translate for the two-leggers, and they should know of something you can do.

The moment she felt the tug of attraction that was her true body, she wished the eagle good luck and separated from him. Instantly he turned south again as she slid into her human self. With regret she changed his farsighted eyes to her own, limited orbs, and his hollow, light bones into a human's heavier ones. Talons became feet; wings became arms. When she opened her eyes, all that remained was a layer of down between her clothes and skin.

"I'm back," she muttered. "Huzzah."

Cloud halted. That crow came by, the mare said. She wanted to tell you she dropped the note into the man's lap. He read it, and the last she saw of him, he was on his way to the castle.

Daine took a deep breath. "I hope he's as trustworthy as Tait says." The girl extracted herself and Kitten from the ropes that kept them on the pony's back. Then, with Daine afoot and Kitten walking or riding, they took the remainder of the day to approach the village, staying clear of outlying farms. They stopped as the shadows lengthened, so Daine could catch and cook some fish and Cloud would have a chance to graze; it was near dark when they moved on.

Everywhere the People were talking. Dunlath's nonhuman residents had much to say about recent events. They spoke to kinfolk, distant relatives, even enemies (at a safe distance). Their opinions and questions were so loud that Daine wondered if the two-leggers didn't guess something was up.

If they did, she saw no sign of it at the village. Hidden in the trees at the spot where she had left her bedroll and saddle, she watched the local people go about their end-of-day chores, then vanish into their homes. Lamps flared briefly in most houses, then went out; farmers rose and went to bed with the sun. Only the inn and the castle windows stayed lit for any time after dark.

Over the night the Song Hollow bats checked in, waking her with news of her friends. Iakoju had made it safely to the ogre dwellings around nightfall, starting a great deal of movement between buildings and a constant hum of ogre voices. The Long Lake Pack busied itself among the mine wagons, working pins that held wheels to axles out of their settings with their teeth, and chewing the reins until only scraps held them together. In the south, wood rats laid dry twigs and grasses at the base of the wall and around all the structures but the gate and the stables. Dogs howled incessantly outside, as little fires erupted in the commander's office, the mess, and the barracks, keeping the men up all night.

At last, with only a few hours left until dawn, the activity ended. The People, and Daine, used the time in unbroken sleep.

She awoke at dawn, aching from tense muscles. In contrast to the racket of the day before, the animals were quiet. Even the birds who greeted the sun were silent, awaiting events. From the trees Daine watched as castle servants crossed the bridge in pairs, small groups, or alone, to enter the village. Parlan waited on the other side of the causeway, steering them to the inn. There were no soldiers to worry about; Yolane relied on Tristan and the forts for protection.

Daine called to the castle mice as the sky

brightened. Soon they reported back to her: only the nobles and Tristan remained there.

The sun rose. In the north and in the south, squirrels were working hard to free the fort horses and do as much damage as possible. The soldiers were finding that their morning bread, tea, porridge, and cheese were inedible. The ogres were collecting weapons and moving their children to safety.

Daine combed her hair and tied it back, then removed her clothes and shook them out before putting them back on. She ate cheese and stolen apples, groomed Cloud, and fed Kitten what remained of their previous night's fish. Last of all, she saddled the mare and tucked Kitten into her carry-sack.

Give them time, Tait had said, but she hadn't known the hours needed by her allies would strain her nerves so cruelly. Her tension was made worse by the fact that she heard little movement in the village. The cows had been milked before sunrise, livestock had been fed, but apart from that, the local two-leggers kept out of sight. It made her feel as if she had a ghost town at her back.

At last, she heard a sound like a huge bell

hit from the inside, as loud here as it had been in the caves. It was followed by another sound from the south, a hollow *thwap!* Billows of smoke appeared on the lake's southern shore. She would have to ask Maura what on *earth* her friend had managed to blow up.

Silver caught her eye from that direction: Stormwings, flying hard and homing in on the castle. She noticed they were as soot-blackened as chimney sweeps as they vanished inside the curtain wall.

She felt the hurrok trio come from the north. One bore a scroll in its left forepaw, and the gems in all their collars burned a bright yellow. They were in pain, clawing at the bands around their necks. Screaming in rage, the hurroks darted into the circle of the castle's wall. Checking the northern sky, she saw faint columns of smoke. Something was afire, but she couldn't tell what it was.

She waited briefly, and the fliers reappeared. This time the hurroks had riders who controlled them with reins and bit. They fought these as they had the collars, with no success. Two flew north. Daine shut her eyes and thought of Huntsong, then opened them to an eagle's vision. The mages on the hurrok pair were Redfern and Gissa. One hurrok tried to turn back, but Gissa was having none of it. Her mouth moved. A cloud of orange fire appeared on the immortal's rump. From the way he leaped forward, the fire must have hurt.

She turned to check the others. The Stormwings bore two humans in rope slings. Tristan rode the hurrok: he too used fire to sting his mount forward.

Daine made her eyes human again, then mounted Cloud. "Now," she told her companions. The pony raced for the causeway. All down its length, past the dock where the nobles kept a few boats and through the gate, Daine cringed, feeling exposed. Only when they were in the courtyard did she dare to sit up. There were no watchers on the castle walls, and the courtyard was empty.

Don't bother unsaddling me, Cloud told her when she dismounted. Find what you came here for. I'll hide in the stables.

"And rob every feed bag you see, right?" Daine whispered as she freed Kitten from her pack and put her down on the flagstones.

Hanging the crossbow on her belt and the quiver over her shoulder, she trotted into the castle, the young dragon close behind.

Blueness and Scrap met her in the great hall. They looked smaller this way, though Daine could see that Blueness *was* a creature of noble bulk, for a cat. Scrap was a dainty thing, and fascinated by Kitten.

Have you seen anything like this? Daine asked the cats, picturing what she thought the model would look like.

No, said Blueness. Scrap! he said imperiously when the youngster, sniffing Kitten's muzzle, didn't reply. Answer the question!

The cat sneezed. No, she replied. But I have not seen all there is to see. We are not allowed in the mages' workrooms.

Show me where those workrooms are, Daine said. Quickly, please.

The cats led the way up a broad flight of stairs to a gallery on the second floor, and down a hallway. Kitten made as little noise as they did: her talons, which Daine thought might click like a dog's, only made tiny scratching sounds.

The new humans sleep here, Blueness said,

stopping at the end of a long corridor. In those two sets of rooms, and those two.

Daine tried one door: it was locked. "Kit, remember how you popped the lock at the inn?" The dragon nodded. "Give this a whirl, will you?"

The dragon sat up on her hindquarters and eyed the lock with interest. She gave a soft trill, as she had at the inn. The lock shone gold for a moment, then went dull. Kitten made a clucking sound and trilled again, breaking the sound into a high note and a low one. The door swung open.

Can she teach me to do that? asked Scrap as they entered the suite.

You do not need to know it, replied Blueness, disappearing into the bedroom. *You are too much of a pawful already.*

The model was not there, nor in the other three suites. Daine frowned as they finished their search. They had seen magical work-rooms, but none had contained models. Also, she had seen nothing that looked like the room where she and Scrap had heard of bloodrain.

"Where are Tristan's rooms?" she asked. "The man with yellow magic?"

They are near the ones of the human female who hates cats, replied Blueness. This way.

They returned to the gallery and circled its rim, then went down a short hall. Scrap's tail twitched angrily when they reached Tristan's door: it was shut. Daine grabbed the knob. It stung her hand, making her yelp. "Kit? This one's magicked. Can you do anything?"

Kitten stood on her hind feet and peered into the lock, then whistled two cheerful notes. Nothing happened. She scowled and whistled again, less cheerfully, more as a demand. Nothing happened.

Daine was trying to decide what to do now when the dragon moved back and croaked. The lock popped from the wood to land at Daine's feet, smoking, and the door swung open. Kitten muttered darkly and kicked the lock mechanism aside as she went in. Daine followed, trying not to laugh.

I wish I could do that, remarked Scrap wistfully as she and Blueness brought up the rear.

Tristan's suite was bigger than those granted to his fellow mages, the furnishings more expensive. The central room was where Scrap had brought her last time. A study and a bedroom opened onto it; a dressing room and privy opened onto the bedroom. Unlike the other mages, Tristan did not have his own workroom. There was no sign of a model of the valley in his study. Indeed, except for a few scrying crystals and assorted books, they found none of the tools commonly used to work magic.

"What are you doing here?" a shrill, furious voice demanded. Daine, Kitten, and the cats faced the unlocked door. Yolane, in a thin nightdress covered by a lace robe, stood there. "Where is Tristan?" With a sneer she added, "I should have guessed you'd be a thief."

Daine put a hand on her bow. It was loaded, but she didn't want to kill Maura's sistser. "I wouldn't call names, if I was you," she retorted.

Yolane backed up. "Tirell! Oram! Jemis! To me! Oram, on the double!"

Daine shook her head. "Yell all you like, they won't come. They're gone."

"What do you mean, 'gone'?"

"I mean it's at an end—the king knows what you're up to. The rebellion's uncovered. You'll never be queen."

"Tristan!" called Yolane. "Gissa! Alamid!"

"They have more important things to do right now," Daine told her. "The southern fort is burning. The ogres in the north are fighting the overseers. The mages went to deal with all that."

"You—" Yolane's face wasn't so attractive, twisted as it was in rage and hate. She turned and ran.

Kitten whistled an inquiry. "We can't," Daine replied. "The model's the important thing right now." Mice! she called silently, and added a picture of the model. Have you seen this? Will you look for it?

All over the castle the mice stopped to think and answer. Soon she knew none of them had seen it. "I don't understand," she muttered. "It's got to be somewhere. They haven't seen anything like bloodrain, either, and I know that has to be cooked in something."

Did they mention the tower? asked Blueness. That is where all the mages gather to do their work.

When he said "tower," she remembered a column of greenish brown smoke, and Huntsong's remark that he did not need to fly through death to know what it looked like. "That's a good question, Blueness. Mice, what about the tower?"

Silence that reached through every nook and cranny of the huge building in which they stood was her answer.

"Mice?" Her eye fell on Scrap. The young cat was backed into a corner, fur puffed out. She was trembling. "Scrap, what is it?"

I know what they mean, she whispered. There is a lizard in the tower, a cold one. Colder than *anything*.

When Scrap said "lizard," the hair went up on the back of Daine's neck. It was the most sensible course, if the mages kept precious secrets in the tower. Tkaa had said a Coldfang would guard a thing until the end of time.

Outside in the gallery she heard Yolane cry, "Belden, wake up!"

There was no time to waste. "Scrap, how can I get into the tower?"

The cats ran out of Tristan's rooms. Daine followed, taking her bow off her belt and checking the bolt already loaded. It was blunt, more to stun than to slay, though it might have killed Yolane at close range. She switched it for a razor-pointed bolt, the tip hardened to punch through almost anything. She hoped it could put a hole in a Coldfang; if it couldn't she was in *real* trouble.

Scrap led them to another gallery, then a spiral stair. They climbed it high above Tristan's suite, passing broad landings that led to other floors. At last there was a window. Looking out, Daine could see over the curtain wall.

Here she felt the first touch of cold. Blueness, Scrap, go back, she told them silently. There's no sense in risking your lives.

But I *want* to, protested Scrap. She was so terrified that all her fur was puffed out and her ears lay flat.

Blueness, take her away, Daine ordered. There's nothing you can do.

Come, Scrap, the older cat said. The fear that had puffed his tail up to bottle-brush size didn't show in his voice. We could only get in the way.

Daine knelt beside Kitten. "You don't have to come," she whispered. Kitten glared and tried to climb past her. Daine shook her head and went first.

Thinking of Wisewing, she changed her ears

to a bat's as they climbed, and listened to each scrap of sound. The cold thickened. Frost gleamed on the walls; curls of icy mist drifted around the small windows. Daine shivered in her thin shirt, and her nose ran. The stair narrowed; the curves tightened. How was she going to get off a shot around a corner?

The sound that made both ears twitch forward was a body, thirty-one feet ahead. Beaded hide brushed stone in a space much wider than the stair.

Fear made Daine's chest tight. When she could bear no more, she yelled, "Coldfang!" The echo hurt her ears: she made them human. "You'd best move—you're standing between me and where I want to go!"

Kitten whistled insults.

She heard a soft thud, then the buzz of a Coldfang rattle. Biting her lip so hard she drew blood, Daine raised the crossbow. "Don't let it catch your eye, Kit. That's how the other one almost got us."

It came tailfirst, on all fours and low, not headfirst or standing as she expected. The sight of the rattle and tail confused her for a second too long. The immortal half lunged, half slid, its weight slamming into her. Daine loosed, but the bolt went high to shatter on the wall. With a yelp the girl fell backward, the bow flying from her hand.

Kitten squeezed to one side. The girl kept rolling down the steep risers, losing arrows from her quiver as she fell. She was lucky the turns in the stair were so close: she couldn't build up any speed. All the same, her rattling progress, bumping into walls and stairs, knocked her silly. Protecting her head and neck with her arms, she kept her body tucked into a round ball and prayed. Kitten, trying to keep away from the advancing Coldfang, scrambled to avoid getting caught under her friend.

At the first landing they reached, Daine came to a halt. She grabbed the knob of a door leading from the stair and shoved. It opened on a hall furnished with suits of armor, old hangings, and wall decorations. Lunging to her feet, she ran in, the sound of talons on stone and that buzzing rattle loud in her ears.

TEП
THE FALL OF TRISTAN AND YOLANE

Kitten darted under a table against the wall, her scales turning the same gray-black as the stone. Daine looked frantically for a weapon of some kind as the Colfang entered. Watching it, she knew coming here had been a mistake: the narrow stair had hampered the immortal as much as it did her. Now the Coldfang had room to move.

Like the one slain by Tkaa, this Coldfang was beaded in bright shades of green. Frost flowers spouted ahead of its advance. It was quicker than the other, and pursued her down the hall. She raced away from it, checking the weapons on the wall. Broadswords were the main choice, but these were the two-handed kind favored by mountain lords—she could never lift one. She saw two maces, but they were higher on the wall than the swords. Trying to get one would slow her down too much.

Looking back at her pursuer, she crashed into a suit of armor. Quickly she rolled out of the way as it went over. From a metal glove dropped a long-handled, double-bladed war ax. She seized it, as heavy as it was, and got up.

The Coldfang stared, long tongue slipping out and in, tasting the air, then sidled to her left. She backed, keeping the blade between them, trying not to meet the thing's eyes. Her arms shook in an effort to hold her weapon up. It was *not* meant for a teenage girl's use.

Suddenly the immortal lunged, far more quickly than she would have dreamed, jaws popping open and fangs dropping down. She squeaked and darted back. The ax proved her undoing, as the long handle tripped her. She threw it to the side and rolled, then scrabbled to her feet. When she looked for the Coldfang, it caught her eyes, and held them. Although she fought, she was frozen in place.

Kitten, now rage-scarlet, jumped from the rear to fasten her jaws in the Coldfang's spine. Blueness and Scrap, behind her, leaped for its eyes. The immortal keened, half rising to its hind feet as it tried to rid itself of the cats with one paw and the dragon with the other. Scrap went flying, to strike the wall.

Free of the Coldfang's grip, Daine seized the ax and moved in close. *"Let go!"* She put all her power into the order. Blueness and Kitten jumped clear.

She swung with all her strength to bury the ax in the Coldfang's skull. It wrenched away, yanking the weapon from her grip, but the ax was firmly seated. The immortal thrashed on the stone floor, weakening with each convulsion. At last it was still.

The girl looked at the mess she had made, at the ax, the shattered immortal, and the gouts of dark blood all around, and vomited.

When she was done, she wiped her mouth and went to Scrap. Blueness crouched beside her, trembling and trying to wash the younger cat's still face.

"No, Blueness," whispered Daine. "Let me." She picked up the small body. It was limp in her hands, without any trace of life.

She is just a kitten, Blueness remarked, sounding lost. She is forever telling me she is a grown cat, but she is only a kitten.

Daine's eyes were streaming as she took the badger's claw from her neck and put it on Scrap's body. "Badger, you owe me. You and Old White and the other animal gods owe me. She would have been alive right now if you hadn't *brought* me here. Now *do* something!"

No reply came, as precious seconds crawled by. She had failed. Hugging that soft body to her chest, Daine rocked back and forth.

—*It is for you, Queenclaw.*— Whoever the speaker was, he wasn't the badger. There was a hint of pack song in his voice, of cold nights filled with wolves singing. —*She is one of yours.*—

—*I am glad you see that, Pack Father,*— purred a new voice, silky and cruel. Blueness jumped to his feet, looking frantically for the speaker. —*As it happens, it pleases me to grant this prayer. A kitten deserves another life. Do not make a habit of asking, though, Daine. The gods are not at* your *beck and call. And finish what you came here to do!*—

Life roared under Daine's hands like a fire. Scrap opened her eyes. *Where is Blueness? I dreamed I was in the fog, and he wasn't with me.*

Daine put her down, tucking the silver claw into a pocket. The tom instantly began to wash his Scrap, purring so loudly he roused echoes. The younger cat screwed up her face and let him do it.

The girl rose, feeling weak in the knees. "You stay here and rest," she said. "I have something to do." Picking Kitten up, she wiped the dragon's muzzle clean of Coldfang blood, and carried her to the stair. As they climbed, she reclaimed those arrows that were unbroken and her crossbow.

The tower door was locked. "Why did they bother?" she asked bitterly, putting the dragon down. "They had their monster to guard it, didn't they?"

Kitten peered into the keyhole, tail twitching. Standing back from it, she croaked. The metal of the lock glowed dull orange. The wood around it began to smoke. Then the color faded, the lock still firmly in place.

Kitten stretched out her neck and croaked

again, holding the note twice as long. She stepped aside just as the lock blew off the door. It fell down the stairs and continued to fall, its rattling audible long after it had gone out of sight. Without a word Daine opened the door.

Inside was a table on which lay the model of the valley, complete with its barrier. Behind that, on a tripod over a low brazier, a small pot of reddish brown liquid bubbled gently. That alone was interesting, because the fire was out. Daine stared at it. Could such a tiny amount of liquid, barely two cups full at best, really cause so much damage?

"Don't go near that," she ordered. Kitten shook her head emphatically, and Daine turned to the model.

What looked like a solid wall of fire in the western pass was a thin line of light that curved over the miniature valley as if a clear bowl were placed on top of it. The "bowl" sparkled with multiple colors, the yellow of Tristan's magic being the most common one. Embedded in the "rivers" into the northern and southern passes were two round, polished black opals.

Drawing her belt-knife, the girl reversed it, gripping it tightly where hilt met blade. She slammed the pommel into the north opal hard, and a crack snaked over the face of the stone. The barrier darkened, then brightened. She struck the opal again, and it cracked in half. Dark lines pursued each other over the curve of the magical light, but she could still see that curve.

"Stands to reason," she told Kitten, walking around the model to the far end. "If you've got two stones holding the thing in place, you have to break 'em both. After all, nothing *else* has been easy since I came to Dunlath, so why should this be?"

She slammed the knife hilt into the second opal, knocking loose a tiny chip. A thin whine filled the air; she glanced at Kitten, who also looked for its source. The whine built in volume, higher than anything the dragon or Daine could produce. It raised the hair on the back of the girl's neck. Gritting her teeth, she adjusted her grip on the abused hilt of her belt-knife.

"For the wolves," she whispered, and slammed the stone again. Whether the previous blow had weakened it more than it had appeared, or whether Old White lent Daine his strength, this did the trick. It shattered explosively. Daine covered her eyes with her free hand, and the room blew up.

Her return to awareness was heralded by a dreadful stench in her nostrils. She gagged and struggled against the iron band that clamped her arms to her sides, then sneezed repeatedly.

"Relax," a familiar voice said. "It's just wakeflower."

She blinked. The dark shape in her blurry eyes sharpened into a long nose, a full mouth, and black-fringed eyes. A bruise puffed up his left cheekbone, and his shirt was ripped. "No flower ever smelled like that," she said.

Numair helped her to sit up and eased his grip on her arms and back. "But it does," he replied innocently. "It grows in swamps, and its scent attracts flies to carry its seed rather than bees, but botanists judge it to be a true flower all the same." He let her go and placed the stopper in the tiny vial he had put under Daine's nose. The vial itself went into his belt-purse. "Are you well enough to sit unaided? I should deal with the bloodrain."

"Go ahead. Be my guest." Daine eased back until the wall supported her. Kitten, who had been poking in the remains of the table, came to examine her, making sure the girl was in one piece. Numair went to the small, bubbling cauldron. "How long have I been out?"

"If your unconsciousness commenced with the barrier's destruction—"

"It did."

"I believe it's some two and a half hours, then, judging by the length of time it took me to reach you. Once the barrier vanished I assumed bird shape and flew here, but I ran into delays. Also, my flight skills are rusty."

"What kind of delays?"

"I believe two of the hurroks managed to shed the magical binding that kept them here. They crossed my path and took exception to me for some reason. It took me an hour to get rid of them."

"What about Spots and Mangle? Did you leave them up there alone?"

"And risk your wrath? I told them to find you, and made sure to lead the hurroks away from them. Now give me a moment here."

His lips moved, though she heard nothing.

A feeling of tension built up in the room, centering on the pot of liquid. Kitten rocked to and fro, intent on Numair, whistling under her breath. His hands moved, to write a letter or rune of some kind on the air in black fire. Just when Daine thought she might scream from the pressure, there was a *pop!* and the cauldron vanished.

"Where did you send it?" she asked when she could breathe again.

"Somewhere else," he replied. "Not a place as you would think of one. I am sorry I did not think to warn you of a backlash from the barrier's destruction. It was Tristan's little joke—a surprise for whomever he asked to undo the spell. He often pulled such pranks when we were in school together."

Stiffly Daine got to her feet. "Some prank," she muttered.

Without warning she was caught up in an extremely tight hug. "You have no idea how glad I am to see you, magelet," Numair said, and put her down.

Daine wiped suddenly leaky eyes on a sleeve. "Maybe a little," she replied, and grinned at him. "It's mutual, you know." She collected her bow, checking to see if the knocking-about it had received broke any important parts.

Numair picked up Kitten. "Now to find Tristan, if he survived the excitement. I hope he did." A cold glint in his eyes made the girl shiver. "I have some things to say to him, and none of them are 'Goddess bless.'"

They went down into the castle, then to the courtyard. Outside, Daine felt an immortal's approach. "Numair, look," she said, and pointed.

Overhead soared a hurrok, Tristan on its back. Sweat darkened the weary creature's sides, and blood flowed from around the bit in its teeth. Crows, led by the one who had carried Tait's note for Daine, mobbed hurrok and rider, stabbing with beaks and claws. Tristan hurled darts of yellow fire at them, which the crows scrambled to avoid.

Move, Daine ordered the birds. They jeered, balked of their prey, and drew off. The girl swung her bow up, took aim, and let a razor-sharp arrow fly. She was fitting another in the notch as the first struck the hurrok in the throat. Tristan threw himself free: yellow fire cushioned and slowed his fall to earth.

Daine's second bolt, as the hurrok dropped, struck home just under his left wing. The creature screamed hatred, wings beating. She grabbed a third bolt and loaded it, just in case. The scream, however, had been a last defiance: the hurrok's wings collapsed, and it plummeted into the lake.

Tristan drifted, like a dandelion seed, to land on his feet near the gate. Numair advanced to meet his foe as black, sparkling fire gathered around his hands. "Tristan, I am *very* disappointed in you," he said amiably.

Tristan pointed. Yellow lightning crackled through the air between them, splintering on a shield of black fire that appeared around Numair.

"C'mon, Kit," Daine said, backing toward the wall. "I don't think he wants help." She swore as she sensed the approach of more immortals—Stormwings, this time. Rikash and his flock were coming in fast.

Ignoring stiff and bruised muscles, the girl raced for the stair that led onto the wall, ignoring an explosion in the courtyard. Kitten, who had climbed enough for one day, stayed to watch the mages with fascination.

A fresh explosion from below made Daine stumble and nearly fall on the open stair. She caught herself and forced her aching legs on. When she reached the parapet, the Stormwings were almost directly overhead, twenty yards up.

From below came a howling screech, and Tristan's furious "You can't beat me, Arram! You never had the belly for combat magic!"

Daine glanced at her friend. Numair stood on a rock spire; except for that, the earth around him was a giant crater. A line of blood ran from his mouth, and he was coated in dust, but he seemed well. Tristan battled the tendrils of a clump of roses that twined around him. Between the crows and those thorns, the mage's elegant clothes and skin were in tatters. His look of amused good nature was gone, replaced by a fury that twisted his handsome face into a mask.

The Stormwings could throw the contest Tristan's way, if she allowed them to interfere. Daine swung her crossbow up and sighted on their chieftain. "Lord Rikash!" she cried in her best parade ground voice.

He hovered, waiting. The others also hovered, watching him. Several had arrows in their living flesh. Others bore wounds from swords, claws, and teeth. All were streaked with smoke and soot.

"I should have seen it would come to this," Rikash said. "What do you want?"

She blinked. What did she want? Once she had wanted to kill every Stormwing she found, but was that still true? It seemed as if, ever since she had come here, someone was telling her that because she didn't like a creature's looks, it didn't mean that creature was bad. She *still* didn't like Stormwing looks, but Rikash seemed almost—decent. And how could she tell Maura that she had killed her friend?

"I'd like to end this bloodshed, I think," she replied. Her voice squeaked a little with embarrassment and nerves. She cleared her throat. "You'n me have no quarrel here—not really. We don't like each other, but you can't go killing everyone you don't like. Isn't that so?"

"Your rustic philosophy amuses me," drawled Rikash. "Go on."

"Kill the ground-pounding bitch!" gasped the brunette female who once had told Maura that Daine was a Stormwing killer.

"Silence!" Rikash snarled at her.

Daine waited for them to be quiet. "Maybe you've heard of my aim. I don't miss often. I put out Queen Zhaneh Bitterclaws's eye, in case you hadn't heard. That was before she pushed me into killing her."

"But that shot was made with a longbow," the Stormwing lord pointed out.

"I'm as good with a crossbow. At this range it's like shooting fish in a barrel. I'm willing to negotiate, though. Since you're a friend of Maura's."

"You boast!" barked a male Stormwing. "Crossbows have no range, fifty feet at best. Don't they?" he asked Rikash.

The Stormwing lord looked at Daine and shrugged. "He's new from the Divine Realms. He thinks humans run screaming at the sight of us."

Daine sighted, loosed, and swung the bow down to redraw the string and load, all before the newcomer had registered the fact that the crossbow bolt had tapped his wing. A single feather dropped away and plummeted into the lake. By the time it struck the water, the bow was back on her shoulder and she was ready to fire again. "I've a two-hundred-yard range on this," she called. "Care to try me?"

Rikash watched her for a long time, metal wings fanning the air. Daine waited him out. When he spoke at last, his voice was quiet. "I am not as old as Zhaneh Bitterclaws was—not as crafty or as powerful. But I believe I may be wiser." To his flock he said, "Let's go, my friends. We must tell the emperor to expect no more Dunlath opals." He looked at Daine and shook his head. "I suppose we're both losing our minds. Please tell Maura I said good-bye and good luck." Gliding to the lake's surface, he banked and turned south.

"No!" yelled the noisy female. She stooped, talons ready to strike. Behind her, in the same fast attack mode, came the male who had lost a feather to her arrow.

The angle they had picked was opposite the sun. Its rays hit their feathers, blinding Daine. She didn't panic, but listened for the nearest moving body, and aimed. Eyes filled with sunspots, she fired: the female shrieked. Down with the crossbow, foot in the stirrup, both hands on the string, *pull* it up over the release.

Something big clacked nearby. She ducked

as the male hurtled over her head. He would return with a fresh attack. Bolt from the quiver into the notch; clip in place; bow to her shoulder. Her vision began to clear: he was coming down, almost directly on top of her. She aimed, shot. The arrow slammed into his chin and up through his skull. The impact knocked him askew. He plummeted into the wall with a crash of metal and slid to its base. The female was already in the lake, sinking as her blood spilled into the water.

The rest of the flock had watched from above. When she looked up to see if they might avenge their friends, they wheeled as one and resumed their flight south. Automatically she redrew the bow and placed another bolt in the notch.

She had locked her attention so hard on the Stormwings that the mages' fight had slipped her mind briefly. Now she looked down. Numair was clothed in a clear, jellylike substance that burned white-hot. His mouth moved inside the burning sheath. It melted away like thawing ice, flame shrinking as it sank into the ground. Tristan was tearing away the strands of a giant silk cocoon.

"You are not taking me to that weak-willed idiot in Corus!" he cried. The cocoon flamed and vanished, leaving him covered in powdery ash. He looked the worse for wear, swaying as he stood, his breath coming in gasps. Lifting his hands, he threw a storm of yellow arrows at Numair, who shielded himself.

"Tristan, enough," the taller mage snapped. "If you rush me, I'll do something we'll regret. Your death would be a criminal waste of your talents."

Tristan glared at him. Sweat made tracks in the ash on his face. "You puling, gutless book-worm." On the gravel at his feet—it had once been stone blocks—a spin of brambles, old cocoon, and leaves caught flame. "You think you'll come away golden, don't you?" The fiery dust-devil roared high to become a tornado of flame. "You and your 'honor code,' your sermons on what we owe the un-Gifted— you made me sick in Carthak and you still do. Well, you will *not* walk away unscorched!" He pointed at Daine, and the funnel leaped for her.

She fired; Numair said a word that made the air scream. The tornado vanished. Her bolt plunged into the tree that was now Tristan Staghorn.

Daine gaped, leaning for support on the bow as her knees wobbled. "So," she remarked, when she had the breath. "Um—thank you. Was that a word of power?"

"Yes. What is he, can you tell?"

"I think it's fair rude to make him a tree and not know what kind he is."

"Daine—"

"Apple. Knowing him, prob'ly a *sour* apple tree. Will this hurt some other part of the world?"

Numair sighed. "As I recall, this word's use means somewhere there is a tree that is now a—a two-legger." He looked around. His stone pedestal was still intact, but the crater around him was at least four feet deep and six feet wide. "How do I get out of this thing?"

Daine remembered one more vital task. "Use a word of power, or something," she called, and ran for the stairs. "I need to find Belden and Yolane!"

Belden was easy to find. He lay on his bed, dressed plainly in black, his face white. The cause of his final sleep had spilled from a tipped-over cup on the bedside table. It was a thick, pale liquid Daine recognized from Numair's poison collection. Beside it was a note written in a sharp, decisive hand.

She knew it was rude to read others' letters, but she wanted to see why he had picked what she felt was a coward's way out of the mess he'd helped to make. The note read:

She has learned the king knows of our plan. Nowhere in Tortall is safe when the king is a mage who knows who to look for, she says—the very trees will reach out to capture us. She said we must get away, that there will be a welcome for us in Carthak. I refused. We gambled, and lost. I will not bring more disgrace to my name. I do not blame her for luring me from the loyal path. I did not have to be tempted. My wrongdoing is my own, and I accept the responsibility.

Daine left the room and closed the door behind her, feeling sick and angry. She could not think about Belden now. The important thing was that Maura's sister was going to escape. Mice! she called. Is Yolane here? Their denial came back instantly: Yolane was long gone.

She left, said Cloud in the stable. It was about the same time as the explosion in the tower. I tried to stop her, but she got away, on horseback.

Daine ran outside to Numair. He had reached the steps, where he sat with his head on his knees. "Yolane's gone. We have to go after her."

"Daine, I can't. I'm used up for the moment." He was gray under his swarthiness. "What about Belden?"

"He killed himself. He's in there." She indicated the castle with a jerk of her head. "If she's to get away clean, she must be headed west. She could see from here the north and south passes are pretty hot right about now."

"Daine?" a voice called. "You here?" Iakoju, armed with a longbow that looked like a child's toy, walked in the gate. With her was the Long Lake Pack. They raced to greet Daine in wolf fashion. Numair was included in the ceremony, and had his face eagerly washed by Short Snout, Fleetfoot, and Russet.

Daine looked at the ogre. Her aqua skin bore collections of bruises, grazes, and soot, and a rip in her tunic revealed a shallow cut on her belly. "What's wrong? Were you driven back? How did you get here so fast?"

"No," replied Iakoju. "We win. My brothers lock up men that still live. Two mages dead—one fall from hurrok when I shoot with this." She held up the bow. "One killed by many little speckled birds."

"Starlings," Daine said.

"Speckled birds," Iakoju agreed. "I take boat to find you. Pack come, too."

There is no more for us to do there, explained Brokefang. Once the ogres chose to fight, nothing could stop them. The humans were scared already, after the work the People did on them. Perhaps they could have fought better with their weapons and horses, but the horses were gone and the weapons were ruined.

"You look bad," Iakoju was telling Numair.

He smiled up at her. "So do you."

Daine had an idea. "If you have Yolane's scent, could you track her? Even if she's on horseback?"

She is one of the two-leggers that brought this on us? Frostfur's eyes glittered angrily.

"All of it was done in her name," the girl replied.

Then we will find her, Brokefang said. Where is her scent?

Blueness and Scrap guided Daine to Yolane's rooms. The girl returned to the pack with a handful of the noblewoman's clothes. Everyone carefully sniffed the delicate gardenia scent that rose from the garments as Daine removed her belt, purse, dagger, and boots. She left the crossbow as well.

"What are you doing?" Numair demanded.

"The pack's going to find her, and I'm going with them, sort of. I have to sit in the lake, though, to help with the magic. I'm awfully tired, and I am *not* going to risk her getting away! Head out, Brokefang. I'll follow."

Numair did not protest as she ran to the docks where the fief's boats were kept. She had learned from him the trick to add to her power when she was tired by getting cold or cold and soaked. She only wished the Long Lake were salt water, since that worked best of all. You can't have everything, she told herself as she tied a rope to the ladder that led to the water. When the knot tested firm, she jumped in.

She gasped: the lake was icy, a product of mountain streams. Tying the rope to her waist, she clung to the last step and reached out, listening for the pack. They were near the end of the causeway.

Her mind blurred when she joined with Brokefang. When it cleared, she knew she couldn't stay in the water, not for as long as pursuit might take. She fought to heave herself onto the ladder, scrabbling at the wooden stair with her paws. The effort to drag her soaked body from the lake was painful. Her muscles screamed; then she was out and leaping up the steps to the dock. At the top something tugged at her middle—a rope tied much too loosely. She didn't need that anymore. Wriggling out of it, she paused and shook out her fur, ridding herself of what felt like pounds of water, then looked for the wolves.

They waited for her where bridge and land met. She raced to join them. Let's go, she said when they would have greeted her all over again.

Brokefang stood in front of her, ears and

tail erect, upper lip barely skinned back over his teeth. Are *you* going to lead the hunt? he demanded.

She looked at him as if he were crazy. You know more about hunting this way than me, she retorted. I'll follow you.

Very good. The upper lip went down. He turned and cast around in the dirt for a moment. She watched, impressed. How can he sort through these incredible smells? she wondered. There were dozens here, a baffling patchwork of scents.

Come, Brokefang ordered, and trotted away. Daine let Frostfur go next, standing well back in case the chief female decided to bite. She followed them and the other wolves strung out behind her. Outside the village, she picked up the first clean scent of gardenia and horse. It was the newest odor on a road littered with yesterday's droppings. For the first time she was glad that the humans had chosen to remain out of sight today: it made Yolane's trail stand out all the more.

At the crossing with the north road they met Spots and Mangle. The horses went to the side of the road farthest from the wolves and waited for them to pass, ears flat, eyes rolling. It was only because they knew these wolves that the horses stayed on the road at all.

She halted. Spots, Mangle, she called, It's me. Don't be scared.

Daine? Mangle took a hesitant step closer. It really *is* you!

Daine? Spots also took half a step closer, badly confused.

Numair's at the castle with Cloud, she told them. Go on—I'll see you soon.

Come *on*, ordered Brokefang. You hold up the hunt!

With a sigh Daine followed.

Time passed, how much she could not say, as they followed the scent and the road to the western pass. Brokefang kept them to a strict schedule of short gallops broken up with longer periods of easy trotting, much as the palace training masters directed those periods of torture known as "cross-country runs." Daine gloried in the power of this strange/familiar body. In her own skin she had been tired; now she was not. She could run all day if the weather stayed like this, with a touch of crispness in the air.

The pack had reached the tree-covered shoulders of the mountains when she began to feel an ache build in her paws.

They are tender because you are new. That was Sharp Nose. *You must build up your pads and your wind to stay with a pack. You will have to practice.*

We had to do that, Runt called from the rear of their column. *You can, too.*

Daine licked a paw, then had an idea. Wading into the stream by the road, she let the water bathe, then numb, her sore feet. *I never thought of that,* Short Snout commented.

So two-leggers are good for something, retorted Daine. He nipped playfully at her, and she at him.

Stop, Brokefang ordered. *And behave.* He had checked each horse pat in the road: this time he called for them to join him. They gathered around the dung, tails wagging, to confer. The spoor was only an hour old. The horse was young, healthy, female, and beginning to overheat.

The pack speeded up. Daine panted as she ran, the day catching up even with her wolf shape. When they next stopped to inspect the mare's leavings, tails wagged harder than ever. This pile was soft and wet, barely five minutes old. Nearby a splash of heady horse sweat marked the ground. The mare's rider was pushing hard. She hadn't rested her mount on the climb to the pass; perhaps she even had tried to make the horse go faster. She had thrown away the advantage of her long head start on the wolves.

They moved out. Now their noses caught the mare's odor on the wind, mixed with saddle leather, oil, and gardenias.

The road topped a crest. When the pack reached it, they saw the horse and rider below. Dark with sweat, the mare was drinking too fast from the stream. Ironically, they had stopped where the trail to the caverns crossed the road.

Spreading out to form a horizontal line, the wolves began to run. With the quarry's scent in her nostrils, Daine forgot her aching feet and ran with them. They knew the mare had to catch their odor soon, but this was a good spot to circle her. She could only run west, and Daine already was calling the marmots to block the road. On either side the horse was walled in by rock and loose earth. Footing that would cripple her was not a problem for the wolves.

The mare smelled them and spun, white showing all the way around her eyes. Yolane, riding sidesaddle, was nearly thrown. She kept her seat and tried to whip her mount into flight. The wolves streamed over the rocks to either side of horse and rider, and surrounded them.

Daine's blood was up. A run meant a hunt to her wolf self; a hunt meant a kill. She wanted to leap for the mare's throat, to bring her down and feast, but caution held her, though she fought it. The mare was shod in hard metal. To lunge in would be to court broken ribs or a broken head. If Yolane had not been riding her, the pack never would have gone after such dangerous prey.

The wolves drew away from those hooves and waited. The mare held still. Yolane screamed and kicked, flailing at her mount with her riding crop. The horse staggered and came within jumping distance of Daine.

Forgetting the danger, the girl-wolf lunged. Battle slammed against her side and knocked her down. Stupid! the pack told her as one. You will get your brains bashed in, and we will lose a hunter!

Sheepishly, Daine flattened her ears and whined, backing to her place in the circle. Once there, she turned to lick her ribs, and thought, What am I doing?

Straightening, she called, Hoof-sister!

The mare faced her, quivering. You are not hoof kin, she said, breath coming hard. You are a hunter. I will not have you in my herd!

I'm not a hunter, not a *true* hunter. The girl freed some magic to connect her to the horse. Briefly her form shifted, trying to develop hooves, but she gripped her wolf shape and held it. Hoof-sister, she said, Dump the human. Run to your stable. You will be safe. It is not you that we want. It is her.

The mare hesitated. Enraged, Yolane struck her mount's tender ears.

The horse had borne enough. She bucked the human off and raced for home. Those wolves between her and the village moved aside and let her pass.

Yolane lay white and still on the ground. Daine trotted over and put her nose close to the woman's face. Her keen ears heard the soft drag of breath: Dunlath's lady was alive.

The pack made themselves comfortable, keeping their circle around Yolane, and Daine walked over to the stream. Sitting down, she began to recover her true shape. It was harder than she had expected. Her body *liked* the wolf shape. Bruises and hot feet notwithstanding, the wolf shape felt good, even natural. The girl had to fight a sense that she was meant to stay a wolf. Every little distraction—birdsong, the pups romping, the call of a distant horn— meant she had to stop and begin again. At last she found her two-legger self and slid into it. Opening her eyes she made an unhappy discovery.

Her clothes were gone. All she wore was the silver badger's claw on its leather thong. "And why am I still wearing you and nothing else?" she demanded.

Where is your flat fur? Are you taking a bath now? asked Runt curiously.

Luckily she had left most of her packs in the nearby caverns. "I'll be right back," she told the wolves. "Don't let her go anywhere."

When Daine returned, wearing clothes she

had wanted to wash before she put them on again, Yolane was conscious. She greeted Daine with a flood of bad language.

Daine listened until the woman began to repeat herself, then said, "Shut up." As it went against the grain to be so rude even to Yolane she added, "Please."

To her surprise, Yolane gulped, then fell silent.

Much better, Brokefang said. The wolves had not moved from their circle around the captive. Will you take her alone, or shall we drive her? I think you will need our help.

"On your feet, milady," Daine ordered. "We're all going to walk back to the village. If you behave yourself, you'll be fine. Just don't try to run, or my friends will bring you down."

Yolane got to her feet. "If they're going to eat me, get it over with."

Daine sighed. "They don't eat humans."

We could try eating one *once*, Short Snout offered. Just to see what she tastes like. It seems this one isn't doing the human pack much good as she is. He walked closer to the woman, grinned up into her face, and licked

333

his chops. Yolane backed away so quickly she tripped on her skirts and fell.

Don't help, Daine chided her friend. "Let's go," she ordered as the noblewoman got to her feet once more. "You walk in front of me."

Yolane dusted her rump and passed the girl, nose in the air. Daine followed. The wolves ranged around the humans as they turned east. It was plain they did not mean for the walk to be pleasant for the captive. They often darted in at her to snap heavy jaws close to her hands, then dashed away. Short Snout liked to draw close to sniff and nibble on Yolane's skirt.

Daine chose not to call them to order: they had worked hard, and they needed a bit of fun. As far as she was concerned, the woman who had helped to bring so much destruction on Dunlath needed harrying.

Halfway to the village, riders came to meet them. In the lead were Numair, the King's Champion, and Sir Raoul. The knights wore armor marked by the day's hard fighting. The warriors behind them, a mixed company of the King's Own and Riders, also looked the worse for wear.

Alanna grinned at Daine when the two

groups met. "I hear you can shape-shift these days."

"Any ill effects?" asked Numair.

"I didn't have my clothes when I changed back. Luckily we were by the caves. How are Tkaa and Maura and Tait and Flicker?"

"Waiting at the castle," said Numair. "The squirrel needs some of your help."

Sir Raoul dismounted and ruffled Daine's hair with one gauntleted hand. "Good work," he said with a grin. "We'll make a king's officer of you yet. Speaking of which—" He went to Yolane and put a hand on her shoulder. Voice formal now, he said, "Yolane of Dunlath, I hereby arrest you in the name of King Jonathan and Queen Thayet of Tortall, for the crime of high treason."

The pack lifted their voices in a triumphant howl. Yolane shuddered. "I am guilty as charged. Now will you get me away from these monsters?"

"They have a different idea of who's the monster here," retorted Daine. "And I think *they* have the right of it. Will someone give me a ride? My pads—my feet—are killing me."

EPILOGUE

Daine was in the castle orchard petting Blueness and Scrap one last time when Maura found her. The girl's eyes were red and puffy. "I wish you weren't leaving," she commented, and sniffed.

Daine smiled. "You'll hardly know I'm gone. You've been that busy, what with Belden's funeral, and working things out so the ogres have farms and all."

"But once the king sends me a guardian, I won't be busy."

"Of course you will. Tkaa and the animals already said they'll deal with no one but you. You're the only noble in Tortall with a basilisk, ogres, bats, wolves, and squirrels as advisers on running a fief. Not to mention a golden eagle." Shading her eyes, she looked at the tower. Branches protruded from the window to Tristan's workroom. It had been specially widened so Huntsong could use it as a nest.

"Don't forget Blueness and Scrap." Maura petted the cats gently.

"Cats aren't *special* advisers. They advise us all the time, whether we want them to or not." Daine gently tugged at her friend's hair. "I'll visit, I promise. *After* the Big Cold, though. Twelve years I lived through mountain winters because I had no choice. That's enough."

"But winter here is *beautiful*," protested Maura. "The lake's all hard for skating, and the trees look like they have sugar frosting—"

Daine shivered. "Enough! You're too good at describing!"

"Will you write? Tell me what you're doing, and Kitten and Numair?"

"I'm not very good at writing letters,"

Daine said. The wistful look in the other girl's huge brown eyes made her sigh. "I'll try. Honest."

Most of their friends—Iakoju, Maura, Tait, the dogs, Blueness, and Scrap—accompanied Daine, Numair, Kitten, and their mounts to the edge of the village, and stopped there. Daine gave Maura and Iakoju a hug and petted each of the dogs. The cats said their farewells to Kitten as Daine took Tait aside. "No more wolf hunting?" she asked him.

"No need to, since Brokefang promised they'd leave th' farm animals alone." The huntsman tweaked her nose. "Weiryn guide your aim, lassie."

"Take care of those dogs, and Maura."

Tkaa, who carried Kitten, and Flicker, who rode with Daine, stayed with them as the small company of horses and humans took the road south. Each time Daine or Numair looked back, the others were still there, watching until the road along the lakeshore took them from sight.

Kitten whistled unhappily. She and the cats had become good friends in the three weeks since the capture of Yolane. Tkaa murmured to her in dragon.

Silently appearing from the trees, the Long Lake Pack fell in step with the travelers. Once the champion and the soldiers had taken their captives south for trial, the wolves had left the populated areas. They had returned to their former habits, now that they had an understanding with the valley's humans.

Dismounting from Cloud, Daine walked among her friends, sharing their thoughts one last time, though she fought to keep her shape her own. Changing to wolf form had taken its toll: she had lain in bed for several days, drinking nasty herbal teas Numair gave her to ease the pain in all her bones. It would be a long time before she tried a full shape-shift again. When she did, she hoped her skeleton would be more accustomed to such changes. For now she walked in a universe of keen smells and sounds shared with her by the pack.

They stopped to eat lunch near the spot where the southern fort had once stood. It was a ruin; no buildings were left inside the blackened remains of the wall. Daine eyed the destruction, awed. "Kegs of *flour* did this?"

"Flour heated under pressure explodes," replied Numair. "They had gotten supplies for the entire valley the day before the barrier came down. Maura couldn't have done better if she'd burned kegs of blasting powder."

Shaking her head, Daine looked at the empty stockade where Blackthorn and his mercenaries had stayed until being taken south with Yolane. With advance warning of their arrival, the King's Own and the Riders had captured Tristan's allies with no blood-shed and only a little magical assistance from Numair and the Lioness. Now all that remained to show that mercenaries had come to Dunlath was this rough and empty fenced yard.

Flicker shared Daine's lunch, handling food gingerly with his left forepaw. It had been nearly severed in the fight at this fort, when the squirrel stopped a Stormwing from killing Tait. Daine had saved the paw, but nothing she could do would ease the tenderness in the bone. Now she let him go through her pockets one last time. His raiding done, Flicker pressed a cold, wet nose to hers. His whiskers tickled.

It was fun, he said. We had excitement before the Big Cold. We fought evil. My kits will know it, and their kits, and every other squirrel in Dunlath through all of time.

"I know. I don't s'pose you'd want to come with us, then?"

No, he replied. Somebody has to tell Maura how us "rodents" feel, and the mice won't do it. They are too afraid of Blueness and Scrap.

"Take care of yourself," she said, wiping her eyes on her sleeve. "You're getting as many lives as a cat, you know."

He gave her a last squirrel kiss, then allowed Tkaa to pick him up and put him in his pouch.

"Take care of my young cousin," the basilisk said in his whispery human voice. "Do not let her eat so many potatoes and cookies. She is getting fat."

Daine smiled at him, lips quivering a little. "Watch over our friends. Don't let the humans bully the People the way they did before we came."

"I doubt the People will allow them to do

so," Tkaa assured her. He touched her cheek gently, and bowed to Numair. "I shall visit when things are settled here," he promised.

Numair smiled at the basilisk. "I'll collect rocks for your welcome feast."

Tkaa nodded—he had expected no less—and set off along the road to the village. Before they were gone from view, Daine saw the squirrel climb onto the top of the basilisk's head, where he could see better. Kitten chirped softly as Daine's eyes spilled over once more.

"Good-byes are sad things," Numair remarked, voice soft.

That is why wolves don't say them, commented Fleetfoot as Daine translated.

"I always knew your kind was smarter than mine," the man replied, smiling.

We knew that, too, agreed Short Snout, making Daine giggle.

"Enough moping," she said, getting up. "Let's move on."

They had reached the wide cleft where river and road left Dunlath—the spot where Tristan had planned to dump bloodrain—when a flash of white on a nearby ledge caught Daine's eye. A giant white wolf stood there, calmly watching them.

"Brokefang," she asked, "didn't you say there are no other wolves here?"

That is Old White, Brokefang replied. The patch behind him, which looks like shadow, is his mate, Night Black.

Calling on a deeper level of her magic, she looked again. When she found Old White and Night Black, they were blazes of silver fire—the same kind of fire that shone from her mentor, the badger. She touched the silver claw at her throat. "I hope you're happy with all this," she called. "Just don't blame me if the People here aren't as obedient to you gods as they were before you brought me in to teach them things."

"Whom are you talking to?" Numair's question made her look at him.

"Old White," she said. "He's up there, him and his mate." She pointed to the ledge, but the wolf gods had vanished. "They *were* there." Checking for the Long Lake Pack, she found that they too had disappeared in a more normal way, fading into the trees that grew on the mountainside.

"Good hunting," she called to them. From the shadows under the trees, she heard her friends wish her the same.

Numair tousled her hair. "Let's go home, magelet."

*Daine's adventures continue
in the next book in*

THE IMMORTALS
SERIES:

EMPEROR
MAGE

His Royal Highness Kaddar, prince of Siraj, duke of Yamut, count of Amar, first lord of the Imperium, heir apparent to His Most Serene Majesty Emperor Ozorne of Carthak, fanned himself and wished the Tortallans would dock. He had been waiting aboard the imperial galley since noon, wearing the panoply of his office as the day, hot for autumn, grew hotter. He shot a glare at the nobles and academics on hand to welcome the visitors: they could relax under the awnings. Imperial dignity kept him in this unshaded chair, where a gold surface collected the sun to throw it back in his eyes.

Looking about, the prince saw the captain, leaning on the rail, scowl and make the Sign against evil on his chest. A stinging fly chose that moment to land on Kaddar's arm. He yelped, swatted the fly, got to his feet, and removed the crown. "Enough of this. Bring me something to drink," he ordered the slaves. "Something *cold*."

He went to the captain, trying not to wince as too-long-inactive legs tingled. "What on earth are you staring at?"

"Tired of broiling, Your Highness?" The man spoke without looking away from the commercial harbor outside the breakwater enclosing the imperial docks. He could speak to Kaddar with less formality than most, since he had taught the prince all that young man knew of boats and sailing.

"Very funny. What has you making the Sign?"

The captain handed the prince his spyglass. "See for yourself, Highness."

Kaddar looked through the glass. All around the waterfront, birds made use of every visible perch. On masts, ledges, gutters, and ropes they sat, watching the harbor.

He found pelicans, birds of prey—on the highest, loneliest perches—songbirds, the gray-and-brown sparrows that lived in the city. Even ship rails sported a variety of feathered creatures. Eerily, that vast collection was silent. They stared at the harbor without uttering a sound.

"It ain't just birds, Prince," the captain remarked. "Lookit the docks."

Kaddar spied dogs and cats, under apparent truce, on every inch of space available. Not all were scruffy alley mongrels or mangy harbor cats. He saw the flash of bright ribbons, even gold and gem-encrusted collars. Cur or alley cat, noble pet or working rat catcher, they sat without a sound, eyes on the harbor. Looking down, Kaddar found something else: the pilings under the docks swarmed with rats. Everywhere—warehouse, wharf, ship—human movement had stopped. No one cared to disturb that silent, attentive gathering of beasts. Hands shaking, the prince returned the glass and made the Sign against evil on his own chest.

"You know what it is?" asked the captain.

"I've never seen—wait. Could it be—?"

Kaddar frowned. "There's a girl, coming with the Tortallans. It's said she has a magic bond with animals, that she can even take on animal shape."

"That's nothin' new," remarked the captain. "There's mages that do it all the time."

"Not like this one, apparently. And she heals animals. They heard my uncle's birds are ill—"

"The *world* knows them birds are ill," muttered the captain. "He can lose a battalion of soldiers in the Yamani Isles and never twitch, but the gods help us if one of his precious birds is off its feed."

Kaddar grimaced. "True. Anyway, as a goodwill gesture, King Jonathan has sent this girl to heal Uncle's birds, if she can. And the university folk want to meet her dragon."

"Dragon! How old *is* this lass anyway?"

"Fifteen. That's why *I'm* out here broiling, instead of my uncle's ministers. He wants me to squire her about when she isn't healing birds or talking to scholars. She'll probably want to visit all the tourist places and gawp at the sights. And Mithros only knows what her table manners are like. She's some commoner from the far north, it's said. I'll be lucky if she knows which fork to use."

"Oh, that won't be a problem," said the captain, straight-faced. "I understand these northerners eat with their hands."

"So nice to have friends aboard," replied the prince tartly.

The captain surveyed the docks through his glass. "A power over animals, *and* a dragon . . . If I was you, Highness, I'd dust off my map of the tourist places and let her eat any way she wants."

At that moment the girl they discussed inched over as far on the bunk as she could, to give the man beside her a bit more room. The dragon in her lap squeaked in protest, but wound her small body into a tighter ball.

The man they were making room for, the mage known as Numair Salmalín, saw their efforts and smiled. "Thank you, Daine. And you, Kitten."

"It's only for a bit," the girl, Daine, said encouragingly.

"If we don't wrap this up soon, *I* will be only a 'bit,'" complained the redheaded woman on Numair's other side. Alanna the

Lioness, the King's Champion, was used to larger meeting places.

At last every member of the Tortallan delegation was crammed into the small shipboard cabin. Magical fire, a sign of shields meant to keep anything said in that room from being overheard, filled the corners and framed the door and portholes.

"No one can listen to us, magically or physically?" asked Duke Gareth of Naxen, head of the delegation. A tall, thin, older man, he sat on the room's only chair, hands crossed over his cane.

The mages there nodded. "It's as safe as our power can make it, Your Grace," replied Numair.

Duke Gareth smiled. "Then we are safe indeed." Looking in turn at everyone, from his son, Gareth the Younger, to Lord Martin of Meron, and from Daine to the clerks, he said, "Let me remind all of you one last time: *be very careful* regarding your actions while we are here. Do *nothing* to jeopardize our mission. The emperor is willing to make peace, but that peace is in no manner secure. If negotiations fall through due to an error on our parts, the other Eastern Lands will not support us. We will be on our own, and Carthak will be on *us*.

"We *need* this peace. We cannot match the imperial armies and navy, any more than we can match imperial wealth. In a fight on Tortallan soil, we *might* prevail, but war of any kind would be long and costly, in terms of lives and in terms of resources."

Alanna frowned. "Do we have to bow and scrape and tug our forelocks then, sir? We don't want to seem weak to these southerners, do we?"

The duke shook his head. "No, but neither should we take risks—particularly not you."

The Champion, whose temper was famous, blushed crimson and held her tongue.

To the others Duke Gareth said, "Go nowhere we are forbidden to go. Do not speak of freedom to the slaves. However we may dislike the practice, it would be unwise to show that dislike publicly. Accept no gifts, boxes, or paper from *anyone* unless they come with the knowledge of the emperor. *Offer* no gifts or pieces of paper to anyone. I understand it is the custom of the palace mages to scatter listening spells through the buildings and grounds. Watch what you say. If a problem arises, let my son, Lord Martin, or Master Numair know *at once*."

"Kitten will be able to detect listening spells," remarked Numair. "I'm not saying she can't be magicked, but most of the common sorceries won't fool her."

Kitten straightened herself on Daine's lap and chirped. She always knew what was being said around her. A slim creature, she was two feet long from nose to hip, with a twelve-inch tail she used for balance and as an extra limb. Her large eyes were amber, set in a long and slender muzzle. Immature wings that would someday carry her in flight lay flat on her back. Silver claws marked her as an immortal, one of the many creatures from the realms of the gods.

Looking at the dragon, the duke smiled. When his eyes moved on to Daine, the smile was replaced with concern. "Daine, be careful. You'll be on your own more than the rest of us, though it's my hope that if you can help his birds, the emperor will let you be. Those birds are his only weakness, I think."

"You understand the rules?" That was Lord Martin. He leaned around the duke to get a better look at Daine. "No childish pranks. Mind your manners, and do as you're told."

Kitten squawked, blue-gold scales bristling at the man's tone.

"Daine understands these things quite well." Numair rested a gentle hand on Kitten's muzzle and slid his thumb under her chin, so she was unable to voice whistles of outrage. "I trust her judgment, and have done so on far more dangerous missions than this."

"We would not have brought her if we believed otherwise," said Duke Gareth. "Remember, Master Numair, you, too, must be careful. The emperor was extraordinarily gracious to grant a pardon to you, and to allow you to meet with scholars at the palace. Don't forget the conditions of that pardon. If he catches you in wrongdoing, he will be able to arrest, try, even execute you, and we will be helpless to stop him."

Numair smiled crookedly, long lashes veiling his brown eyes. "Believe me, Your Grace, I don't plan to give Ozorne any excuse to rescind my pardon. I was in his dungeons once and see no reason to repeat the experience."

The duke nodded. "Now, my friends—it is time we prepared to dock. I hope that Mithros will bless our company with the light of wisdom, and that the Goddess will grant us patience."

"So mote it be," murmured the others.

SONG OF THE LIONESS QUARTET

Discover how it all began
in Tamora Pierce's
Song of the Lioness quartet.

SIMON PULSE
Simon & Schuster Children's Publishing
www.SimonSaysTEEN.com

THE
✦ IMMORTALS ✦

MAGIC LIVES ON IN
THE KINGDOM OF TORTALL.
Experience all of its legends!